SIX WORDS

Becky Wolsk

Text Isle Patchwork

Washington, DC, USA

ISBN 978-0-9829981-1-3

Printed in the United States of America.

This one is for the teachers.

"If you bring that sentence in for a fitting, I can have it shortened by Wednesday."

~ **Captain Benjamin Franklin "Hawkeye" Pierce,** *M*A*S*H*

HINT:

A Table of Contents lists clues.

TABLE OF CONTENTS

First Scavenger Hunt: Sixth Grade Hike

1) Introduction: Share the question you want answered.

2) Tree ID: Sassafras (Jake), Tree-of-Heaven (Kira)

3) Berry ID: Bayberries (Tamika), Wineberries (Maria), Pokeberries (Harold)

4) Foraging for pokeberries and twigs (led by Nelson and Davon)

5) Bird ID: Chestnut-sided Warbler (Hassan), Ovenbird (Malcolm), Vireo (Gail), Yellow-bellied Flycatcher (Rochelle)

6) Creek bed ID: Rocks (Aretha), Mosses and Algae (Nicole)

7) Map ID sites before retracing our steps: Key and Scale (Susan), Terrain (Larry), and Labeling (Victor)

Chapter 1: The Secret Is Not a Secret

"I will ignore Harold's outfit—or lack of an outfit," Barbara Ford, the art teacher, told Sophia Green before they joined the sixth graders in the clearing beside the Nature Center.

"I'm down with that like a limbo dancer," Sophia agreed. She had known Harold for one week and already disliked him.

Sophia and Barbara passed out clipboards and pencils while every student, other than Harold, consulted their handouts.

None of the students looked excited, and some looked nervous. They rarely left their neighborhood, where the streets were full of traffic and the stores weren't.

"I don't have a list," Harold whined. His yellow flannel pajamas glowed like traffic lights. Everyone else wore long pants, and the sky blue t-shirts Barbara had designed. On the front of the t-shirts were six words: "George Washington Carver Public Charter School." The words encircled a navy blue and green Earth. Carver was a middle school with three grades, so all sixth graders were new students.

"Did you leave your backpack on the bus?" Sophia asked Harold.

"Unnhmm."

"Get it."

"Awww, maaann!" He slapped the dirt hard, then stormed off.

"Shouldn't I go with him?" suggested Maggie, the director of Carver's kitchen garden program. Maggie had volunteered to be the field trip's parent chaperone despite her daughter Tamika's objection.

"Thanks," Sophia said, realizing too late that she shouldn't have let a troublemaker walk off alone, especially across a parking lot.

Sophia turned back to the group. "Let's get started with Step 1. We'll go around the circle, and when it's your turn to introduce yourself, please share the question you're curious about."

When Sophia introduced herself as Carver's curriculum director, she explained that she designed the biggest lessons of the school year as scavenger hunts, to encourage students to become environmental stewards without lectures. She also promised never to use the word "veggies," though many scavenger hunts focused on organic produce and the sustainable foods movement.

"I can't keep you all from using that word, but it's my pet peeve," Sophia told them, glad they were giggling.

The first two children to introduce themselves, Nicole Furlani and Larry Beale, asked variations of the same question: how long do we have to hike? Neither mentioned miles, because they didn't measure distance that way. Nicole wanted the number of hours and minutes. Larry wanted to know if they would eat lunch later than they did back at school.

"The hike will take an hour and a half," Sophia answered immediately, in spite of the four goals that she kept pinned to the inside cover of her journal:

1) Don't answer too quickly.
2) Fuel kids' curiosity.
3) Prepare them so they won't feel put on the spot and can begin thinking about lessons and tasks ahead of time.
4) Help them discover their own route to answers.

Sophia assumed, from her own strict upbringing, that children in unfamiliar surroundings desperately needed a time-defined schedule. She identified with kids who used hours as guideposts. Sophia never sneered, "Time passes, will you?" the way her Godmother Connie had. Sophia helped new students keep track of hours, so they could divide and conquer their first un-anticipatable month at Carver.

For years, at Connie's prompting, Sophia had divided all her plans and projects into numbered lists of goals. Numbers divided and conquered the flood of creative ideas and impulses coursing through her brain, so she would have something tangible to steady herself and to show others.

"We'll hike for two miles as we follow the steps of the scavenger hunt," Sophia told the group. She wondered which child would be the first to notice the blue trail markers. Those spray-painted circles were another means of breaking long trails into smaller, manageable steps.

It was time for the next student in the circle to introduce herself. Sophia smiled at bespectacled, pretty Kira Hughes.

"Hi, I'm Kira, and...." Kira stopped to watch Harold's return. He tossed down his backpack before sitting down. The bulk of it slammed against Larry Beale's thigh.

"Watch it!" Larry said, scooting as far to the right of Harold as space allowed.

"Sorry," Harold mumbled.

"It's Kira's turn," Sophia said to minimize the undeserved attention that Harold attracted.

"I have a question about Step 2 of our scavenger hunt," Kira said.

"What Step 2?" Harold asked while everyone else looked down at their sheets.

"Larry, would you share your list with him?" Sophia asked.

"Step 2 is Tree ID," Kira told him. "And I'm assigned to find the 'Tree-of-Heaven.' In last night's homework, I read that the 'Tree-of-Heaven' is also called a 'Stinking Sumac.'" She grinned, and snickers radiated around the circle like electricity. "The question I'll be looking to solve is: why does one tree have two names?"

"Cause it's stanky," Harold said. More snickering.

Sophia frowned at him. "Don't interrupt."

"That's all right, I'm done," Kira said.

Victor Jones was next. Sophia asked him to go ahead.

"Wait!" Harold said. "Miz Green, you forgot to answer Kira's question!"

"No, Harold, I did not forget. Okay?" Sophia winced. She knew she sounded shrill and ineffectual when her defensiveness flared. "Right now we're just introducing ourselves, and sharing one question each. You missed your turn, so we'll come back to you at the end."

"No fair!" Harold exclaimed. "It's not my fault I left my bag on the bus. I want my question answered now. Why are there only seven steps on this scavenger hunt? There are sixteen kids here. We should each get our own step. The list should be numbered 1 to 16. One for each kid. So we don't have to share doing the ID's together 'cuz we don't know each other very well yet."

Sophia was about to protest but Victor Jones beat her to it. "Harold, don't barge in, dawg. I'm up now." Victor didn't sound annoyed. He and Harold were friends and had sat together on the bus.

Victor held up both arms like TV antennae. "I am the fabulous, someday-to-be-world-famous Victor Jones. My question is something I heard from a seventh grader. He said there's a surprise at the end of every scavenger hunt. Is this hunt going to have a surprise? Because, well, Step 7 says we're going to do stuff to a map. No offense, but that's not like, as enjoyable as earning some candy or something."

Sophia and Barbara exchanged amused glances.

Sophia cleared her throat. "At this point, I will only confirm that all scavenger hunts have surprise endings."

Tamika Lewis introduced herself. "Miz Green, you know what I'm curious about? Can you give us a little hint about the surprise?"

"No, but Mrs. Ford will," Sophia answered too quickly.

"Ooh, what is it?" Tamika asked Barbara.

"I won't speak out of turn," Barbara replied. "Jake, go ahead."

"My name's Jake Foreman. Can I change my question?"

"Sure," Sophia said, expecting him to rephrase Tamika's question.

"Harold, why you wearing pajamas to school?" Jake asked.

"I'm not at school right now," Harold said, grinning.

"Oh yes you are," Sophia countered.

"Well, no one told me I couldn't wear pajamas. And I live so near Carver I can roll out o' bed and right into class in these."

"You look like the Gorton's fisherman," Victor said.

"And you smell like him too," Larry Beale sang, which opened the floodgates for everyone else's jokes.

Sophia intervened. "Enough with the standup. Save your best material for the bus ride back."

Maria Arevalo's question returned everyone to the checklist.

"My question is about Step 3: Berry ID. Are wineberries used to make wine?"

"Are you serious?" Harold's voice cut like a chainsaw. "Maria wants to get drunk!"

"Stop it," Sophia snapped. She hadn't meant to snap. After working with kids for over ten years, Sophia still reacted to teasing as if it were poison. Her godmother had sugared teasing with addictive advice.

Sophia tore her gaze from Harold so she could smile at Maria, hoping to lift the girl's lowered eyes. "You've asked a great question. Most people make wine from grapes, but you can make wine from wineberries. They're a type of raspberry, and they are more sour than commercial raspberries. We would grow them in the school garden if they weren't invasive in this area."

Maria barely nodded. She was staring at her hands. Luckily, Maggie was next, and she deflected the kids' attention.

"My name is Maggie Lewis. I run Carver's kitchen garden program, and I'm Tamika's mom. Today I will be curious to see if I can avoid embarrassing Tamika."

Harold, who was sitting next to Maggie, laughed louder than anyone else. Tamika just rolled her eyes. "Go on Harold," she said. "It's finally your turn."

"Okay. I'm Harold Tompkins, best and the brightest. Yeaaayy yeayyy yeayyyy yeayyy yeayyyy—" he mock-cheered, with no end in sight.

"What's your question?" Sophia asked.

"I told you already. I don't understand why there are only seven steps on the scavenger hunt list when there are sixteen of us. You said when we got on the bus that everyone of us was going to be in charge of something."

"You still are," Barbara assured him. "Each step has smaller steps within it. Because Sophia—I mean, Ms. Green—never creates a scavenger hunt with more than eight steps."

"Why?" Larry Beale asked.

Sophia was eager to explain why, but Victor interrupted. "Harold, don't you see your name on the list? Under Step 3: Berry ID. You gotta find the pokeberries."

"Which will bring us to Step 4," Barbara said. "The foraging step. You're each responsible for filling the wax paper bags that Devon and Nelson will hand out. You'll fill them with one fallen twig, and as many fallen pokeberries as we can find on the ground. We've got to follow the rules of our educational permit, so we aren't allowed to rip anything off living plants."

"What are the twigs and berries for?" Tamika asked. "I don't see how we'd need them for the last three steps." Step 5 focused on Bird IDs, Step 6 on a creek bed, and Step 7 on map reading.

Kira Hughes asked, "Do the twigs and berries have anything to do with the surprise?"

Sophia was impressed and couldn't resist blurting: "Kira's right. You'll use the twigs and berries once we get back to the art room this afternoon."

"Aha." Kira said. "So there's a step 8…a secret Step 8!"

"Not so secret anymore," Barbara said. She glanced at Sophia, who detected a frown. Sophia assumed Barbara was disappointed by Sophia's impulsive giveaway. Sophia quietly apologized as soon as the group started walking toward the trailhead. "I know you didn't want them to know we're winding up in the art room. But I still think they'll be excited."

"I wasn't worrying about that. Look, I know Harold is annoying, but you could do a better job of disguising the fact that you want him to disappear."

Sophia's stomach jolted. She hid her chagrin. "You know how it is with troublemakers. It's better to start out harsh in September and lighten up later. I'm glad my criticism was obvious."

Barbara laughed. "Obvious like the glare of his pajamas."

Chapter 2: Novels Are Veiled Self-Help Books

At the trail head, the sixth graders lined up in pairs. Sophia and Maggie handed out identification cards with photographs and bullet points. Nelson and Devon distributed the wax paper collection bags for twigs and pokeberries.

Harold squinted over his photograph. "Pokeberries look like blueberries."

Later, Sophia would wish she had responded to this observation by pointing out that pokeberries were poisonous. In the moment, however, she only heard Harold's voice, she didn't listen to his words. The loud voice inspired her to walk behind him for supervision's sake.

To start off the hike, Sophia, Barbara, and Maggie cheered, "On your mark, get set, grow!" The kids groaned over the wordplay but started walking with more energy than they had shown on the brief path from the nature center to the trail head. As Sophia had hoped, the dorky phrase distracted them from their reluctance to hike.

Maggie joined Sophia after Tamika said "Mom, this path isn't wide enough for three people, why don't you go be Miz Green's partner so she won't be lonely."

"Miz Green, I don't want to get dirt on me," Harold whined. "My mom'll kill you if I mess up my pajamas."

Sophia flinched at his disrespectfulness.

"Don't tell me your mama let you wear those to school," Maggie teased him. "You're the one whose gonna get busted, buster."

Chatter filtered down the line when Jake Foreman announced the first tree ID, sassafras.

"My card says sassafras leaves come in three different shapes," he told the others. "Here's the leaf that looks like a mitten. Is that why its common name is 'mitten tree,' Miz Green?"

"Right."

"And here's the oval shape, and the claw shape." He bent over to smell one of the branches.

"I smell something sort of sweet," he said.

Kira smelled the leaves, too. "It smells like the air freshener in my dad's taxi," she observed. Kids crowded in.

"People used to make root beer with sassafras," Jake told them after checking his card again.

"But then some bigwig lawyer at the FDA decided the leaves were carcinogenic," Sophia said. "So now it's illegal to make real root beer."

Maggie cleared her throat as if to change the subject. "Hey kids, why do you think Ms. Green made sassafras the first ID on the list?"

Several kids guessed that Maggie was going to help them make illegal root beer as soon they got back to school.

"Whoo hoo! Root beer floats," said a boy named Hassan. "That must be the surprise!"

"Nope," Sophia said. She had been thinking that her crack about the FDA lawyer had been dumb. Her dad's anger toward lawyers had rubbed off on her, but she didn't want to make derogatory remarks like that in front of students. Sophia also felt rankled because they were behind schedule. She wished Maggie hadn't derailed the kids by asking them to guess why sassafras was the first tree ID.

Maggie fielded the students' more serious guesses until Sophia's impatience flared.

"I made sassafras the first ID because the leaves have three different shapes," she explained. "Sassafras was the first plant I ever thought of as interesting. Before I stood still long enough to notice it, I had unconsciously assumed that all leaves were the same color green, and that they were all shaped like tears. So nature bored me to tears, and I hated hiking."

"Really?" Nicole said.

"So why're you making us hike?" Jake asked.

"Because we're the new Carver students," Victor told him. "So now we have to learn to get good at hiking and growing stuff in the school garden, and be all organic and recycling everything. We're gonna save the earth, and we get to nag our parents to not use so many paper towels and shi—I mean, shoot."

Sophia grinned at Victor for catching himself before he cursed. "Victor just summarized why we're here. And today you all will learn the names of the most interesting plants on this trail, and we'll see and smell and touch them. I hope that the more sensory details you notice today, the more curious you'll feel about nature's diversity and—"

She stopped herself from barreling into lecture mode.

"Tell them about your godmother's brilliant experiment," Maggie suggested.

Sophia didn't want to share her past with the group. "No. It's too long a story. We should stick to our schedule."

"It isn't a long story. It was a simple, two-step experiment."
Maggie turned back to the kids. "Ms. Green's godmother taught
Ms. Green to feel curious and protective of our environment
when she brought her to the sassafras tree...."

Sophia remembered her godmother's words as though they
had been Connie's exact words:

*"Step one: Stand still long enough to sense what it feels like
to be still. You think stillness is boring but it's actually an
interesting sensation.*

*Step two: Transform your eyes into a video camera and
capture the details. Pretend you will win an award for Best
Nature Documentary if you can impel your audience to discover
beauty that they would otherwise overlook."*

A girl named Gail asked Sophia what a godmother was.

"A godmother is a fairy godmother," Nicole answered.

"And a godfather is a gangsta!" Victor added.

"Not always," Sophia said, taking a deep breath. "A
godparent is a trustworthy adult—or usually trustworthy—whom
your parents ask to take care of you in case anything bad
happens to them."

"But bad things rarely happen to parents," Maggie lied,
looking meaningfully at her daughter.

"Right," Barbara said. "A godparent is a family friend or a
relative."

And sometimes a critic, Sophia added silently. She had told
her colleagues that she had a resourceful godmother. But they
didn't know the tragedy that had befallen Sophia's mother, and
they didn't know Sophia's godmother was a notorious guru.

"Countess Connie" became a household name in the early 1970s, thanks to her bestseller *Live Like Your Days Are Numbered*. It wasn't Connie's first book. She had been an unsuccessful novelist, but gave up novel-writing because of an epiphany (and because she couldn't get her third novel published).

Connie decided that all novelists were cowards. They created characters to fulfill their own desires and nightmares. Sympathetic characters imparted advice that the author didn't have the gumption to offer directly. Novels were veiled self-help books.

In *Live Like Your Days Are Numbered*, Connie told readers how to emulate her slenderness and creative productivity. She attributed her success to an "enumerative balancing act." Every day, she matched her word count to her calorie count. At minimum, she wrote 1000 words and ate 1000 calories. At maximum, she wrote and ate until she reached the number 2000.

Thanksgiving was a heavy writing day.

Connie claimed you could achieve any goal if you framed your pursuit with numbers. She loved the number two, said it was the most powerful:

> *Any obstacle can be understood and surmounted once you identify its Two Opposing Forces.* (*Live Like*, p. 2)

Connie also claimed that all people should pair up or die upon reaching adulthood. Sophia, who was thirty-four and newly single couldn't stand Connie's latest book, entitled *Noah's Ark: Would Your Relationship Make the Cut?*

Connie urged reporters to describe her as an Enumerative Guide. In a televised interview, she described herself as a spiritual Albert Einstein:

"I have discovered the unifying scaffold that binds together Christianity, Judaism, Eastern spiritual teachings, Islam, and all nations that model their government after the U.S. Constitution."

"So show us the scaffold," asked the rakish interviewer. "Where is it?"

"You see it each day," Countess Connie replied. "On any numbered list of goals."

"You mean, like the Ten Commandments?" the interviewer asked.

"Yes," Connie agreed sweetly. "On the Ten Commandments, and on anybody's to-do list."

Connie became the target of late-night talk show jokes in 1982, when she announced she was working on a spiritual manual entitled *My Spiritual Quest: Revising Buddhism's Four Noble Truths and the Eightfold Path.* She resented a reporter who pointed out that Buddhism helps its practitioners transcend the self. "Countess Connie, in contrast, is a self-help siren."

Another reporter dismissed her advice as fashion-magazine numerology. Connie responded with an angry letter to the editor:

Confusing my Enumerative Guidance with numerology is like confusing astronomy with astrology. I am both Mathematician and Scientist. I wield numbers to unleash human potential. Not since the discovery of DNA's double helix has anyone done more with pairings and other numerical patterns than I have done. In the tradition of Prometheus, my numbered guidance is fire and fuel.

Connie's next book was a heartwarming (for her) memoir of her son Ryan's birth story. She devoted four chapters to a description of how she had counted breaths to correspond not only with contractions, but also to match how many centimeters she was dilating. She titled the book *From My Uterus to Your Universe*. Few people would admit they had bought it, and everyone made fun of the title. Ryan was a freshman in college, and mortified by the unwanted spotlight that his mother attracted.

Connie ran away from the United States, except she didn't describe it as running away. She and her husband, Bo, hiked the pilgrimage to Santiago de Compostela in Spain. Then they moved to an orchard in Castile.

Connie might have stayed abroad forever, but on April 22, 1989, Sophia's mother, Persephone, was struck by a car while running across the driveway at Sophia's school. The accident left her paralyzed from the waist down.

Connie and Bo rushed back to Ithaca where Sophia's parents were Cornell professors. Bo bought an orchard with more pear trees than apples. He and Connie christened it Harmonious Pairs Orchard, to draw attention to Connie's love of pairs.

Sophia was startled back to the present by the sound of a distant waterfall, and the sound was growing louder. Where was this coming from? There were no waterfalls around here. She spun around. Harold had iPod headphones on, turned up so high that the sound leaked like cascading water.

"Hand it over."

"No way. Get your own." He darted away, and Sophia came after him.

"You'll get it back on the bus," she barked at his scowl. Only then did she remember Barbara's suggestion to tone down her manner toward him.

When the students entered the clearing that local birdwatchers called "The Ridge," Kira found a Tree-of-Heaven.

"Smell the leaves," Jake called out.

"Salty," she said, as everyone gathered around her.

"The male trees will smell like peanut butter in the spring, when their flowers are in bloom," Sophia explained.

"Told ja boys stink," Nicole Furlani muttered to Kira and Tamika. Sophia felt grateful to her for not saying it louder.

"This tree isn't that tall yet," Kira told the group after consulting the laminated ID card, "but some of them can grow as high as 80 feet or more, and they grow fast. That's where the reference to heaven in the name comes from."

Sixteen pairs of eyes looked upward, including Harold's. Every scavenger hunt provided this treasure at some point during the lesson. The whole class was united by constructive curiosity.

"It can be fun to learn the names of plants," Sophia began, trying to sound like she was just thinking a new thought out loud, "because the people who have encountered these plants over the centuries gave them two kinds of names. Some names are positive and some are negative. So, as Kira observed earlier, this tree is both a 'Tree-of-Heaven' *and* a 'stinking sumac.'"

"The 'stinking sumac' is its glass-half-empty name, and 'Tree-of-Heaven' is the glass half full," added Maggie, as if on cue. "I wonder if the positive names came from observers who investigated the plants more closely. Sometimes negative observations hit a person quicker than positive observations, which is why impulsive reactions often cause mistakes."

"My godmother used to talk about that," Sophia said, as the group started walking again. "She told me the mind has a negativity bias. It tries to be protective by forcing us to notice negative outcomes. The painful thoughts we sense are mental red flags, but if that jabbing transmission comes on too strong or too often, people get chronically stressed, and even do things that make them feel ashamed of themselves."

"I'd like to meet your godmother one day," Maggie replied. "The few times you've mentioned her she sounded wise and saintly."

"Connie is wise and saintly, I guess," Sophia said. Connie had helped Martin and Persephone care for Sophia from the time Sophia was in middle school until she started Cornell.

Sophia hitched up her yoga pants because the forgiving waistline had slipped below her flabby belly. She called these yoga pants her "Yo! Gut!" pants. Sophia's Buddha belly reminded her that she hadn't answered Connie's latest email yet. Connie had been going through her closet in preparation for her *Noah's Ark* book tour, and had some size six pants that were too roomy for her size four figure. Would Sophia like Connie to mail her the pants?

Sophia sighed. She hadn't been a size six since she was about 26. Connie's emphasis on physical appearance struck Sophia as embarrassing and competitive. Sophia dressed functionally. Her brown eyes looked smaller behind the glasses she shoved on every morning because inserting her contacts took long. Her blonde hair was the color of light dimmed by a cheap lampshade from the 1970s. She hid her hair in a braid.

In every email sent to Connie, Sophia made a subtle attempt to remind her vain godmother that the proverbial apple had fallen far from the tree. Sophia emphasized her commitment to teaching inner city kids about environmental stewardship.

In accordance with the advice Connie gave her readers, Sophia acted as if she was confident, and most of the time, she was confident, and absorbed by Carver and the students. It helped that Sophia always had a boyfriend until a few months earlier. Her latest adoring suitor, Jack, had accepted his dream job (which happened to be in Indonesia), after she told him she would never want to get married or have children. She blurted this out one evening after they had hosted a dinner party. Jack was drunk. He had tottered down onto one knee to propose, just when she wanted him to help her tackle the post-party mountain of dirty dishes and platters.

"Miz Green?"

"Yes, Harold?"

"I think I found the pokeweed bush."

"You did. Good detective work."

Most of the pokeweed leaves were green, but some were dappled with red, as though they'd been dipped in cranberry paint. The shiny purple berries were so dark they looked black, and they studded their dark pink stems in neat rows.

"See these berry clusters?" Sophia asked the kids. "The way they're lined up? The botanical term for these is 'raceme.' You can remember the name by imagining all the berries on a starting line, ready to race." Sophia remembered the term "raceme" differently. It reminded her of the word "racy," and she was relieved none of her students had ever made that connection.

Sophia's journal began with a spreadsheet of the hundred or so terms that she sprinkled through the school year, like Hansel and Gretel's breadcrumbs. The terms were numbered, and listed in alphabetical order. Each time she mentioned a term during the course of a scavenger hunt, she'd write the hunt's date beside it. She tried to mention each term two to four times, so the kids would retain it.

"Can I taste one?" Harold asked her.

"No, no way," Sophia said. "Pokeberries are poisonous. Hey, oh gosh, I forgot to pass out the gloves."

"So how come we're gonna collect these berries if we can't eat 'em?" Harold asked.

"Now I will give you a hint," Barbara told him. "Pokeweed berries are also known as ink berries."

"Oohhh, we're gonna make ink!" Jake said as most of his classmates erupted with excitement.

"I don't think so," Harold said. "I'm sure these are blueberries."

"No, Harold." Sophia said. "These are darker than blueberries, and blueberries have crowns at the top. See how these tops are indented?" She knew most of the students wouldn't know what 'indented' meant, so she added, "They look poked-in at the top. And that's why people call them pokeberries, or pokeweed."

Sophia held out one of the fallen branches to Kira Hughes, so Kira could pass it around while Sophia explained that "in general, berries that are blue or black are safer to eat than red or white ones, but pokeberries are poisonous. They show us you can't rely on generalizations."

"Generalizations are bad," Kira said, and the way she caught her breath made Sophia think she wanted to say more.

"Shhh, everyone. Go on, Kira."

"Well, generalizations usually aren't true. Like with stereotypes. So judging berries by their color is like judging somebody by what color their skin is."

"Excellent observation." For the rest of the hike, Sophia walked with Kira and ignored Harold.

Back at the art room, where the long tables were swathed in newspaper, each child had a twig and a wax paper bag of pokeberries.

"Here comes the surprise, Step 8," Barbara said as she and Sophia handed out glass baby food jars. Nadia Badavi, Carver's social studies teacher and the mother of a one-year-old, had donated them.

Barbara passed out latex-free gloves. "You shouldn't handle the berries without these." She showed the students how to use the twigs to stir the dark purple berries into chunky purple ink. Then the class used the twigs as pens to practice writing on scrap paper.

After the children had had the chance to get a feel for the scratchy, viscous textures of twig points dipped in crushed berries, Barbara slowly lifted the lid of a cardboard box. "You all have earned your surprise," she said. Sophia and Barbara passed out the brand-new journals that the students would use primarily use in English class. Sophia explained the origin of the schoolmade journals.

"Before last year's eighth grade class graduated, they made the rag paper covers for you and pasted them onto donated notebooks. You can write your name on the cover, and decorate it any way you want."

"Wait," Barbara called out, making stop signs with both hands. "After you've written your name, put your pen back in your jar and think for a minute before you add anything else. You will use these journals all year, so take your time. Don't just give into your first impulse."

While the students decorated their journals, Sophia snapped photographs, so she could email the images to last year's eighth graders. She wanted them to see how much the new sixth graders appreciated their handiwork.

Sophia didn't want to photograph Harold, so she heard but didn't see him when he began retching. She whirled around. Barbara was already beside him. His light brown complexion had turned gray and blotchy, and he was looking down at his body in disbelief, as though someone had hurled a bucket of paint at his stomach. Purple stained his shirt and pants and the floor underneath him. He tried to walk forward but fell to the ground instead. Sophia's sense of mastery collapsed with his thin body.

Chapter 3: The Secret That Hung Over Eden

September came again. It had been one year since Harold's accident. Whenever Sophia remembered him, she shoved that horrible day and her guilt to the back of her mind. If she was at home when she remembered, she drank a shot of Jack Daniels.

Harold had been okay. The doctors at the hospital said he couldn't have eaten too many berries. He hadn't had to spend the night at the hospital, but his parents, the Tompkinses, had been furious and pulled Harold out of Carver.

Sophia decided to replace the sixth graders' hike with an orientation on campus. The seventh and eighth graders would introduce the new sixth graders to the seven wonders of Carver's school garden:

1) Kitchen garden

2) Babylonian hanging garden

3) Medicinal garden

4) Compost heap

5) Rain garden

6) Butterfly patch

7) Cover crop station, where seedlings of black-eyed peas, sweet potatoes, and soybeans would soon be planted in accordance with George Washington Carver's promotion of these green crops to replenish the soil with nitrogen over the winter.

Sophia didn't want to start until Dawn Jordan, Carver's principal, arrived. During the first few days of school, Dawn was especially punctual. She and the rest of Carver's staff wanted to model good habits for the students, and especially for the new sixth graders. Ten minutes passed. Where was Dawn?

Sophia couldn't keep the kids waiting without risking chaos. She told them to count off "1 through 7, 1 through 7, 1 through 7," until all were efficiently divided into seven smaller groups, one for each of the seven wonders. Each group's scavenger hunt list had the same content, but a different sequence for the seven different starting points. Sophia wanted to avoid swarming the kitchen garden, which was everyone's favorite because it produced good food and sales at the neighborhood's farmers market.

Sophia gave the kids as brief an introduction as she could. Victor Jones, proud to be a seventh grader, shot his hand up. "Ooh, Miz Green? Can I tell the sixth graders something about the surprise? I mean, I won't tell them what it is, just that they gotta *earn* it."

"A surprise? My list doesn't have a surprise," a sixth grader named Candace said.

"Mine either," a boy complained.

Victor grinned. "Okay shorties, listen up. Miz Green never puts the surprise on the lists because otherwise it wouldn't be a surprise, but you always get 'em. As soon as all of y'all have been through the Seven Wonders, and checked off everything on the lists, you get to break out of your groups and look for the surprise."

"But what're we looking for?" a girl named Teresa asked.

"I can't tell you that now," Victor said. "Otherwise you'd be looking for the surprise and nothing else."

"And there's a lot of cool stuff to see first," Kira told them. "We helped the eighth graders tend to all these plants."

"Your enthusiasm is wonderful but we should get started," Sophia suggested.

"Don't forget to say 'On your mark, get set, grow,'" Tamika Lewis reminded her.

"You can say it." Sophia's attention was diverted by Dawn's entrance through the back gate. Sophia was about to wave, but the sight of Dawn's frown stopped her.

Dawn sifted through students and teachers. Surely she must be coming over to relieve Sophia's curiosity.

"Come by my office as soon as this ends. We have to talk," Dawn whispered.

"What's wrong?"

"I can't go into it now."

Sophia was about to ask for a hint, but some kids stood too close to them. Sophia hoped these eavesdropping eighth graders didn't think she was in trouble with "the boss." Dawn and Sophia were good friends underneath their relationship as principal and curriculum designer. Sophia was pretty sure she wasn't in trouble with Dawn, but she was feeling touchier than usual because her passive-aggression toward Connie had turned more aggressive three weeks earlier.

While visiting her family in Ithaca, Sophia had reluctantly gone to lunch at Connie and Bo's orchard. Connie spoiled Sophia's enjoyment of the great food by going on and on about low-calorie recipes. Bo sensed Sophia's annoyance, and tried to change the subject a few times. Sophia was sure Connie knew what he was trying to do and wouldn't take the hint. Finally Sophia changed the subject, though her new topic was more loaded than Connie's low-calorie monologue.

"So, you know how I collect quotes?" Sophia asked rhetorically. "This summer I've started collecting six-word quotes."

"Why six words?" Bo asked.

"Because brevity is powerful." Sophia looked pointedly at Connie. "I learned the six-word concept from Lucy Dell, Carver's English teacher. She told me Hemingway's shortest story: 'For sale: baby shoes, never worn.'"

"That story packs a punch," Bo said.

"Yes, and most of Carver's students are reluctant writers, so Lucy wants to use that story, and other evocative six-word sentences as story prompts. She wants to illustrate the wide variety of ideas that authors can convey with less than a handful of words." Sophia looked at Connie and said, "Your fans are so addicted to your work that they would be disappointed if you began writing succinctly."

Connie chuckled. "I'm surprised to hear you value brevity. You're not exactly Calvin Coolidge either."

"But I keep my scavenger hunts as brief as I can," Sophia countered.

Two days before school started, Sophia received an aggressive email from Connie.

Sophia dear,
Just checked out the Carver website and it looks stale. Why are faculty bios the only new content as your school year begins?
Congratulations on the new science teacher—you should encourage your principal to hire more Black male teachers. How brilliant that he's Muslim as well! Nadia Badavi must be relieved about that.

Sophia knew that was true. Carver's student population was 7% Muslim, 93% Christian, but Nadia, the social studies teacher, was the only non-Christian adult.

I wonder if the fact that Tariq Ali has a PhD in Environmental Science will motivate you to dust off your unfinished dissertation? Since you value brevity, you could always make it a short dissertation.
Remember when you told me you wanted to promote environmental stewardship more widely? Do you ever feel like you're hiding yourself in one low-profile school? I hope not! Those kids love you, and you make a difference at Carver. I envy your altruism.
Also, did you see that Tariq Ali was the captain of his college football team? You ought to encourage him to do something about Carver's anemic sports program. And while we're on that subject, I will close with this slogan for your six-word quote collection: Healthy bodies lead to

healthy minds! Here's to hoping you're starting off the
school year right by exercising regularly!

This email raised Sophia's hackles like seedlings shooting up toward a grow light. As usual, she replied too quickly, sending it before reading over her response:

I agree that Tariq is perfect, and what a wonderful world it
would be if we were all as perfect. With regard to the
website, we don't have a big budget and even if we did we
wouldn't choose to spend it on an extravagant site like
yours. We also don't have the resources for a full P.E.
program. I do yoga with the kids and some other teachers,
and often bike to work. It's so great that you're still able to
exercise despite your advanced age.

Sophia cringed as she read over that mean last line. Connie was as sadistic as an eighteenth-century French aristocrat, and Sophia had just added fuel to her fire. She read over Connie's email. At least Sophia's brevity pitch seemed to have stuck in Connie's craw.

Connie hadn't responded to Sophia's mean message. Sophia had been worrying about this, which also made her worry about Dawn instead of just feeling curious.

Sophia walked over to Nadia Badavi, who sometimes learned gossip faster than Sophia did. Nadia, Carver's social studies teacher, was supervising the "Babylonian Hanging Garden." She had designed this Second Wonder of the school garden with walls of trellised peas, grapes, and hyacinth bean vines.

Could Sophia distract the kids somehow, so she could pull Nadia aside and ask her if she knew what was going on with

Dawn? Even if she didn't, Nadia might have a theory that Sophia could chew on to tide herself over.

"I found the tunnel you told me to look for," a girl named Keisha was telling Nadia. Keisha stepped under the arch of "Ruby Moon" hyacinth bean vines. The spade-shaped leaves were green with purple veins, and the blossoms were both pink or fuchsia. She ran fingers over a flat, magenta pod. "This feels like leather."

"Ruby Moon," a girl named Teresa read off the plastic label that had once been a yogurt lid. "That's a real nice name."

Keisha stepped back to make room for the rest of their group, then made a discovery from her new position on the other side of the archway.

"I found the constellation!" she exclaimed, pointing to the red, star-shaped flowers that dotted the light green fronds of a cypress vine. While the children admired the sight, Sophia wished she had written up more time-consuming steps so the kids would be absorbed enough to provide her a quick and quiet conversation with Nadia. She wished one of the steps had been "Estimate and then count the number of vines." The effort to piece apart all those intertwined tendrils would take a long time.

"I'm surprised you're not circulating," Nadia said in her lowest teacher-to-teacher voice.

"Oh, sorry."

"No, not to be sorry," Nadia murmured in her Persian-accented English.

Sophia realized the kids were too close for her to ask about Dawn's curious behavior so she forced herself to orbit around each of the seven wonders. Finally the student groups had answered their questions and located their items. It was time to reveal the path to their surprise.

"Victor, would you do the honors?" Sophia asked him. Dawn had once complimented her on her habit of shifting the limelight to a child. Sophia wished she were as succinct as the kids often were.

"You guys gotta spread out," Victor was saying," and look for a rolled-up piece of newspaper. It's supposed to look like a diploma scroll. It's tied with a scallion, which is like a little bulb onion with a long green part that looks like a giant piece of grass."

"That's all we get?" a boy named Lincoln said. "A fake diploma?"

"Nooo," Victor said. "There's something inside the newspaper. You gotta unroll it to find it."

"Search gently," Sophia cautioned them. "The surprise is on the edge of one of the beds, so you won't have to disturb the plants."

"I saw it already," a boy named Garry said. "Next to the corn stalks." He retrieved it, then satisfied his classmates' curiosity by unrolling it quickly and reading aloud:

"'By spring, you will be able to switch places with your parents and teachers."

"For real?" Lincoln asked Sophia.

"Of course for real, or Miz Green wouldn't have said it," Kira told him. "Only you won't find out what she means until spring."

Sophia hoped that whatever worried Dawn would disappear soon, and she hoped it wouldn't prevent her from keeping her promise to the kids.

Chapter 4: The Opposite of a Pizza Delivery

"What's up?" Sophia asked after Dawn opened her office door.

"I have terrible news," Dawn said. She handed Sophia a document that had narrow margins, double spacing, and capital letters.

It was a legal document, Sophia realized. Poor Dawn. She put out legal and financial fires all day long. Sophia was glad her work as a curriculum designer was mostly academic and creative. It insulated her.

Or at least Sophia had been insulated, until she saw that her name was at the top of this document. Listed under the horrible word DEFENDANTS. And Carver and Dawn were defendants, and oh no, Barbara Ford, the art teacher, and even the Foundation for Urban Environmental Learning, which made Carver possible.

About an inch above their names were the names

HAROLD AND MARTHA TOMPKINS, as Parents and Next Friends of Minor Child, HAROLD TOMPKINS, JR., Plaintiff.

Under that line, separating the Tompkinses from the Carver names, was an ominous, lowercase "v" for "versus."

"I can't believe this," Sophia said, though her nauseous stomach believed it already.

"We should have known Harold would come back to haunt us," Dawn replied. "I wish I could have gotten his parents to stay in touch with me. We paid the hospital bill. I did everything Peter said we should do." Peter was Peter Resnick, an active Carver trustee and a senior partner at Bygones and Cromwell.

"Where's Harold now?" Sophia asked.

"Shaw. With his sister."

"That's a good school. More male teachers than we've got."

"Uh huh. He shouldn't have come here in the first place. I will never forget his mother coming up to me after Back-to-School night to say she hoped Harold's teachers wouldn't be so busy hugging trees that they neglected the basics."

"Ugh. Charming."

"She made it clear they had chosen Carver because they lived two blocks away," Dawn continued. "She said Harold had been unfairly accused of lateness by the principal of his previous school."

"Yeah, on the hike, he bragged about rolling out of bed and into class in his pajamas."

Dawn snorted. She rarely snorted.

"He wore pajamas on the hike," Sophia recalled. "I bet he found some sneaky way to put them on behind his mother's back."

"When I ran into his sister this summer she said he was doing well at Shaw," Dawn said. "Seemed like it was for the best, the transfer to another school, I mean. Not the poisoning."

Sophia winced, wishing she hadn't assigned the pokeberry ID to Harold. She hadn't supervised him properly. Sure, she'd been on his case the moment he did something irritating, but she hadn't been at all protective of him. He was just a child. She realized she had burdened Harold with an unconscious expectation. She had wanted him to consider the world from a teacher's perspective, AND refrain from annoying her personally.

How effective had her spiel been about the pokeberry's dangers? She knew she had been distracted, eager to introduce the vocabulary word "raceme" so she could check it off her list.

After twelve months, Sophia's repressed guilt flooded back. She turned back to the pages before her. As far as the Tompkinses and their lawyer were concerned, her misplaced focus that afternoon was "negligent and reckless conduct." The legalese in the complaint careened from impersonality to harshness and back again. She began scanning the document instead of reading it, because a slow approach to each harsh point hurt too much, and she had to take a deep breath before slowing down for the section that described Harold's condition:

Plaintiff Harold Tompkins, Jr. suffered gastrointestinal and respiratory distress and severe emotional distress, requiring ongoing psychological treatment. As a result of such exposure, plaintiff is at an increased risk of contracting stress-related illness, and is entitled to recover the costs of a comprehensive annual and physical exam in addition to medical costs already incurred.

A dull ache within her ribs became more noticeable. Harold might feel permanently wounded by this incident, as his parents would, and now she would, regardless of the outcome of the lawsuit. Every September, from now on, the excitement and promise of a new school year would be sullied by the memory of Harold.

Sophia looked at the date on the first page: September 7, 2009. "Why do you think they filed this now?"

"I don't know," Dawn replied. "Maybe to prevent us from doing the Rock Creek Hike activity again?"

"But why not send it to us sooner? For all they knew, we could have already done it."

Dawn shrugged. "Maybe something came up, and it got filed late."

Sophia's attention was diverted by a provocative heading at the top of the last page:

PRAYER FOR RELIEF.

"Are the Tompkinses religious?" she asked Dawn.

"Are you looking at that Prayer for Relief phrase?" Dawn asked back.

"Yeah."

"I have that on my list of questions to ask Peter. I will ask him what it means."

Sophia hoped the Tompkinses were religious—very, very religious. Their prayer for relief might weaken their case in a secular courtroom. She hoped they would compromise the strength of their case by demanding mandatory prayer to start each class. The School Board would never go for that. Charter schools were public. But then she read the list of demands, and they had nothing to do with religious accommodations. The Tompkins wanted "compensatory damages in the amount of $100,000, punitive damages in the amount of $50,000, plus costs of this action."

"A hundred and fifty thousand dollars?" Sophia shook her head. "Wait until they see my car." She imagined the setting of the deposition as a street-level conference room with a picture window. She would park in front of the window so she could point out her ancient Volvo when the Tompkinses' lawyer asked about her salary. The Volvo's rust patches resembled eczema. Sophia's mood was lifting when Dawn explained the obvious.

"They're going after the foundation with those numbers."

"Oh right. Of course." Sophia flipped back to the defendants' list at the top of the first page. Stephen Lanham had been so generous that Dawn was spared most of the fundraising responsibilities that challenged other charter school founders. Sophia shut her eyes, which only sharpened the painful image of Stephen's dismay.

"Look at the last item on the Prayer for Relief list," Dawn said. "They want to establish a parents oversight committee to review your scavenger hunts before they're presented to the students, and they want hunts restricted to school grounds. No more field trips."

Sophia's chest tightened at the thought of anyone limiting the scope of her scavenger hunts. How dare they interfere? Not to mention the burden of having to seek parental approval. She remembered Louie Simpson's dad freaking out over the rain barrels the students had built to collect stormwater runoff for use in the garden. John Simpson had crashed a faculty meeting to accuse them of creating a West Nile Virus risk. Sophia explained that they had put mosquito screens over all openings, but it took days to return voice mails from parents that Simpson had panicked before getting the facts at the meeting.

"Can you imagine what a nightmare it will be to have to clear hunts with parents first?" she asked Dawn.

"That's the least of our problems."

"Oh." Sophia looked down at her clasped hands.

"You have to admit, restricting scavenger hunts to school grounds isn't such a bad idea," Dawn said in a gentler tone. "It's safer, and you've got more than enough to work with in the school garden."

"Yeah, maybe. But I don't think we should link what happened to—"

The phone interrupted them.

"Peter, thank goodness," Dawn said. "Thanks for getting right back to me. Sophia, I'm going to be a while. I'll see you later."

Sophia rose slowly, to express her reluctance to leave. She was dying to find out what Peter Resnick would say.

"Call me as soon as you get served," Dawn added.

Served? What did Dawn mean? And then it dawned on Sophia. She hadn't even thought of that—the fact that somebody would come after her with her very own copy of the lawsuit complaint. Getting served by a process server was the opposite of looking forward to pizza delivery. You didn't want a summons to come anywhere near you, especially not to your front door.

Chapter 5: A Numbered List Subdues Any Problem

Sophia made it back to her office and slumped into her oversized leather chair. Carver was full of donated office furniture from the last time Peter's law firm had redecorated. In the corridor, children called to one another and slammed locker doors. She shot up from her chair to close her door. On the back of it hung a poster of seventy-five stairs that had been christened "*The Exorcist* steps," after the 1970s horror movie. The staircase was in Georgetown, one of Washington, DC's whitest and fanciest neighborhoods. Yuppies ran up and down it for exercise. To Sophia, their Herculean drive represented the Washington, DC she didn't want to compete against. She avoided the movers and shakers who worked on Capitol Hill or K Street. She told herself they spent their careers prevaricating, pretending to push for values that transcended their own ambition. Just looking at the Exorcist steps filled her with overwhelm.

Sophia limited Carver's scavenger hunts to eight steps or fewer. When Dawn hired her to help launch Carver, Connie emailed Sophia a numbered list she had discovered in a biography of George Washington Carver.

Carver suggested his students pursue eight goals:

1.Be clean both inside and out.
2.Neither look up to the rich or down on the poor.
3.Lose, if need be, without squealing.
4.Win without bragging.
5.Always be considerate of women, children, and older people.
6.Be too brave to lie.
7.Be too generous to cheat.
8.Take your share of the world and let others take theirs.

Sophia presented this list to Dawn without mentioning Connie had found it. When members of the school community complimented Sophia for unearthing it, she took credit for the discovery.

Sophia could still hear the six words Dawn had said when they shared the list with their trustees: "Our school will treasure these goals." Sophia told everyone at that meeting that she would limit her scavenger hunts to eight steps to honor Dr. Carver's eightfold list. But Connie's Enumerative Guidance was Sophia foundation.

Sophia glanced at the family portrait on her desk. Sophia wasn't included because she'd take the photograph. Connie sat in the front row next to Sophia's mother, Persephone. Persephone's lap was draped with an ankle-length afghan. In contrast, Connie's miniskirt showed off her tanned, lotioned shins. The three men, Martin, Bo, and Ryan, stood behind the women.

Ryan, Connie and Bo's golden boy, was nine years older than Sophia. Sophia admired him and became a curriculum designer to follow in his footsteps, though he was a much bigger fish than she was.

Kind, aloof Ryan had helped launch the 'Math Is Everywhere' curriculum, an award-winning program that enabled children to learn math skills by concept instead of by rote. Sophia had neither seen nor heard from him in two years. She was under the impression that he stuck to a never-ending string of girlfriends. He kept his distance from Connie.

"You're better about answering my emails," Connie wrote Sophia once. "But then, Ryan was never a mama's boy. I miss him."

Now Sophia turned on her laptop to check her inbox, bracing herself for a harsh email from Connie, and a passively-worded, professional message or two about the lawsuit.

No sign of the lawsuit in her inbox. Not yet. But there was a Connie email:

Your demeanor has been frosty recently. As I've told you at least fourteen times, you should not be upset by my criticism. I get tired of being treacly as I answer fan letters. I write you without sweetening my opinion. I don't even read over my emails to you. I am sorry if I activate your defensive inner core, but I do love you.

And because I love you, I have to express my concerns about your Ack!-tions because who else will? You're like Ryan. Such a workaholic. Neither of you have ever had a best friend, and the scores of inferior people you date are not true companions. I trace your recent hostility back the publication of Noah's Ark. I can read between the lines and am certain that you are secretly afraid of winding up a spinster.

Now I have apologized to you. You owe me an apology in exchange for implying that I am older than Methuselah.

Sophia sighed. She covered up the last part of the email, wishing Connie had ended it after those beautiful four words: "I do love you." But Connie never knew when to stop.

In reply, Sophia typed two words:

I'm sorry.

Sophia didn't ponder whether or not to mention the lawsuit. She had to keep it secret from Connie. If Connie found out, the fountain of unsolicited advice would overfloweth.

Sophia jabbed the Send key quickly, as if her fingers might type something to incriminate her.

She glanced at the clock and saw it was 5:45, which was later than she expected. Cally would be getting home soon. Cally was a research neurologist and Sophia's landlord. Sophia rented Cally's basement for the price of the city's cheapest studio apartments. In exchange, Sophia tended to the yard and housesat during Cally's frequent business trips for the National Institutes of Health.

What if the process server rang Cally's doorbell to ask for Sophia? He or she might ask for Sophia in some official way. Cally was sharp and worldly. She might realize Sophia was being sued. Sophia couldn't risk Cally's pity.

Sophia raced home, to the extent that she could in her primeval Volvo. Thank goodness she hadn't biked to work that morning. She forced herself to do yardwork, so she could be productive in the midst of distraction. After an hour of ripping up bindweed and raking leaves, she ran over the pile several times with the mulching mower. When she got to the most rewarding part of the process, folding the shredded leaves into the compost bin, she imagined she had received her copy of the lawsuit already, and had shredded it in with the leaves. Then she heard the melody of Cally's wind chimes quicken. She headed for the front of the house to intercept a woman in a khaki trenchcoat.

Sophia read her copy of the complaint while drinking a bottle of red wine that she had promised herself she would use as cooking wine. She brooded about the way lawyers had hurt her father. "Lawyers clump words into quicksand," Martin had written her recently, after the health insurance company's in-house counsel again denied the most expensive costs of long-term care for Sophia's mother. Martin obsessed about lawyers the way she obsessed about Connie. Sophia hoped that Peter Resnick, who was a Big Swinging Dick senior partner at his law firm, would make the lawsuit disappear. By the laws of karmic justice, Sophia's family deserved that, she thought.

She also hoped that Peter would predict how long the lawsuit would affect her and her colleagues' days and weeks. She remembered that on the hike with Harold, Larry Beale and Nicole Furlani had asked how long they would have to walk. Right now, as they had, Sophia craved the protection of a time-defined schedule. She dreaded the path ahead. How valid were the Tompkinses' claims about Harold? So many unknowns. Curiosity maddened her.

Before going to bed, Sophia eyed her journal without opening it. Journal writing was her nightly regimen, but she knew that when she was upset, the fast flow of words took a long time to scrawl. She would lose track of time, get to sleep too late, and feel gross the next day.

Sophia wished she had a best friend she could call. She was reluctant to call her mom. Persephone would be supportive, but Sophia never liked to complain to her mother. Sophia felt grateful and guilty that she could walk. Every day she remembered her mother dropping her off at school on April 22, 1989. Sophia jumped out of the car so quick, not checking behind her. Persephone leapt out to run after her daughter with the lunchbox, so Sophia wouldn't have to have saltines for lunch again. Like her daughter, Persephone didn't adequately check behind her, and another parent who was pulling out at that moment ran into her. Persephone would spend the rest of her life confined to a wheelchair.

"I'm not confined by my wheelchair!" Persephone would have exclaimed. Her mother had a constructive perspective. She often observed that she was only confined physically, and that she had never met a person who wasn't confined by something. In a commencement address at Cornell, Persephone said, "I'm calmer and freer than 99.9 percent of you, especially since many of you are academics."

Persephone's definition of happiness was peace of mind, and she said she enjoyed peace in every way except financially. Martin said he couldn't bear to accept the money Connie kept offering and Connie taunted him for what she thought of as excessive pride every time he declined.

Sophia checked the time. Then she wrote the day's date and decided not to write any sentence that included the word "lawsuit." It would stain the page. Instead she made a list, because list-making temporarily abated fear.

1) Nauseated
2) Dizzy
3) searing, scary trepidation
4) uncertainty

Sophia wrote these words over and over again, so the list ran up to eight items long, then twelve, then sixteen, up to forty-eight. The concrete action of numbering these repetitions dulled the meaning of the words.

Sophia slept fitfully. The next morning, she felt too tired to bike to school, though she usually didn't let herself drive in two days in a row because biking was environmentally friendlier.

Dawn met her in the lobby, looking as tired as Sophia felt. They ducked into the library for privacy. Sophia felt pained by the sight of book spines with tantalizing titles. She wondered how long it would be before she could anticipate her schedule again, so she could pencil in her daily thirty minutes of reading for fun.

"I got um…served," Sophia told Dawn.

"Barbara was too."

"How did she react?"

"She's fine. You know how she is. And she has less to worry— hey, do you remember that Prayer for Relief phrase that we were wondering about yesterday?"

"Please tell me it means the Tompkinses are fundamentalists and the judge will be skeptical."

"No. Unfortunately. It's a standard phrase in complaints."

"Shoot."

"Peter got us a great lawyer. An associate from his firm who will represent us pro bono. I want you to meet with him as soon as possible."

"Okay." Sophia avoided meeting Dawn's eyes. Her gaze landed on a shoe box of due date cards. She longed for the days of her early childhood, when her only sense of transgression was from overdue books.

Dawn continued, "Peter says we need to collect everything in writing that's even remotely related to the incident. For the discovery process. Emails, and anything in your or Barbara's or my files. Don't you keep a teaching journal? To document the kids' reactions to each scavenger hunt?"

"Yes," Sophia said tentatively.

"I remember you said you write about every hunt in detail, so you'll know how to revise them for future lessons. I'm sure you wrote up that hike, since it was the first hunt of the school year?'

"Uh. Right."

"Okay, so you should photocopy that whole entry, and any other pages in your teaching journal that mention Harold or the pokeberries."

Sophia's stomach lurched.

"Oh, and make some extra copies," Dawn said, thinking aloud. "For Stephen Lanham, and of course for the lawyer. He has your number and will call you directly."

"Okay."

"Are you all right?"

"Yeah."

"This whole thing is awful," Dawn said. "But I feel calmer than I did yesterday. Peter and I talked again this morning. He says that as long as we can prove you pass the reasonable professional standard, they won't be able to prove negligence. No one's more dedicated to the students than you. Your teaching journal account will convey your devotion."

"Thanks," Sophia said abstractedly, wishing she had never bragged to Dawn about keeping a teaching journal. Her journal was really a ventilator for everything. Although most entries were full of lesson plans and goals, the pages were also stuffed with overlong screeds about Connie. Those parts were inconsistent expressions of gratitude punctuated by rage. More straightforward complaints decried the sins of students with bad manners, or teachers who didn't think on their feet as quickly as Sophia did.

Sophia had bitched and moaned plenty about Harold. She was pretty sure she hadn't written anything that would make her appear sympathetic like, "…thank goodness he healed quickly."

"I should get to my office," Sophia said. She couldn't wait to shut the door, pull out her 2008-2009 journal, and assess the damage.

"Do you want to come to my office for lunch?" Dawn asked.

"I'm not hungry."

"You probably just finished one of your insanely healthy, ecologically responsible breakfasts."

"Yeah," Sophia said. She had lost her appetite forever. Dawn, Stephen Lanham, and Barbara Ford the three people in the world Sophia most wanted to protect from her rant. Then she realized she was equally loathe to have Carver parents and her parents, and Connie, read it. At least the chances that they would see it were slim.

As Sophia closed the door to her office, she glanced at the section of her bulletin board that she had studded with Countess Connie quotes. A sun-bleached line hit too close to home:

They are children, not immature adults.

Connie had written this to scold Sophia for making fun of a whiney student. Now Sophia noticed it was a six-word sentence, and that coincidence gave it the force of a magic spell.

She tore it down. Then she ripped the weathered paper into shards before tossing it in the recycle bin, because she felt paranoid enough to imagine some nosy student unearthing the quote if she left it whole.

Sophia opened the previous year's journal and rifled pages until she found what she remembered:

Harold took up a surprising amount of space on the trail, considering how scrawny he is...

In those bright yellow pajamas, he might as well have been a marquee: "Now Playing: Here Comes Trouble!"

I don't want to be stuck with this pint-sized asshole for three years.

...that hooting laugh made me want to smack him.

What a morbid way for the other sixth graders to have to begin their school year and their Carver experience. That little shit.

How unkind to have written these things just hours after Harold had barfed his brains out all over the art room.

She wished she'd been far-sighted enough to anticipate that the Tompkinses might sue, and that if they did, this journal entry, as an account of Harold's injury, would be relevant. Hmm. Relevant? That wasn't the right word. She scanned her memory for "Law and Order" episodes. "Discoverable." The journal entry was probably discoverable, and when the Tompkinses discovered its contents, they would be furious.

Their lawyer would be delighted. Dawn would be horrified, no, not just horrified, disgusted.

What if the students found out? Wouldn't they hear if the case went to trial? How likely was a trial?

Until right now, Sophia had always been grateful that her personal and professional life were inextricable. Her identity as an educator was her soul. Carver gave her such a sense of purpose that she woke up each morning without an alarm, and kept her journal by her bed because she often got ideas before drifting off to sleep. Now, the lack of boundaries between her private foibles and professional responsibility threatened the school community.

Sophia looked back down at the horrible entry, and noticed something she hadn't seen before. Most of the mean things she'd said about Harold appeared on the pages before the section on the pokeberry bush. And the last mean remark she had made, about Harold ruining things for everyone, came after the passages where he took ill and went to the hospital. This unplanned structure meant the mean parts could be separated from her account of the events mentioned in the lawsuit. Excellent. She'd just photocopy the midsection of the entry. She'd explain that, contrary to what she had told Dawn before, the teaching journal was equally a private diary, and that the beginning and ending of the entry weren't relevant to the case. Sure, that's how she'd handle this. It would save everyone a lot of upset. Okay. Fine. A solution.

Sophia took a deep, centering breath, as Connie called it. Funny how Sophia never remembered to take a deep breath until after it would have helped her. Then she remembered Dawn's exact words:

"...you should photocopy that whole entry..."

Sophia covered her face with her hands. The protection of her palms on her cheeks and temples gave her a warming tingle up her back. The warmth made her feel better. There was a bright side to the way Dawn had worded her request, for the *whole* entry. That wording would protect Sophia from her impulse to be sneaky. How would she have lived with herself, knowing she'd gone down the wrong path? And maybe the mean parts of her journal entry could be hidden by attorney-client privilege, a delicious "Law and Order" phrase.

Sophia looked back up at her bulletin board, at the empty beige space where the ripped-down quote had been. She regretted ripping it down and sighed. She told herself to chillax, a word she had heard her students use over and over again. She liked that word, and wished she could chillax about Connie. It was tedious to obsess about family drama, the way her students obsessed about their crushes and their enemies. Her gaze shifted to a another Connie-ism:

REGRET is the price you pay for wasting time wishing you could rewind time.
FRUSTRATION is the price you pay for wasting time wishing you could fast forward time.
Live here, now, to conquer both.

But Sophia was already slipping out of the present moment. She was unable to keep herself from reliving the regret and frustration she had felt as a seventeen year old, when she had been doubly caught—first, caught by impulse, then caught as a consequence of the impulse.

On the second floor of Sophia's childhood home, Connie had turned an old sleeping porch into a meditation space that she

55

used, rain or shine, because she said meditation rendered her impervious to temperature.

In *My Spiritual Quest: Revising Buddhism's Four Noble Truths and the Eightfold Path,* Connie recommended augmenting Buddhist vipassana mediation with techniques from early Christianity and Catholic "mental prayer."

At Connie's lectures, many people had asked her to describe her daily meditation regimen. *"Which one of those three do you think is best?"* and *"Do you combine those three?"* were two questions asked over and over again.

Connie never satisfied their curiosity. She said, "You're approaching meditation mechanically, as though it were a physical workout, like doing two sets of eight pushups."

"But Connie," Sophia once protested after a lecture, "you just finished telling those people that they should use your two favorite tools, numbers and lists, to control themselves."

"Two minutes, four minutes, eight minutes. Not long enough for daily meditation," Connie murmured, like a Zen master speaking English as a second language.

"So how do you meditate?" Sophia asked, echoing Connie's fans.

Connie cryptically said, "There are two types of actions: those you count on to control, and those that transcend control. But I'd never write about that distinction, or tell my audience about that, because it is something they have to discover for themselves."

A few weeks later, on a warm day in May, Sophia went up to the attic to bring down some summer clothes. Her flirtatious driving instructor was cute, and she was looking forward to wearing a sundress to her lesson. She happened to glance out the attic window, across the lawn to where the woods began. "The woods are full of great climbing trees," Connie often observed.

Sophia realized that one of those trees faced Connie's meditation porch. On impulse, Sophia decided to use that tree as a ladder, to spy on Connie while she meditated.

Except that when Sophia climbed up and found herself a perch, she saw Connie wasn't meditating.

Connie was reading a magazine while eating something that resembled a submarine sandwich. Actually, it *was* a submarine sandwich. The sight was ironic, given the draconian weight loss advice in *Live Like Your Days Are Numbered.*

Sophia ogled Connie's private moment until the tree sap on her palms became cloying. As she washed her hands at the basement sink a few minutes later, she resolved never to spy on Connie again. What she had just seen was satisfying enough to last forever. Sophia would never envy Connie again. She felt powerful, for the first time in her life, because she knew Connie's secret. Even if this afternoon had been an aberration, how wonderful to imagine that it wasn't an aberration. How wonderful to imagine that Connie was just like the seekers and snackers who flocked to her book readings.

Connie was both hider and seeker.

If only Sophia had stuck to her resolution. Instead, she began spying on Connie regularly. Each time, Connie was reading and eating. Fritos were her frequent snack of choice. Sophia could only see the color of the magazines and books, not their titles, but they were usually thick paperbacks. Sophia recognized one lavender-colored volume as a mass-market self-help book that Connie had ridiculed. Connie was highlighting passages in it and nodding to herself. Sophia giggled. And then, Connie stood up. Maybe this was coincidental, Sophia assured herself. Connie could not have heard a giggle. But if Connie had not heard Sophia, she must have sensed the teenager's presence the way one senses an unwanted gaze. Connie looked out the window. Sophia froze like a scared squirrel but it was too late. Connie locked her into a staring contest.

Chapter 6: A Hot Lawyer Invades Sophia's Privacy

Sophia couldn't remember a time when she hadn't lived in Connie's shadow and in Connie's light. Connie said painful things, Connie said insightful things. Some of Connie's advice was outstanding, though her books were absurd.

Connie never mentioned the spying incident. She acted as if Sophia had never done it, and even became nicer for a long time. She gave Sophia tips about boys and homemade beauty potions. Thanks to Connie's advice, Sophia had never been dumped by a boyfriend. She attributed her stainless romantic past to Connie's Queen Guinevere Rule: Don't date anyone more attractive than you. Conservative advice, well-suited to Connie's belief that everyone should pair up or die as soon as they possibly could.

The first thing Sophia noticed about Carver's pro bono lawyer, Daniel Giordano, was that his curly brown hair seemed too sexy and shaggy for lawyer-hair. His dark eyes reminded her of Connie's and Ryan's dark eyes. Oops. Giordano was staring because she was staring. Stop. She pursed her lips. He grinned flirtatiously.

Men never flirted with Sophia until they became familiar with her hip career and her confidence about it. She believed this was because her physical features were bland, and her ex-boyfriends had bland looks too. They were virtuous men who shared her politics. They were environmentally friendly and read every book that she read first. If Jack hadn't pressured her for more, and then moved to Indonesia to revamp a Peace Corps field office, she would have stuck with him—at least for another year or so.

"Thanks for taking our case, Mr. Giordano," Sophia said.

"Mr. Giordano's my dad. I'm Danny," he replied. "And I should thank you. This will be a good break from my usual soulless grind."

Huh? A good break? Harold had been hurt, and now Carver and her career were endangered. The discovery process was going to reveal she was a jerk. Sophia looked over her shoulder, scanning carrels and stacks. She was glad Barbara Ford hadn't come in yet, and that Ms. Ruiz, the librarian, left by one-thirty every afternoon. No one else had witnessed how glibly this hotshot had referred to the lawsuit. When should she warn Dawn that he was arrogant and might be careless? Before or after the shock of Sophia's no-holds-barred journal reportage? She took a deep breath. "Reportage" wasn't the right term. "Reportage" referred to an account that had been written to be shared. Her journal should be hers alone. Except it wasn't.

"We should get started," Danny suggested.

"Shouldn't we wait for Barbara Ford? I assume she will be joining us?"

"She and I spoke already. Barbara's role in this is peripheral and simpler than yours. The pokeberry activity wasn't her idea, after all."

Sophia nodded and was about to speak before Danny continued.

"She felt bad about having to admit that."

"Barbara's an amazing teacher and artist," Sophia said quickly. "She shows the kids how to make art supplies out of containers and other things that usually wind up in the trash."

Danny opened his laptop and turned it on. "It's good you two get along so well, because I'm sure Priscilla Mathers, the Tompkinses' attorney, will try to intimidate Barbara into pointing the finger at you."

"Oh."

"Yes. And I should also warn you that Mathers will compliment your botanical expertise at the deposition, but she will do it to turn your knowledge against you."

"Oh." Sophia frowned. "Well. I'm not even sure I'd call myself a botanist."

"Doesn't matter. For the purposes of this case, you might as well be. My impression is that Harold was known to be a troublemaker."

"Yes." Sophia agreed. Those bright yellow pajamas screamed Caution! Caution!

"I need to show you something," she told Danny. "Because Dawn said I needed to give you everything related to the, um, incident."

"Right." He looked as smooth as paper.

"The day after that hike...I wrote about what happened in my teaching journal. But, my teaching journal is also my diary."

She handed him the pages, and clasped her sweaty hands together.

When he finished reading, he seemed about to speak, but then he picked the pages back up and scanned them.

"You're funny enough to be a comedienne, but that won't help you in this case, no pun intended."

Her eyes filled with tears. She looked up at the lights on the ceiling, as if the light could dry them.

"Oh my gosh," Danny pulled a handkerchief from his pocket and held it out to her. "I don't usually make women cry this fast."

"I wasn't crying," Sophia said. "I suffer from seasonal allergies."

"Okay, but there's nothing to cry over," Danny said. "You were smart to bring this to our first meeting. The sooner I can deal with it the better."

She nodded.

"Are you going to cry again or can I continue?"

"I was not crying," Sophia muttered. "Can we hide the journal from the Tompkinses? You could use the phrase 'attorney-client privilege', couldn't you?"

"No." He smiled. "Because you wrote it for yourself, not for a lawyer."

"Oh."

"According to discovery rules, I'm afraid you'll have to give me the journal to review and photocopy for Priscilla Mathers. I'll messenger it over. We need to give her everything related to Harold, the hike, and everything you've done for the school. You don't drink too much or do drugs, do you?"

"No drugs but uh, what do you think is too much drinking?"

He grinned. "Well, if you were a celebrity, and someone did an episode of 'True Hollywood Story' about you, how many minutes would they devote to your drinking habits?"

"Oh. Not too much. Sometimes I drink a glass of wine over the course of a weekend," she lied.

"No DWIs? No mornings waking up in a stranger's bed, or covered in vomit and wedged behind a dumpster?"

"Nope. None of that." Then a mortifying realization turned Sophia's stomach. "Wait a minute. If I have to give you the journal, does that mean you get to read the whole thing?"

"Yes. I have to. In order to represent you properly," Danny said. "But I won't relish the task."

"This sucks."

He nodded sympathetically.

"You don't get it. I'm a private person. A lot of people say they are but I really am. This is worse than having you poke around through—" She was about to say "underwear drawer," but that would be a tad too vivid. What had she written about sex with Jack? What about her slight crush on Tariq, that brilliant new science teacher who hadn't yet noticed her brilliance?

And then she realized that Danny would find out her godmother was Countess Connie.

"There's something I need to let you know right away," she said.

"Another bombshell?"

"No, it has nothing to do with the case, but my godmother is famous, and I say a lot of mean things about her in my journal. Private things."

"Who is she?'

"Countess Connie."

"The new age lady?"

"Yes. None of my colleagues know I'm related to her. And I don't want them to find out."

Danny considered this for a minute. "If your boss or Stephen Lanham asks to see the whole journal, I have to give it to them, but I won't volunteer it, and I'm sure they would honor your privacy, especially sensitive passages about your family."

"That's true," Sophia nodded. Dawn and Stephen were not gossipy. Stephen would never bring up Countess Connie in Sophia's presence. He wouldn't think about it twice. Dawn might bring it up but in a gentle way. Though it might hurt Dawn's feelings that Sophia had kept such a big personal secret.

When Dawn founded Carver, Sophia was her first hire. Shortly after meeting, they went out to lunch and made an error that entwined their lives in an unusual way.

Two months after their lunch, Sophia had her credit card out to make a student loan payment when she realized her Capi-City credit card wasn't her card. It looked the same as hers, but the card number was different and so was the name on the card: *Dawn Jordan*. Sophia's stomach flipflopped. How had her new boss's card gotten there? Would Dawn think she had stolen it? And, oh God, how long had Sophia been using this card, thinking it was her own? She fled to her computer, grateful to have online access to her account. Two purchases had been made that afternoon, at a gas station and at Luscious LoCal, the yuppie organic market that Sophia went to for foods she couldn't grow, or find at farmers markets, or through her contacts with local meat and dairy producers. Sophia felt worried to see these purchases because she hadn't been to either place that day, and she hadn't made the other purchases that she saw on her online statement. Curiously, all those purchases were from vendors and restaurants that she liked, and whoever was using her card was as frugal as she was. Sophia drank a vodka tonic to get her courage up, and then called Dawn to let her know she had her Visa card.

"That's impossible…" Dawn said. Confusion perforated her words. "I just used it a few hours ago. It's in my wallet. I think…Just a sec."

Dawn had Sophia's credit card. Both women were mystified

until they mentally retraced their steps. They must have switched cards when they had lunch together. Sophia had insisted on splitting the tab because even though Dawn had invited her out to as part of the job offer process, Sophia never felt comfortable letting someone else pay her way.

Dawn called Sophia back after reviewing her most recent statement. "You know, I think the reason I didn't notice this switch earlier is because your spending habits mirror mine. And you shop at the exact same places. We must have a lot in common."

Since that comedy of errors, Dawn had been Sophia's best friend at Carver. Dawn admired Sophia's spontaneity, and Sophia admired Dawn's equanimity.

Danny told Sophia that he would get a protective order so that anything in the journal that wasn't relevant would be kept confidential. "And Mathers will have to return her copy of the journal or certify that she destroyed it."

"What are the chances that the case will go to trial?"

"Can't say at this point. And there's another problem, aside from the fact that you slammed this kid in your diary."

She winced.

"You mention at the end of the entry how concerned you are about the effect the poisoning would have on the other sixth graders, since they know nothing about the natural world, and you talk about doing risk assessment activities with them, and a lesson about safer sources of natural dyes. You list raspberries and red cabbage and beets, and two medieval-sounding plants: dyer's greenweed and woad. Why didn't you use one of these safer plants in the first place? What's so special about pokeberries?"

"I know," Sophia said. "In hindsight, I wish we'd used something else to make the ink, but I had several reasons for choosing pokeberries." She pulled a paper out of her folder to refer to it. "First, I have a list of several other environmental education programs which make pokeberry ink with kids as part of their curriculum. Second, I have three books of nature projects to do with children that mention writing with pokeberry ink, and their directions and precautions are consistent with the ones I took."

Danny nodded as though she was going to continue and she did. "The last reason is a personal one. My godmother and I used to make pokeberry ink when I was very little, and I used the ink to write words on homemade paper. So I guess you could say my godmother led me astray."

"Not a helpful fairy godmother, eh?"

"That's the perfect way to express my relationship with her. Not that I don't love her, and I'm grateful to her for—"

"You're getting off track," Danny said.

"Sorry. Won't it help my case that I've done pokeberry ink projects so many times before without incident?"

"The problem is that once you knew you had a troublemaker in your midst—and the diary entry makes your awareness painfully clear—you should have modified the activity on the spot. And, the permission slip makes no mention of poisonous berries. That's another big problem."

"Right. Dawn's been over that with me."

"I agree with her that the parents oversight committee that the Tompkinses requested must be convened as soon as possible."

"Darn."

"Don't worry about it. From what I've heard, you are popular with the parents."

"That's true, but I worry that the type of parent who joins an oversight committee will be one of our squeakier wheels." She was thinking of John Simpson's paranoia and suspicion. "Maybe it could be a parent-teacher oversight committee."

"That should work," Danny said. "I heard from your colleague Barbara that you are wildly creative. She told me about your scavenger hunt format. She also said you came up with the school's motto, 'Curiosity is Fuel.'"

Sophia squirmed with pride and embarrassment. "It's pointless to do a hunt for something kids aren't curious to find."

"Are you modest?"

"Huh?" That was a bold question. Like a rake's line from a nineteenth-century British novel. But then Sophia realized he wasn't talking about sexual modesty, because he added, "If I were a teacher, especially at a school as worthwhile as this one, I'd brag about my work all the time."

"On the contrary, I am comfortable bragging about myself," Sophia said. "But it's more productive and honest for me to brag about Carver and the students. Successful teaching requires a three-legged stool, I mean, not a real stool, but you have to have both an administration and parent body that supports innovation. And bright kids who haven't been turned off of school yet."

"Your scavenger hunt idea is a great way to channel the kids' hunter-gatherer impulses."

"Exactly. That's my priority. I keep things simple, no more than eight steps per hunt. Otherwise I'll lose them. They'll collapse into chattering, mostly about sneakers and video games."

"Everyone's a hunter-gatherer," Danny said.

"Well, the hunts are my framing device," she said matter-of-factly but not too matter-of-factly. She was cueing him to flirt again, but not too soon.

"I like that phrase, 'framing device.' Maybe that's what I like about writing legal briefs," Danny said. "I find them much easier to complete than the papers I had to write in college because they've got a formulaic structure. I just plug in the facts, or rather, the way I want to frame the facts, and the briefs write themselves."

"Picasso said something about that."

"About legal briefs?"

She laughed. "Nope. He said, 'Forcing yourself to use restricted means is the sort of restraint that liberates invention. It obliges you to make a kind of progress that you can't even imagine in advance.'"

"Is that from a speech that your students memorized or something?"

"No, I memorized it. I collect quotes and that's one of my favorites. It's on the wall in my office."

"'Restraint liberates invention.' I like the sound of restraint." Danny winked at her.

"Picasso was referring to structural restrictions," Sophia replied, tinting her voice with irritation. She would not flatter him by flirting, the way so many women probably did. But the guy looked sharp in his suit, all buttoned up. Although he probably never had time to exercise or even get outside much. He was pale, and might have a paunch from working long hours, she assured herself. The suit fit so well because he frittered away thousands of dollars on expensive clothes instead of donating it to nonprofits that didn't have enough money to help people whose lives were unbearable. One of her father's anti-lawyer rants echoed in her mind.

"Dressers of language," Martin had scoffed. "Educators explicate, lawyers complicate."

"Explicate's a complicated word," Persephone had teased. "But it does rhyme." Persephone didn't hate lawyers. She agreed with Connie and most pop psychologists that when people couldn't stand a character trait in another person, it was because they shared that trait. Persephone had once told Martin that he didn't like lawyers because "you overdo wordplay, and lawyers play on words like musical instruments." Persephone's figures of speech were often musical. She was a professor emeritus in Cornell's music department, and played the jazz clarinet before her accident.

Another time, when Martin's anti-lawyer rant was fueled by wine, Connie cryptically mused, "Words lie, but numbers never lie."

"What on earth does that mean?" Martin barked at her. "Even for you that makes no sense."

"Stop it, Martin," Persephone said quietly. "Or at least don't speak that way to her when I'm in the room."

Connie and Persephone had been friends since they met in elementary school. Connie's mother had run away with another man when Connie was a baby. Because of this, Persephone felt sorry for Connie no matter what Connie did. She smiled sadly whenever Connie made grandiose comments. For better and for worse, Persephone allowed Connie to treat Sophia like the daughter she would never have. When Sophia, as a teenager, had complained that Connie was too strict, Persephone said, "She never learned how to mother a daughter because her mother abandoned her. And strict is good. Connie dotes on you."

Only years later would Sophia find more accurate words than "strict" to describe what bothered her about Connie. "Shaming" and "sadistic" came to mind. Words too powerful to share with her parents, because she didn't want to make them feel bad for saddling her with an ungentle godmother.

At the end of Danny and Sophia's meeting, he asked her if she had time to show him around before he left. "It would help me paint a heartwarming description of the school."

She raised an eyebrow.

"What?" he asked.

"You're the most glib person I've met in as long as I can remember. It's disconcerting."

"Sorry."

"That's okay. Carver *is* heartwarming, among other qualities. I would be happy to show you the school garden, and our curriculum revolves around it. The students in the after school program will be out there."

How good it would be to get outside. Wholesome, unlike what she had written about Harold in her journal entry.

Chapter 7: Is That Guy, Like, Your Boyfriend?

As they marched down the stairwell, Sophia checked out Danny's spotless loafers. "The ground will be muddy. You probably don't have sneakers with you."

"Yes, in the trunk of my car I have running shoes and squash shoes. I play squash a few times a week. You probably don't play it." She noticed he had echoed her words.

"No, but I eat squash a few times a week."

"Cute. Thanks for suggesting sneakers, but I'm not going to bother to change shoes."

"We have a bunch of plastic grocery bags in the shed, and rubber bands. You could rig up some booties."

"I'm more into booty than booties."

"You wouldn't feel self-conscious, if that's what you're worried about. A lot of the kids wear plastic bags so they won't get their sneakers dirty. And I'm sure we'll see some of the adult volunteers wearing all manner of grotesque rubber clogs. The volunteers used to own this garden, before they donated their community garden plots to us. They're so devoted to our mission that a lot of them drop in on their way home from work without changing out of their work clothes first. The garden is fashionista-free."

"I don't mind dirtiness." Danny said. Sophia thought the innuendos were wearing thin and telepathically suggested he cut them out.

Danny didn't speak at first sight of the garden. She waited.

"Eden," he said finally. She looked where he was looking, at the grid of raised beds, sprouting green in all shapes and heights. She told him the garden was organized into Seven Wonders.

"Our social studies teacher, Nadia Badavi, chose the allusion to the seven wonders of the ancient world because George Washington Carver promoted so many organic farming methods that are thousands of years old. Most people who know about him know about his innovations, but they don't realize he recycled knowledge as well."

"Roots and wings," Danny murmured.

"Exactly. How do you know that phrase? I associate it with needlepoint cushions."

"I did needlepoint in law school to relax."

"No you didn't."

"True. But my mother does many needlepoint pillows. She made me pillows with my college and law school insignias. I didn't have the cajones to put them on my bed in college or law school, but they suburbanize my living room now." He crouched down to read the label beside a patch of spaghetti squash.

"Hasta La Pasta? Did your kids make that up?"

"That's its real name. We have five criteria when we choose plants: nutrition, natural disease resistance, heartiness, funny or interesting names, and rich beautiful colors. To attract the kids."

"What makes the dirt smell so good?" Danny asked.

"Health. Our soil's well-composted."

"Whoa." He bobbed back up again, lifted his foot to inspect the bottom of his shoe. "What's in the compost?" he asked quietly. "Is it, um..., manure?"

She was sure the words "shit" or "poop" had come to the forefront of his brain while he groped for the politer term.

"Not our compost," she assured him. "Manure would freak out our city kids. We compost with garden clippings, kitchen waste, paper products, and sawdust. The pile is set off from the rest of the garden by those hay bales. See over there? The hay degrades to make the mix richer."

"Hi Miz Green," Victor called to her from the pizza patch.

Sophia introduced him to Danny. Victor showed off the tomatoes, onions, sweet peppers, sage, and oregano.

"Maggie, our kitchen garden director, teaches the students how to make and preserve tomato sauce, so we have plenty for pizza parties during the school year," Sophia said.

"None of our vegetables are GMOed," Victor said proudly.

"Does GMO mean genetically-modified?" Danny asked.

"Yeah. GMOed food is Frankenstein food." Victor grinned. "Hey Miz Green, for this year's Halloween party, why don't we serve Frankenfood?"

Sophia rolled her eyes. "Yeah right. We would have to revoke our charter. Will you tell Mr. Giordano about the cauliflower?"

The yellow-orange cauliflower plants were Victor's favorites.

"This variety is called cheddar or citrus. They sell out in five seconds at the farmers market. 'Cause of the name. And they're healthier, and they're good when you make them with real cheddar cheese sauce, not the Velveeta glue my family used to eat. The white ones they sell in supermarkets look gray next this kind. So I don't want to eat those white ones any more,"

Victor admitted. "They look nasty like brains sawed out of the top of a victim's head when they're still alive. By a mad scientist."

"Are you already looking forward to Halloween?" Sophia said.

"I've been looking forward to Halloween since July."

"What grade are you in, son?" Danny asked.

"Seventh."

He was Harold's age, and as boisterous as Harold.

"Thanks for showing me the garden," Danny said, turning to Sophia. She wondered if he sounded abrupt because he, too, had related Victor's youth to Harold's.

"May I bring you back to the lobby through our kitchen? " she asked Danny. "We've got a cold pantry which the kids help build."

"Holy Little House on the Prairie," Danny quipped. "I would like to see that."

"Our kitchen director teaches the kids to preserve fruits and vegetables by canning them. They also dry apples and herbs, and store about 200 pounds of stone ground flour from a mill in Raphine, Virginia." She wondered if Danny realized what a blow it would be to get rid of field trips, and added, "I wish I could bring the kids to that mill, so they could see where their wheat is ground and learn how to do it." Maybe hint-dropping was too subtle. She mentioned her concern outright. Danny's reaction was negligible. She would have to bring it up again at a future meeting.

"This looks like a loft," Danny said admiringly when they reached the kitchen. Plate glass lined the right wall, filling the white room with natural light. Appliances and two sinks lined the left, and there were several butcher block islands in the middle, one of which was occupied by Bernard, Maggie's son, his friend Rashid, and the contents of their knapsacks. It wasn't clear from the messy table whether they'd just been doing homework or playing videogames.

"Hi Miz Green," Rashid said, while Bernard nodded. Rashid, whose knapsack was bigger, slid his DSi behind its bulk.

"Does Franklin know you're down here?"

"Yeah, we signed out," said Bernard. His voice wasn't as friendly as usual. Was this because he didn't know Danny? Or had Bernard overheard Maggie and her husband discuss the lawsuit?

"Bernard, Rashid, this is Mr. Giordano. I'm showing him around." She didn't think she'd need to say anything else. Students were used to being observed by donors and visiting teachers and administrators from other urban environmental programs. So why was Bernard frowning? After he and Rashid exchanged glances, Sophia decided against asking one of them to tell Danny about the cold pantry.

"The pantry is at the bottom of these stairs," she told Danny. She took her keys out and opened the thickly insulated door for him, gesturing for him to step inside ahead of her.

"There's no electrical source of refrigeration in here," she explained, pride lifting her mood. "The kids and several teachers dug seven feet down to create it, but we refer to it as a 'cool pantry' instead of a cellar because it's drier than most root cellars, so we can store a greater variety of foods. Oh, and the door has a safety release, so no one can get locked in, and we don't keep perishable items like dairy products or meats in here. It's not cold enough."

Danny didn't seem to be listening. He was standing by a group of two-foot-high clear plastic canisters. "I haven't seen this much white powder since the 80s."

She grinned.

After he'd admired the sugar and flours, Sophia pointed out an alcove at the back, where the canned goods were shelved. Danny admired the colorful labels the kids had designed.

"Come up whenever you're ready," she said, and went back up the stairs. She hoped Danny would linger in the pantry, so she could see whether the boys would be friendlier without him.

Bernard and Rashid were whispering, and stopped as soon as she reentered the kitchen.

"What's up?" she asked them.

"Is that guy, like, your boyfriend?"

"Bernard! Shut up, man," Rashid hissed. "Sorry, Miz Green."

"You boys are full of beans," she replied, feeling relieved now that she understood. Her kids had never seen her alone with a guy before. Donors and visiting teachers came through in groups. She bet Bernard and Rashid assumed she was a spinster, though she doubted they knew that word.

"I'm not her boyfriend, unfortunately," said a deep voice behind her. Sophia whirled around. She liked Danny's boldness, though it was unfortunate that he'd said "unfortunately" he wasn't her boyfriend. Rashid and Bernard were gossipers and would tell everyone that "we met this dude who's crushin' on Miz Green."

"I'm a new volunteer," Danny was telling Bernard and Rashid.

Sophia's stomach lurched at this description. Danny was not a new volunteer. He had lied, just as her father said all lawyers lied.

"I'll show you out," Sophia told Danny. "See you boys later."

"Later Miz G," Rashid echoed.

Only after Sophia had said goodbye to Danny did she realize he hadn't lied. As the school's pro bono attorney, he *was* volunteering. Now she wished she had not ushered him out so fast.

It was time to face Dawn with the world's meanest journal entry.

Chapter 8: I'll Never Keep a Journal Again

Behind the closed door of Dawn's office, Dawn read Sophia's journal entry while Sophia sat across from her. Sophia read Dawn's facial expressions and gestures because she couldn't bear to look away. Dawn grimaced. She read more, then grimaced more. At times she shielded her eyes from the pages, or from Sophia.

Finally Dawn spoke. "Has Stephen gotten a copy of this yet?"

"No. Just Daniel Giordano."

"What did he say?"

Sophia pulled out a page of notes.

"Oh, didn't you have a chance yet to fully document your meeting with him in your diary?"

It was the first time Dawn had ever spoken to her sarcastically.

"No. My notes from the meeting are just a numbered list." She slumped back in the chair, and debriefed Dawn.

When Sophia had finished, Dawn said, "I have to call Peter and Stephen about this right now, then I'll fax them copies because I can't summarize it."

"I'll do it. I owe it to you to take care of this mess myself."

"You can't," Dawn said, shaking her head. "They'll be angrier if they don't hear it from me."

Sophia nodded.

"I wish you had anticipated you might have to disclose everything you wrote down about Harold's injury. Didn't I ask you last year to give me anything you had written about Harold?"

"Yes, but after I drafted the incident report for Peter I focused on printing out emails that I had exchanged about it with colleagues."

"Stop journaling about anything having to do with Carver. And while you're at it, well, I don't know if this is fair to request, but you might want to think twice about writing down anything that would make you look dysfunctional."

"Okay."

" Of all my friends, you drink the most. Were you drinking while you wrote that rant about Harold?"

"No," Sophia said though she couldn't remember if she had been. "I'm not a big drinker, Dawn. And I've never driven after drinking more than a glass of wine."

"That doesn't mean you couldn't stand to drink less."

Sophia assured herself that Dawn wasn't a good judge of alcohol consumption since she didn't drink and the people closest to her probably didn't drink either.

"You should take off," Dawn said. "I need to call Stephen." She looked at her phone, then back at Sophia. "And I need to be at all your meetings with Giordano from now on. I want to make sure nothing falls through the cracks that could hurt us at the deposition."

"I think Danny's going to work hard for us," Sophia said as stood up to leave.

"You call him by his first name?" Dawn raised an eyebrow.

"He said he prefers to be called Danny."

"He didn't tell me that." Dawn sounded suspicious.

"Well, after I told him about the wretched journal entry, I wanted to shift focus by showing him how great Carver is. So I gave him a tour. And he met Victor, Bernard, and Rashid. They impressed him. I think he'll like us."

"I don't care if he likes us or not," Dawn said through gritted teeth.

"But he's more motivated now. To protect us."

"To protect us? Or just you?" Dawn gave her a hard look, then turned away to pick up the phone.

Sophia had to concentrate on making it out the door, then down the hallway, and down the stairs to the parking lot. She was determined to drive away before the tears came. Salt stung her eyes. And then she saw Tariq.

"Hey," she said.

He nodded and walked past her, also heading for the parking lot. She did not think it was collegial for him to walk ahead when they were going the same way.

Tariq was parked a few cars down from her own. He slid his briefcase onto the passenger seat and was headed for the driver's side door when she caught up with him.

"Nice wheels!"

"Thanks."

"Prius?"

"Uh… yeah."

She felt sort of silly. She didn't want him to think she didn't know what a Prius was.

"'Bye," he said, opening his driver's side door.

"Once the new aquarium's set up, would you assign some students to save its waste water for the garden?"

"Of course."

"Thanks." Sophia was disappointed that she hadn't knocked Tariq's socks off with her resourceful idea to reuse fish tank waste water. He said "Of course" derisively, as if she had just suggested that recycling paper might be better than throwing it in the garbage. She missed her mom, and wished she could be comforted by her mother in person, but she didn't want to face Connie, and her mom wouldn't visit DC. Since the accident, Persephone feared of the loss of independence she might encounter while traveling by train or plane, and she wasn't wild about spending a lot of time in cars either. She confined herself to Ithaca the way the mythological Persephone was confined to Hades between growing seasons.

An hour after getting home from work, Sophia had dined on two bowls of granola and was curled up on the living room couch. Through the telephone, her mother was saying all the right things. "Please don't torture yourself with guilt, darling. The only people who don't make mistakes are the people who don't do anything substantive, and despite your anticipation, I know this episode will turn out better than you expect—just a minute." Sophia could hear her parents conferring. Or bickering.

"Hold your horses, Martin," her mother said.

Persephone sounded exasperated when she got back on the phone. "Your father's dying to talk to you. He's ripping the receiver out of my hand."

Sophia heard her dad apologize to her mom. "I'm sorry for being impatient, Perse, but you're sugarcoating reality like a snowfall." It was true. Persephone was not a worrier. Despite what had happened to her.

"Sophia? You can talk to Mom again later. We gotta strategize. First, you need your own lawyer," Martin insisted. "Can't that social studies teacher's husband recommend someone?"

"Farhad Badavi? Yes, he could, but I don't need anyone else. This pro bono guy seems good."

"Don't let pride make you foolish. I'll lend you the money."

Sophia wondered if Connie had said the same thing to him.

"No."

"But Dawn Jordan's first priority is the school's welfare, not your friendship—"

"That is obvious." But this hadn't been obvious to Sophia until right now.

"Dawn has got to be on the defensive," Martin said.

"There's a lot of that going around," Sophia said. "Are you pacing?"

"No." His breath changed, so she could tell he had stopped pacing.

"I shouldn't have told you about this until the lawsuit was over. I hate to get you upset." She rolled onto her back as much as the narrow couch would allow.

"Don't worry about me. Though I would feel better if I knew you had your own representation. How are you going to feel if they ask you to resign?"

"I'm not going to lose my job over this," she answered with fake certainty.

"Maybe you will. Once word of the lawsuit gets out, they might ask you to leave, in order to wipe the slate clean."

"Oh Dad." She wanted a drink, but didn't want her father to hear the sound of the bottle opening. "I've got to finish some schoolwork. Would you do me a favor? Please don't tell Connie about the lawsuit, and please ask Mom not to tell her."

There was a long pause.

"Dad?"

"I won't." Then he whispered, "Connie's mouth is bigger than an airplane hangar, bigger even than a lawyer's mouth."

"Dad! Don't let Mom hear you say that. Isn't she still right there?"

"No. She's gone to the music room. So I want to tell you something I'll deny later. I make lawyer jokes because Persephone won't let me make Connie jokes. I've got to vent somehow so I scapegoat a whole profession. Though I am really mad at those health insurance company lawyers."

"Maybe that's why I get such a kick out of your lawyer rants. Thank you for letting me know that." Sophia wished he had told her this when she was a teenager. They could have been secret allies when Sophia was still living at home.

That night before bed, Sophia couldn't wait to write about her father's revelation in her journal. Then she remembered that Danny might at this very moment be perusing the copy of the journal that she had sent him. She didn't want to do any more journal-writing. The privacy risk was too great.

The next morning, Sophia checked her school email account from home before driving to work. Dawn had sent an ALL FACULTY/ALL PARENTS message inviting parents to participate in the new parent-teacher oversight committee.

While I wish I could invite all parents to join in this process, conference room space limits us to the first ten respondents.

Committee members will serve for one semester, to give as many parents as possible a chance to participate in this community-building venture.

Sophia wished Dawn had limited the invitation to parents with scientific credentials. But Dawn wouldn't feel comfortable with that restriction. Sophia imagined John Simpson neighing: "I'm a concerned father. That should be the only credential I need."

Worries tussled Sophia's mind like a cackle of hyenas. As a curriculum designer, she appreciated ambiguity, possibility, and discovery. But she couldn't stand these "opportunities" now that she was a plaintiff.

"First, Stephen said a lot of bad words," Dawn told Sophia in a teacher-to-teacher whisper, because the hallway was almost, but not empty, in the wake of the second bell.

"Yikes." Sophia had never heard Stephen curse.

"And then he said you were an idiot."

Sophia closed her eyes. Did Dawn have to be specific?

"Hi Miz Green, Miz Jordan," Larry Beale said, with a little wave.

"You planning on getting to class?" Dawn asked him.

"On my way."

"Let's take this outside," Dawn said.

Sophia wished she were wearing her jacket. The morning hadn't warmed up yet. She folded her arms for warmth and leaned against the iron railing.

"I've never seen Stephen so angry," Dawn continued. "This mess comes at a particularly bad time because the financial meltdown discouraged our donors. We're still waiting and hoping that the biggest names will reappear. We cannot afford negative press coverage."

"I'm so sorry."

"I know. But if it's any consolation, I'm not as mad at you anymore."

"You're not?"

"My mind was changed. By the last two pages of that mean journal entry."

Sophia remembered she had concluded the entry with two scavenger hunts, but she didn't remember their names.

Dawn grabbed her hand. "I've got the pages in my office. Let's go. It's freezing out here."

On the first of the two photocopies that Dawn handed Sophia, INSURANCE AGENT was scrawled on top. Beneath it was a numbered list, with cross-outs and additions.

"Your brainstorms are almost illegible," Dawn said, "but here are the final versions you gave me two days later." She handed Sophia two paper-clipped pages.

The first of the two scavenger hunts, the INSURANCE AGENT hunt, showed the kids how to research and then graph risk probabilities. That hunt's surprise was the opportunity to role-play a game modeled after Donald Trump's reality show, "The Apprentice." The students competed to see which insurance agent could best argue which risks to prioritize.

The second hunt focused on safer sources of dye.

"These were great hunts," Dawn said. "Remember how excited the kids got? So as terrible as your journal entry was about Harold, you weren't just stewing in negativity. These notes on the last two pages led to wonderful activities for the children. I'm going to give Stephen the final draft versions. I want him to see these hunts clearly, they're like the rainbow at the end of your stormy diatribe." Then Dawn remembered something else she'd wanted to say: "Wait for Stephen to make the first move before contacting him. It will make things easier for both of us, and more importantly, for Carver."

"Thank you so much."

Dawn sighed. "Your creativity is your saving grace."

Chapter 9: Steer Today To Make Tomorrow Easier

Sophia shopped for food on Thursday afternoons to avoid weekend crowds and because Thursdays were her break point between lesson prep and odd jobs for Cally. She conducted a multistage grocery run that wasn't as wasteful of gas as it might have been because she could stop at the butcher's and the Penn Quarter farmers market on her route home from work. Her last stop was Luscious LoCal, the questionably organic supermarket a block from her house.

Luscious LoCal's layout, like all store layouts, was a scavenger hunt. Profit-driven designers made the route circuitous. The more the customers saw, the more their impulsivity flared. Sophia couldn't afford to give into temptation, but often people-watched as other shoppers filled their carts in hopes of satisfying the everlasting cycle of their desires. *Samsara*, she thought, remembering the term from Hinduism and Buddhism that Connie had taught her. She was grateful to know the word and the concept behind it. She thought this knowledge would inoculate her from desire to the extent that anything could.

Sophia always mapped her grocery list in the shape of a figure eight. This shape galvanized her not only because eight was one of Connie's magic numbers, but because the figure eight minimized backtracking. Backtracking made Sophia feel vulnerable. "Steer today to make tomorrow easier." That was Connie's way of putting it.

She found the few items she needed, then hunted for Brendan, the store's buyer. Sophia wanted to tell him about a local, sustainable dairy, Loudoun Creamery. It was the real deal, not faux-organic.

"One of these days I'm going to take out a restraining order against you," Brendan told her because she always tracked him down to shill for small food producers. She held brochures in front of his nose until other customers started looking at them both funny and he got too self-conscious to refuse.

"You could work out an arrangement with Loudoun Creamery's owner, Mimi," Sophia suggested. "She just opened a wine and cheese shop on U Street. They make most of the cheeses they sell."

"I already have cheese coming out of my ears," he protested.

Sophia winced over this disgusting notion: fettuccine-like strands of cheese flowing from Brendan's ears. "My students could make you hand-lettered signs: 'Keep local cows in business!'" She shook imaginary pompoms in her attempt to make this phrase sound catchy.

"Don't quit your day job, Sophia."

"What do you mean?" Little did he know she might be forced to resign.

"Your slogans always sound forced," Brendan told her. "Or maybe I just don't like the way you force them on me."

88

Brendan's criticism didn't bruise Sophia. She was in her environmental stewardship mode. Besides, Sophia thought her slogans and quotes were great. She was flattered by how many of her students decorated their notebooks with sayings she had dreamed up or culled from her quote collection.

"Wait!" Sophia called after Brendan as he attempted escape. She couldn't stand it when he walked away from her before she had her full say.

"Mimi would be generous about providing samples."

Brendan rolled his eyes. "Don't talk to me about samples. They don't help sales as much as the top brass thinks they do."

"Did I mention how pretty Mimi is? And single. Well, divorced. Amicably. It was all her husband's fault. And she's got big gazoongas."

"Shhhh," Brendan whispered.

"Better than calling them 'tits.'"

"Shhhh." He flapped his arms up and down.

"That reminds me. Her cows are in great shape. Great milkers."

"For the love of God, Sophia."

"The cows, I mean. Now I'm talking about the cows. Not her boobs. When was the last time you had a date?"

"You're keeping me from one right now," Brendan said, scowling. "A date with one of my deliveries."

"Sorry."

"No you're not," he called back as he disappeared into *Employees Only*.

Brendan was right. Sophia wasn't sorry for challenging him. At Carver, she used the name of the grocery chain, Luscious LoCal, to help her define greenwashing. Brendan stocked the supposedly "LoCal" store with far-flung, fossil-fueled offerings. Not that she had anything against supermarkets stocking a wide variety of international foods—she loved rice vinegar and frijoles as much as the next sophisticated Washingtonian. But why not devote some shelf space to local and sustainable brands, amidst the vegan and the gluten-free?

The word blend "LoCal" was doubly dishonest because most of their products were as densely caloric as the foods you would find in any supermarket. The shelves were stuffed with nut butters, granolas, and bulk bins of every different kind of dried fruit under the sun. Their deli's prepared food display featured groaning boards of meatless lasagnas and enchiladas, baked potatoes stuffed with feta, ricotta, and sour cream, and vegetable side dishes that glistened with excess olive oil. Globs of fresh mozzarella abounded.

Back at home in her kitchen, Sophia ate globs of mozzarella from the Penn Quarter farmers market while brooding over Stephen Lanham's fury, and that remark Dawn had made:

"Your creativity is your saving grace."

The compliment was a double-edged sword, like one of Connie's compliments. Sophia knew she would never forget it, even after the lawsuit ended. Whenever that would be.

She worried that her anxiety about the lawsuit would interfere with her creativity and productivity.

If only she could write in her journal. But she wouldn't let herself because journal-writing no longer felt private. She decided to call Nadia.

Nadia's plummy Persian accent and friendliness always heartened Sophia. Instead of admitting the true reason for her call, Sophia pretended she had questions about the next day's social studies lesson.

They brainstormed a while and then Nadia said, "Don't be all work and no play, sweetheart. You want to go on a hike this weekend? Farhad's business trip was canceled and he's going to take Amir to the zoo."

"I'd love to. It will get my mind off...."

"The lawsuit?" Nadia guessed.

"Yes. Well, I should go now. I think a pot's boiling over."

The next morning while eating breakfast, Sophia turned on her laptop to prepare for her meeting with Tariq.

Instead of opening "Sciencescavengerhunts.doc," she clicked open her email and read a new message from Connie:

Haven't heard from you in a while. I learned the hard way, from Ryan, that the first few weeks of a new school year are particularly busy, and not a time for chit chat, even via email. But I have been thinking of you and hoping your school year is starting off well.

Hi Connie,
School's great. I decided to replace the sixth graders' first scavenger hunt with a tour of our school garden instead of the hike. This shift highlights Carver's current priorities: urban gardening and greening, and sustainable food production. And field tripping is too expensive since the recession.

Sophia couldn't help noticing the similarity between the words "recession" and "repression." She hoped her godmother wouldn't read between the lines.

Now I'm off to run a scavenger hunt.

Of course, she wasn't off to a scavenger hunt, though she had been thinking about Danny quite a bit. Impulsively, she clicked open a new email, feeling on the prowl.

Danny,

On Sunday I'm hiking with a Carver colleague, Nadia Badavi, through the part of Rock Creek Park where I took Harold's class. Any chance you could come? Might be a good idea for you to see the area, especially because the foliage is at the same stage it was then. Feel free to bring a friend.

She reread the email after already sending it. She hoped she didn't sound like she was asking him on a date. At least Nadia would be there to chaperone. Sophia emailed Nadia to let her know Danny would join them so he could see where the accident had occurred.

Danny accepted Sophia's invitation.

Then Nadia emailed:

Okay.

That single-word reply, "Okay," looked curt. And then Sophia realized she hadn't put herself in her friend's shoes. Nadia had probably hoped for a relaxing hike. She had little time for recreation between schoolwork and motherwork. Revisiting the poisonous pokeberries might be almost as stressful for Nadia as it would be for Sophia. She wished she had asked Nadia first before inviting Danny. She wished she had thought this through before acting.

An hour before Sophia was supposed to leave for the hike on Sunday morning, Nadia phoned.

"Amir is sick, and although I know Farhad can handle it, I want to stay here with them. I'm sorry to bail on you at the last minute. Will it be awkward to be on your own with that lawyer? I know you don't trust lawyers."

"Oh, no problem," Sophia said. Only after she hung up did she wish she had said she hoped Amir would feel better soon. She was always on the lookout for ways to subtly indicate that she wasn't self-absorbed.

Chapter 10: It's A Journal, Not a Novel

Sophia had offered to pick Danny up at his brownstone in the expensive downtown enclave of Kalorama. There was a small French sign above his doorbell: *Attention Au Chien*. Sophia, who had taken Spanish in high school, wondered if this meant *Beware of Dog* or *Pay Attention to the Dog*.

When Danny opened the door his head was bent to one side, nestling a cordless phone. "Almost done," he mouthed, gesturing for her to come in. His apartment had shuttered floor-to-ceiling windows. The dining area and kitchen were part of one big living room. She picked up the Sunday paper and pretended to read while eavesdropping.

"It isn't a big deal unless you make it a big deal," Danny told the phone.

As soon as they got into Sophia's Volvo, Danny said, "This is just the kind of car I'd expect a teacher to have."

"Gee thanks."

He ignored her sarcasm. "Sure. I know from your journal how proud you are of your frugality. I envy your virtue. Except for the mean stuff you said about Harold, but other than that you're a solid citizen."

"I'm glad there's a bright side to your invasion of my privacy."

"Hey, I'm doing this case pro bono."

"I appreciate it," Sophia replied.

"Can I say something bold?"

"Don't you always?" She couldn't wait to hear what he was going to say.

"I like your personality. And it's surreal that your godmother is the infamous Countess Connie."

"Remember, I don't want anyone to know that."

"I know. It isn't relevant, other than the fact that you learned about pokeberries from her. Her name will be kept confidential."

"Thank God. No one who doesn't know me from Ithaca knows."

"Why? Because you're a bohemian snob? Embarrassed to be connected with a self-help guru?"

"Don't call me a bohemian snob. I don't care what Connie does for a living. I care about how difficult it's been to grow up with her."

"Oh yeah. I can't believe you transcribed your email exchanges. And no offense, but you are repetitive about her…"

"Repetitive? Well excuse me. It's a journal, not a novel. I can be as repetitive as I want. If I can't yammer to a journal, who can I yammer to?"

"You could yammer to me. If we become friends."

"Do all lawyers talk to clients this way?" Sophia asked him.

"No. But I can't speak for all lawyers. I'm a maverick. And not in the John McCain-Sarah Palin-like sense of that word. More like James Dean."

Sophia rolled her eyes. "Don't flatter yourself."

"Okay. But seriously, you seem cool in a geeky way. I'm not going to beg you to be my friend or anything," Danny said playfully. "Though it wouldn't interfere with the lawsuit. It's not like we'd be dating or something."

"Have you ever dated a client?"

"Most of my clients are white-collar criminals, and they are fat men of my dad's age."

Sophia grinned at him. She started driving again, and pushed the button that was always set to public radio.

Danny reached over and turned the volume down. "How long will this hike be?"

"We'll do the two miles that Barbara, Maggie, and I did with the kids, beginning near the park's Nature Center. The area's full of migrating birds right now." Sophia had decided to downplay the pokeberries until they actually got to them toward the end of the hike.

"So, in addition to being a treehugger, you're a birdwatcher, eh?" Danny asked.

"Please don't use the words 'treehugger' or 'veggies' in my presence. Birdwatching is an inherited interest. My dad's an ornithologist."

"An eye doctor?"

"No." She looked over to see if Danny were joking and he was.

"All I know about your dad is that he hates lawyers. I guess that's an inherited trait?"

"Dad's a professor at Cornell. He can't afford to retire because the lawyers from his insurance company shield their clients from having to pay anything more than the minimum for my mother's long-term care."

"Right. You wrote in the journal about her being sick."

"Not sick. Paralyzed and in a wheelchair."

At least the journal made no reference to Sophia's role in Persephone's accident.

"Mom works part time," Sophia said. "She's a professor, too, and used to play jazz clarinet in a band."

"What was the name of it?" Danny asked.

"They didn't have a name," Sophia replied, grateful to be asked an easy question.

"I thought all bands had names," Danny mused.

"I've always thought it was strange that they didn't think up some catchy name. My mom and I come from a long line of unusually-named women. My grandmother studied Ancient Greek and Roman culture, so Mom's name is Persephone, and my real name is Sophonisba."

"That must have been an awkward name on the playground when you were little."

"No. I always went by 'Sophia.' No one other than my mom calls me Sophonisba, and she doesn't use it very often."

"Did she name you after a Greek goddess?"

"No. Sophonisba was a noblewoman who drank poison to avoid being humiliated by the Romans."

"Poisoned, eh? That's ironic."

When Sophia flinched, Danny noticed. "Sorry, my bad," he said. "You know what? I'm going to Google the name Sophonisba. I already Googled your name. For professional reasons." He gave her a sidelong smile, which she pretended to ignore.

"If I had a band, naming it would be my favorite part," she told him after a few beats of silence. "I'm not that interested in music."

"It's refreshing to hear you admit that. I'm not into music either, but I'd never let anyone know I'm unmoved by it. People already think lawyers are soulless."

She turned onto Glover Road. "Oh look. See that meadow? That's garlic mustard. I wish I could pick some to make pesto, but it's against the law to forage in Rock Creek Park without an education permit. But don't worry. I had one when I brought Harold's class here."

"I never worry," Danny replied.

About twenty minutes later, Sophia showed Danny one of her father's favorite songbirds.

"Can you see that one? With the brown stripe?"

"The one that looks like it's got a green Mohawk?" Danny asked.

"Yes. That's a Chestnut-sided warbler."

The bird cocked his head, then responded to an acquaintance with six resolute chirps.

"It's got a tongue-twister of a Latin name, 'Dendroica pensylvanica,'" Sophia said.

"Whoa. I guess it isn't in a bird-watcher's best interest to create easy names, like 'Mohawk bird.'"

"Why?" she asked.

"Well, if they used fun names, they'd probably attract more people, and I bet they don't want to do that. You know, crowds scare the birds off."

Sophia laughed. "No way. The more people learn about birds, the more likely they'll be to protect their habitats. In New Jersey, a former colleague of mine just launched a K-12 foundation so kids can actively help preserve green space along the Atlantic Flyway by recording nocturnal flight calls." Sophia decided not to mention that Paul had been one of many ex-boyfriends. In addition to being an award-winning teacher, administrator, and fundraiser, Paul loved animation as much as he loved birds. His fondness for clay animation, in particular, led Sophia to break up with him.

For several months of late nights, Paul had painstakingly constructed a clay cartoon about the perils of bird migration, despite Sophia's suggestion that clay animation might not be the best format to use.

"You should have more faith in me," he protested one night when she said she thought he wasn't getting enough sleep.

"I'm trying to," she told him. She didn't find out until it was too late that he had decided to focus on the danger that skyscrapers and communications towers posed to birds, who were distracted from their proper path by aviation warning lights.

Paul's cartoon premiered at an elementary school. About a minute into the five-minute show, the auditorium erupted in laughter as a zaftig Swainson's Thrush splattered onto the plate glass of a brightly lit office building. The claymation had made the bird's death look hysterically funny.

"Stop laughing!" Paul had hissed at the students who were closest to him, as if they were the ringleaders. Even the teachers couldn't restrain their giggling. Sophia was too horrified by Paul's mistake to find the laughter infectious. She dreaded having to go home with him at the end of the day. That night in bed, she put her arms around him, and he thanked her for not saying "I told you so." She lay awake for hours, wondering how long she'd have to wait to move out. She would never be able to have sex with him again without imagining that exploding bird. She made her escape a few weeks later, hoping Paul wouldn't attribute her flight to the flight of his splattering birds.

Sophia and Danny came upon a patch of wineberries, the same berries Harold had teased Maria Arevalo about. Wineberries, like raspberries and blackberries, were from the rubus genus, more popularly known as brambles. Brambles grow aggressively, binding and crowding out other plants, and scratching berry pickers with their thorns. Sophia's father loved to tell people that for hundreds of years in England, lawyers were called brambles and brambles were called lawyers or lawyer bushes. For reasons he couldn't explain, the slur was especially common in New Zealand. "I've got to get myself there for a visit," her dad would say. "Kindred spirits down under."

"This is a wineberry bush," Sophia said simply. "Around here, they fruit in late June or July, and they look just like raspberries, but they're more sour and their stems are bristled."

Danny reached out to touch one of the furry red canes. "Pretty soft."

"I teach the kids to I.D. them by thinking of the bristled stems as fur coats. Wineberries are invasive in this region, which means they harm the native ecosystem, and fur coats are invasive and harmful everywhere."

"I bought my mom a fur coat for Christmas. With a hat to match."

"Oh, sorry if I offended you." Sophia wasn't sorry though. She was just thinking: *Eew. Strike two against Danny.* Strike one was his occupation.

"I'm just kidding," Danny said. "I wanted to see how you'd react."

"Oh yeah, taunt the treehugger. I'm used to it."

"My parents live in Florida. Mama would melt in a fur coat."

It was cute that he said "mama" instead of "my mother."

Sophia and Danny didn't talk much while they ate. Then she noticed him pouring the rest of his bottle of spring water on the inner part of his wrist.

"My wrist's itching," he explained.

"Yikes. I bet there was poison ivy near the wineberries. I should have warned you. They tend to grow near each other."

"Can I use some of your water?" he asked her.

"Sure, but water won't help. I'll be right back. I'm going to try to find you some jewelweed."

"Um, I'm not really in the mood right now for another plant I.D," he called after her, sounding more amused than annoyed.

She whirled back around. "I'm getting it because it will relieve the itch."

It didn't take Sophia long to find some shoots. She came back to Danny carrying several stalks, and began showing him how to split the stems and crush the leaves to yield the most juice.

"Will you put it on for me?" he asked evenly.

"Sure."

"I can't believe you broke the law."

"What?"

"You don't have a permit for today, right? So you weren't supposed to pick anything."

"Oh. I think under the circumstances, the rangers would understand."

"Why is it called jewelweed?"

"The leaves are water-repellant, so water beads on them, like little crystals. They're also called touch-me-nots, because their seeds pop out so easily. We grow jewelweed in our medicinal garden."

"At Carver? You've got a medicinal garden?"

"Yes." She didn't like the look on his face.

101

"You or Dawn should have told me about that."

"They're just herbs."

"That's what my roommate in college said when he got caught growing marijuana plants under grow lights in our dorm room closet."

"The herbs we grow are legal. And benign unless you eat a bathtub full of them. We use yarrow for lotion, and several plants as natural remedies for gardening problems. Chamomile disinfects seedling flats. We grow culinary herbs too, but they're in one of the vegetable plots—"

"I'll need a list of the medicinal plants." He frowned. "I've got a really smart friend at the FDA who will be able to help me assess their risks."

"I can get you any information you need."

"No. Don't. That will just complicate matters. And I need her to do it. I mean, she knows how to do a formal risk assessment, and she can approach this from a legal angle."

"Oh. Okay. Well, your wrist should start to feel better in about twenty minutes."

"That soon?"

"Yeah. It works fast."

"I'll remember that for our next hike." His grin was handsome. "You haven't showed me the pokeberries yet. Are you procrastinating?"

"Uh, … not intentionally," she said. "We'll see them on the way to the parking lot."

A few minutes later they came to a grove of several bushes.

"Here they are," she announced.

"Harold was right. They look just like blueberries," Danny said.

She sighed. He reached over to ruffle her hair.

Sophia stepped back. "My car's right up this path."

"Was I too forward?"

"No. I'm just not into having my hair ruffled."

"Duly noted," he replied.

"And I'm really edgy because of the lawsuit."

"That's natural. I guess I forget how traumatic lawsuits are for laypeople," he said.

"Geez."

"What?"

"You're more flip than a gymnast, Danny."

"There are worse things I could be."

"Right." She didn't know what he was getting at. She only knew her fate was in his hands, legally speaking. She hoped she could leave a door open for hooking up with him without having to step through that door too soon.

The following week, Sophia had a meeting with both Danny and Dawn. It ran smoothly at first. But then Sophia handed Danny the list of medicinal plants that he had requested. Dawn looked confused.

"I should have told you earlier," Sophia explained. "Danny thinks the medicinals in the school garden might be a liability."

Dawn's confusion turned to concern.

"Not exactly a liability," Danny said. "I just wanted to look at the list. It's nothing to worry about. Hey, did Sophia tell you about our great hike last weekend?"

"No," Dawn replied. "Sophia didn't tell me about that."

Danny told Dawn that Sophia had cured his poison ivy with jewelweed, making it sound dramatic and funny.

Dawn shot Sophia a disapproving glance. Sophia felt like a middle schooler. Was Dawn was jealous, that Sophia had gotten to hike with this cute guy? And then Sophia remembered what she'd conveniently forgotten. She'd promised she wouldn't meet

Danny without Dawn present. *Sorry*, Sophia mouthed. Dawn rolled her eyes. *Too little, too late.*

Danny either missed or ignored their exchange. "...I'm now planning to argue that because Sophia identified so many species for the children that day, the pokeberries appeared in the context of a wide variety of plants, rather than as a food."

"That sounds like a good approach," Dawn said. "But it's harder for me to judge not having been out there with you. Next time, please include me in any of your *field trips*, Sophia."

Sophia flinched, and Danny noticed. He leapt to her defense.

"You would have been bored," he told Dawn.

"Mr. Giordano, you don't know me well enough to assume whether I'd be bored or not.

"All I meant was that I'm sure I strained Sophia's patience with my stupid questions."

"No," Sophia protested automatically.

"Sophia went above and beyond the call of duty." Danny insisted. He put his hands flat on either side of his clipboard with the earnestness of a politician. "I learned so much from being in the woods with an environmental educator. Now I understand how important it is to give kids that opportunity. And if this case goes to trial, I'll point out to the jury that pokeweed berries aren't any more dangerous than the industrial cleaners used to clean school bathrooms."

Dawn nodded. "We don't use those products here. Mostly Borax, baking soda, and vinegar. Some bleach. Because the conventional cleaners haven't been tested properly."

"All kids are exposed to dangerous chemicals of some sort, in the industrialized world and in the natural world," Sophia said. "At least with Carver's curriculum, we're warning our kids about manmade environmental hazards."

"Right," Danny agreed. "And through the field trips and the school garden, you're saving them from the hazard of NDD."

"Have you been reading Richard Louv's *Last Child in the Woods*?" Sophia asked with a knowing smile. The book's subtitle was *Saving Our Children From Nature-Deficit Disorder*, which the author also referred to as NDD.

"Yeah. I picked it up the day after the hike," Danny said. "I was going to give it to you, as a thank-you gift for the hike, but I couldn't resist reading it first. It's brilliant. Do you like Louv's ideas?"

"That book is one of our favorites," Dawn said primly. "I'm glad you had a chance to read it."

"Well, I wouldn't have if it weren't for Sophia's taking the time to show me the importance of green space. Now I'll be able to represent her better."

"Don't you mean, you'll be able to represent Carver better?" Dawn asked.

"Of course. Your interests are the same."

Sophia wished her father could have heard that. But maybe Martin would have said Danny was mollifying Dawn. Dawn looked skeptical.

Sophia went back to her office after the meeting, and had just begun drafting a new hunt when Dawn knocked on her open door.

"Hey," Sophia said.

Dawn shut the door behind her. *Shoot*, Sophia thought, and braced herself by sitting up in her chair.

"Did you sleep with him?"

"Are you kidding?"

"Don't give me that innocent look."

"We haven't done anything yet. I mean, we haven't done anything, period."

"Oh my God," Dawn said. "Doesn't take a fortuneteller."

"What do you mean?"

"You're going to hook up with him for a while, and then break up with him abruptly. The night before the deposition or something. Because you have this weird complex about lawyers. He's slicker than an oil spill, and your lack of respect for him will win out you're your hormones. Heaven forbid you should give a man another chance to be anything other than perfect. Oh, and then, once you've impulsively broken up with him, you'll regret it some night and impulsively hook up with him again, and then it will become a mess that you'll wind up blaming on him. Then you'll brood about it instead of telling me or any of your other friends how you are truly feeling."

"Slow down. I wish you had told me you were feeling this way about me, I mean, before now."

"I'm worried, Sophia. And your impulsivity worries me the most."

"Impulsivity?" Sophia repeated.

"You heard me."

Sophia played back a mental tape of Connie criticizing her impulsivity.

"Sophia?"

"I'm deflecting Danny."

Dawn sighed. "Promise you'll deflect until the case is over?"

"I promise, but…" Sophia looked down at her hands.

"No buts," Dawn said. "No buts and no butts, especially if they're lawyers' butts."

"Is it so bad if he's attracted to me?"

Dawn looked even more annoyed. "No. It's great. For you."

106

"But Danny said Carver's interests and my interests are the same."

"Wrong. Maybe I need to show both of you the Venn diagram in the math department. Carver and you overlap but don't match. He shouldn't have said our interests were the same. I'm no lawyer, but I think that was a sloppy thing for him to say."

After Dawn left, Sophia stared at the quotes on her bulletin board for a while, not really seeing them because she was upset. When the intensity became unbearable, she daydreamed.

Sophia replayed memories of hiking with Danny. It wasn't the first time she had numbed herself out with memories of his banter and sexiness. She hadn't daydreamed about men much before meeting him, maybe because as an adult, she hadn't needed mental shelter until this school year.

Danny's glibness about the lawsuit comforted Sophia like nothing else. If he didn't think the sky was falling in, it couldn't be falling in, because he was the lawsuit expert. And because he had read her journal, she believed he knew her more intimately than her ex-boyfriends had. On the hike, Danny disconcerted her by referring to private matters that she had only journaled about. Although she felt disconcerted, these moments bonded her to him.

She wished she could write about Danny's influence in a new journal.

Chapter 11: Good News, Followed By Bad News

Stephen Lanham, the head of the foundation that made Carver possible, summoned Sophia to lunch. She didn't have to tell Dawn they would be meeting. Stephen was a stickler for hierarchy and always let Dawn know before contacting Carver employees. In friendlier days before the lawsuit, Dawn always gave Sophia a "when and why" heads-up, but not this time. Sophia thought of this as she fed the parking meter outside the restaurant. L'Eco Bistro was the foundation's unofficial cafeteria.

Her cell phone rang, an abrasion muted slightly from her jacket pocket. When she saw the phone number on the display, her heart sped. It had been two months since her first meeting with Danny and she had memorized his number. She let the call go to voice mail so she could look forward to listening to it after lunch.

Stephen beckoned from a back table.

"I hope you weren't waiting long?" Sophia asked, though she knew she was early. She had checked her watch compulsively all morning.

"Not *too* long," Stephen said. His face was gaunt, with a beige moustache like half a bird's nest. Sophia imagined food stuck to it. Disgusting. She made a mental note to maintain eye contact without glancing below the bridge of his nose.

"I'm so sorry to have put Carver through this. Thank you for meeting with me over lunch," she said.

"Lunch was the only time I had free."

"Well, you're kind to give me the opportunity to... to let you know that if there's anything I can do to make up for—"

"You can't make up for it."

Stephen took a deep breath and released it as an aggravated sigh. "But there is something special in January that you can do for Carver's benefit, and we'll discuss that in due course."

She wished that he would just tell her already, but he sipped at his tea and looked aggrieved for what felt like five minutes. Finally he finished the tea, looked down into the cup to make sure there was no more, then looked out across the restaurant. She wondered if he were checking for people he knew who might overhear. Then he turned back to her.

"I have reached a settlement with Priscilla Mathers."

Sophia's jolt knocked over the cruet of olive oil that accompanied their breadsticks. Luckily, it had one of those well-engineered lids that only flows when shaken.

"A settlement? Of part of the lawsuit?" She didn't want to presume the horror was over.

"A settlement of the whole lawsuit."

"What? Does this mean the lawsuit's over?—I mean, done? Or, uh, I guess it wouldn't end overnight or anything. So…when might we know when it's going to be, you know, fully done?"

"Depends on your definition of 'done.' If everything goes as planned with the paperwork, the case will not go to trial. You see, after reading the cruel things you said about that poor boy in your diary, I lost sleep worrying about your performance at the deposition, let alone before a jury."

Sophia closed her eyes and willed herself not to cry or tell Stephen that she resented his sadism.

Stephen sounded particularly pompous as he said, "I asked Daniel Giordano not to tell you I'd decided to settle—I wanted to tell you myself. Also, I did not want you to hear the news from Dawn. I know you and she are friends." He grimaced. "This is not a time for celebration."

It was time for Stephen's salade niçoise and Sophia's quiche, however. "Sorry for interrupting," the waiter said unapologetically.

"This enormous financial burden couldn't happen at a worse time, not that there would ever be a good time," Stephen said. "Our liability insurance will cover most of the expense of the settlement, but our rates will go up. I'll be speaking to Dawn later today to find out where we can cut corners."

"May I participate in that discussion?"

Stephen hesitated. Sophia guessed he wanted to say no, but school policy required him to consult her about programming details.

"Given your role as curriculum director, you'll have to participate," Stephen said. Then, without warning, he added, "I've told Dawn to reduce you to part-time status. And instead of an annual salary, you'll be paid by the hour. You'll be on probation for a year, which means Dawn will have to add a memo about the lawsuit to your file."

"Will I lose my health insurance?" Sophia stammered.

"Not if you agree to add your name to our substitute teacher list. Then you can maintain the 40-hour week requirement for the benefit plan. Dawn suggested substitute teaching for that reason. If it weren't for her support of you, I would have asked for your resignation. Frankly, I think Carver no longer needs a full-time curriculum designer."

Sophia reeled. Stephen wasn't done hitting her with bad news.

"… recently heard through the grapevine that the promising new science teacher, Tariq Ali, wishes you would give him more leeway. You are aware he has a PhD, aren't you? We're lucky to have him and I don't want to lose him to another school."

Sophia held back tears.

"Why don't you go to the powder room and freshen up," Stephen suggested. He looked around nervously.

When Sophia came back to the table, she had to dig her fingernails into her palms to keep from bursting into fresh sobs. So much for her determination never to cry in front of a male boss.

She searched her mind for a response, coaching herself to be polite and constructive. When she got home she could throw darts at his picture. At least figuratively. The only photo she had of Stephen was in Carver's yearbook, and she wasn't an accurate enough dart player to hit a target that small.

"Feeling better now?" he asked.

She cleared her throat and spoke. "You mentioned earlier that there was something I could do to help Carver in January. What were you thinking of?"

Stephen looked relieved. "Daniel Giordano's drawn up a confidentiality agreement," he began, "and Priscilla Mathers says the Tompkins will honor it as part of the settlement, but we can't enforce it. I'm worried they're going to feed reporters an inflammatory account of Harold's injury and the lawsuit. We can only counter negative publicity with positive stories. And I've thought of one. Do you know of the grocery store, Luscious LoCal?"

"Yes."

"They are holding a chili cookoff in mid-January. I'd like you to enter the contest with a team of students from the after school program, so it won't interfere with class schedules. Get Maggie to help you make up a recipe."

Just before Stephen released Sophia he said, "There's one more thing. We will adopt the 'Math Is Everywhere' curriculum. Effective next fall."

"What?" This hit like a bombshell blasting out of Sophia's past. She thought of Ryan, Connie's aloof son.

"Don't tell me you've never heard of it."

"I have. My godmother's son helped create it. But I'm surprised to hear you suggest 'Math Is Everywhere' for Carver. I don't like the precedent we'd be setting. All major lessons in each subject should reflect our commitment to environmental stewardship. Sherri—I mean, the head of the math department—and I do that easily, in accordance with DCPS learning standards when we make up the lessons ourselves."

"All the private schools converted to 'Math is Everywhere' years ago," Stephen argued. "If we adopt it for the 2010-2011 school year, we'll make education news headlines as one of the first charter schools to offer low- and middle-income students the same advantage as at the most affluent schools."

"We're already giving our kids as good an education as they would receive at any private school in the country, and I can't think of a single prep school that integrates its school garden into the curriculum to the extent that we do."

"Carver needs the favorable publicity that a switch to 'Math is Everywhere' would attract. And now you're only a part-time curriculum director, so you won't be able to supervise the math lessons in the way you've done previously."

Sophia felt like Stephen had just told her she would need to give up an arm or a leg.

"Don't be a lone ranger," Stephen said in place of "Goodbye."

"I won't."

"I'll look forward to trying the chili at Luscious LoCal."

"Thanks, Stephen. This will be a great way to showcase local organic ingredients."

"Just make sure it tastes good enough to win the cookoff."

A few minutes later, Sophia sat parked a few blocks away from L'Eco Bistro and Stephen's clutches. Danny, via cell phone, was filling her head with reassuring, complimentary words.

"Don't worry about Stephen, I will let him know that you were responsible for how quickly we reached a settlement. Pricilla Mathers was putty in my hands once I started using all the phrases I borrowed from your donor presentations."

"Which phrases worked?"

"Green space, environmental stewardship, and--"

"I didn't coin those phrases."

"How about 'hands-in-the-dirt learning'?"

"That's my corny tweak of the cliché 'hands-on learning.'"

"Don't be modest. Your modesty's like a facial tic. If you learned to promote yourself more you could become a lobbyist or a politician. You could make a difference on a larger scale."

"Washington has enough lobbyists and politicians," Sophia said. She remembered Connie criticizing her lack of ambition in an email:

As long as you stay at Carver, you'll get ego strokes from working with underprivileged kids, but you could help more of them if you aimed higher. You're too defensive to challenge yourself.

"What are you thinking about?" Danny asked her.

"Just how miserable I'd be as a politician. Every interview would feel like an interrogation."

"Depends on what you've got to hide from your past."

Sophia thought of Connie.

How much did you party in college?" Danny asked.

"Not much."

"You weren't following the Grateful Dead around?"

"No," she scowled. "I worked my way through college. I was too busy to go to concerts."

"Did you do any drugs?"

"I drank a lot."

"Who didn't?" He hesitated, then said, "We should celebrate the settlement. When can I take you out to dinner?"

"I don't feel like celebrating. Stephen told Dawn to reduce me to part-time status, and though I'll be able to supplement my income with substitute-teaching, I'll make even less than I make now." Sophia's stomach tightened at the thought. At least the amount she had to contribute to her landlord Cally's utility bills was low. Sophia had retrofitted as much as she could to conserve energy in her basement apartment and the two floors upstairs where Cally lived.

"You can do well with less," Danny protested. "I bet you just eat homemade granola, rice, and beans anyway."

"I have to worry about money, Mr. Fancy Pants Corporate Lawyer," Sophia snapped. "And I have to figure out how I can start saving money toward an emergency fund. Stephen might tell Dawn not to offer me a contract renewal this spring. He's a grudge-holder."

"Look, you no longer have the lawsuit to worry about. Don't replace one worry with another."

"Stephen also told me he's worried the Tompkinses will brag about the settlement and trash Carver to reporters."

"That won't happen." Danny's comforting certainty evaporated her irritation with him.

"Why do you think the Tompkinses won't brag about the settlement to reporters? I'm surprised they haven't been publicly trashing Carver. Also, Stephen said the confidentiality agreement was unenforceable."

"He's right, but the Tompkinses don't know that," Danny replied.

"Won't Priscilla Mathers tell them? She won the case. I would think she'd welcome the publicity."

"She didn't win the case, she settled it. For peanuts. Didn't Stephen tell you the amount?"

"He said it was an 'enormous financial burden.'"

"Stephen is an asshole. The Tompkinses accepted our opening bid of ten-thousand dollars."

"That sounds like a lot of money to me. Though it isn't as bad as 150,000."

"Right, and ten-thousand is nothing compared to what Priscilla would have gotten in court. She's a talented litigator. A little bird told me she begged the Tompkinses to hold out for more, but they were too excited by the prospect of an immediate payout. They're remodeling their kitchen and bathroom. Which is why they filed the lawsuit when they did."

"So that's it. I was wondering why they waited so long. Dawn thought they filed when they did to prevent the September hike."

"Dawn gave them too much credit."

Sophia wanted to believe him. "Are you sure about this?"

"Yes. My source has a big mouth but she's as accurate as a game of telephone at a court stenographer's convention."

Hmmm, Sophia thought. Danny's network of friends seemed densely populated with helpful "shes." She recalled trawling through the pages and pages of his Facebook friend list. More photogenic blondes than a beauty pageant.

"Mathers won't want the press to find out the Tompkinses are spending the settlement money on granite countertops and a Jacuzzi. Trust me. She won't let them know the confidentiality agreement's weak. And the reason they haven't been chirping to the media all along is because she told them early on to keep their mouths shut. Both Mr. and Mrs. Tompkins are loose cannons. They wouldn't interview well, and most reporters are limousine liberals who eat up all your eco-babble."

Sophia winced.

"Pardon my bluntness. You still there? You need me to filch you some Valium?"

"No. I'm starting to feel better."

"Harold Tompkins didn't spend the night at the hospital. And if news of your diary entry got out, which is the worst case scenario, there are a lot of people out there who will identify with you. You think you're the first grownup to ever find a smartass kid annoying? It's not like you hit him."

Sophia slumped back in her seat, knowing that teachers were held to higher standards than lawyers. "I'm exhausted," she said. "I usually don't get this tired until later in the school year."

"Whatever. You need champagne. On me, literally and figuratively."

Sophia rolled her eyes. "You are cheesier than mozzarella. I'm getting off the phone now."

"What are you doing Saturday night?"

"I don't know yet, but, uh, thank you for all you did with Priscilla Mathers. Really. This day has been a roller-coaster. I'll call you once I've been able to process all this news."

Sophia didn't call Danny. He emailed her a few days later to ask her out that Saturday night.

Okay but it can't be a date, Sophia emailed back. *I don't want to stress Dawn out anymore than I already have.*

Danny emailed back, as quickly as if they were texting.

Why? Does Dawn want to go on a date with me? Do you think she will be jealous?

Ha ha, she wrote back, then clicked her email closed.

Sophia worked slowly on her curriculum paperwork. Soon it would dwindle. That thought was hugely depressing, and before she knew it she was watching "Keeping Up with the Kardashians" on the couch, eating a pint of locally-produced Loudoun Creamery ice cream. The Kardashian sisters were talking about boys, and Sophia started thinking about how attractive Danny was. He came on too strong, but she adored the fact that he was worry-free.

When she checked her email later that night, she saw he had emailed her back already.

Don't worry about Dawn. The lawsuit's history.

Sophia recalled Dawn's request. The lawsuit was over, so Sophia could date him. She felt flattered by his persistence.

Chapter 12: Feeling Thorny about the Rose Queen

Danny picked Sophia up at her apartment before their date. His tie was as scarlet as a pokeberry stem, and he smelled like prohibitively expensive aftershave and leather. He kissed Sophia hello on the lips, but a quick kiss, as though they'd been together for months. Very smooth, getting the first kiss out of the way so there wouldn't be any awkwardness after dinner. Not that Danny could ever be awkward. He was frequently and attractively over-the-top.

"I couldn't get a reservation at Atman Palace," Danny told her as he drove, "but there's another Indian restaurant, in Glover Park, that I thought we might try, if you can stand visiting a yuppie neighborhood?"

"If I must dine with a lawyer, I can dine with a lawyer in a yuppie neighborhood," Sophia replied.

When they pulled up to the valet, Sophia was amused to see that the name of the restaurant was Samsara.

She started to tell Danny why it amused her at dinner, but he wanted to hear more about Connie. He asked a lot of questions, which Sophia answered enthusiastically. It was such a fun release to bitch about Connie. Sophia loved the attentiveness with which Danny questioned her.

After dinner, while they waited for the valet to come back with Danny's car, she said, "I wish I'd asked our waiter if he knew why they named it Samsara. That's one of Buddhism's darkest concepts. It means—"

"Where is the fucking valet?" Danny asked, then blew on his hands to warm them up.

Neither of them were sober, she thought through the haze of her ginger martini buzz.

The valet pulled up to the curb in Danny's BMW. They had only driven a block when she asked him to pull over.

"I feel nauseous. Can we walk a bit? I need some fresh air."

"Okay. If we walk along Massachusetts Avenue we'll be at my place in about twenty minutes," he said. "It's all downhill from here."

The word "downhill" echoed in Sophia's head so she over-analyzed it. Did he mean the walk back to his place was downhill, or that this budding romance would go downhill fast?

When they got back to his place, they made out on his couch. She stopped him so she could call a cab.

"Why leave now?" he asked her.

"I'm tired," she said.

"And you're too savvy to sleep with a guy on the first date."

"No. I don't worry about rules like that," she patted him on the shoulder. "I'm the boss of my relationships."

When her cab came Danny asked if he could pay for it.

"Nope. Thanks for dinner."

"When do you usually wake up on weekends?" he asked her. "Can I take you out to breakfast tomorrow? Or lunch or dinner?"

"Your schedule is too flexible for a corporate lawyer," Sophia told him as she closed the cab door.

Danny and Sophia saw each other several times over the course of the next two weeks. When Sophia finally slept over, she discovered that Danny was good at sealing the deal, but he could have used a gym membership. He also overdid the dirty talk the first time. Fortunately, she knew how to reduce the chattiness.

The morning after their first sleepover, Sophia woke to the smell of roses. There were three yellow blooms in a rectangular crystal vase next to his bed. The petals looked like curls of butter, with a few scarlet edges.

She watched Danny sleep, and when he woke up, she asked him if he had gone out earlier that morning to get the flowers.

"No. They were right there last night."

"I'm surprised I didn't notice them," she said.

"We were both pretty drunk. Aren't they beautiful?"

Sophia expected him to flatter her, to say something like: "I bought them yesterday, hoping we would wind up in my room so I could impress you with them." But instead he said, "My best friend, Margaret, grows them. She has a key to my place and pops in sometimes when I'm not home to surprise me with these."

Ah. His best friend was a woman. Who grew roses and popped in to leave him some. Sophia was suddenly aware of stomach-based unease, for reasons unrelated to hangover and fitful sleep.

"I can't wait for you to meet Margaret," Danny said. "You two will get along like peas in a pod." He nudged her. "Get it? A gardening joke."

"Ah."

"She and Ben are so into roses that they converted half their back patio into a greenhouse."

121

Thank goodness there's a Ben, Sophia thought. Because she didn't want this rose-growing Margaret woman to be competition. Sophia wanted to sleep with Danny over and over again, until the desire for him wore off. She wondered if Margaret's Ben were a boyfriend, fiancé, or husband.

Three weeks later, Danny was driving Sophia to Georgetown, where Margaret and Ben were hosting Danny's birthday party.

They stopped at a red light. Danny traced a figure eight on Sophia's forearm.

"You and Margaret are similar," he said.

Sophia waited.

"You're both free spirits."

"Is that how you would describe me? In that clichéd way?"

"Doesn't it fit?"

"No. My mom has always teased me for being the least spontaneous creative person she knows. Every day I adhere to all sorts of routines, in my work and at home—"

"Recycling."

"Yeah, and gardening tasks." In her mind's eye, Sophia saw her office bulletin board and remembered Connie motto "Steer today to make tomorrow easier."

"I force myself to stick to a schedule," Sophia said smugly. "So I'll have the time and mental space to create the most substantive hunts for the kids—and not just for them, I mean, but with them." The thought of Connie's motto had made her nervously chatty, she realized, as if she were interviewing for a job.

"That's something else you have in common with Margaret," Danny mused. "You're both attractively absorbed by your work."

"What does she do?" Sophia wondered if Margaret also worked with young people.

"She's an attorney at the FDA. We met in college and then wound up at George Washington together for law school. And we liked DC so much that we decided to get jobs here. Most of the people you will meet Saturday night are friends from GW."

"Mm."

"You seem unenthused. Don't worry. No one will bore you with old school stories."

"I wasn't thinking of that. It was just funny to hear you say 'GW' because at Carver that's our nickname for George Washington Carver. In fact, our faculty never refers to George Washington Carver as 'G-Dub' or Dubya' or 'George W,' because we associate those nicknames with the Wicked Wizard of Waterboarding."

"He deserved that title." Danny's voice sounded sincere. Whenever Sophia brought up George W. Bush (which was pretty frequently, considering he was out of office), she noticed Danny was quick to disavow the former president. At least in her presence. She assumed most corporate lawyers were Republicans, even if they had to hide this because most people in DC are Democrats.

"I wouldn't mind hearing some old school stories about you," Sophia murmured.

"Well, I hate to disappoint you, but like you, I studied too hard to do anything memorable. Now Margaret, on the other hand, was always up to something."

"Then I'll look forward to meeting her. And Ben. Is he a lawyer also? "

"No. Ben's a hairdresser."

Hmm, Sophia thought. She realized that as a child, she would have assumed all male hairdressers or dancers or interior designers were gay. She hoped Ben was straight and that he and Margaret were a monogamous, sexually compatible couple.

Ben and Margaret lived in a red brick townhouse on Q Street in Georgetown. Two pale pink rose bushes bracketed the front steps, and botanical prints of roses lined the front hall and dining room.

Sophia was startled by the touch of a hand on the back of her arm. She turned, expecting it to be Danny. He had been mobbed by well-wishers as soon as they had arrived, and she escaped to the buffet so he wouldn't feel obligated to interrupt everyone's enthusiasm with a round of introductions. But the person who had touched her so intimately was a woman in a white pantsuit.

"You must be Margaret," Sophia said, offering her hand. But Margaret hugged her instead. Sophia thought this was ballsy because Sophia was holding a glass of red wine, and almost tipped it onto Margaret. What a shame it would be to stain that ostentatious outfit.

"When I saw you walk in with Danny, I knew you were Sophia from the darling way you'd wrapped his gift." Margaret's Southern accent sounded as breathy as Marilyn Monroe's. "Waste not want not!"

Sophia thought it was weird that Margaret, the party's hostess, would have taken the time to notice Sophia's gift.

Sophia had wrapped Danny's present, a copy of Frank Luntz's *Words that Work,* in last Sunday's comics. She used ribbon from a spool she'd accumulated by knotting together leftover ribbons. She drew a picture of a balloon with a D on one of the comic squares, then realized that the balloon's wavy tail made it look like a jaunty sperm. To remedy this, she added a layered birthday cake, then zigzagged lines of confetti, to make clear that the balloon was one of several non-spermy birthday symbols.

"Danny wants me to show you the greenhouse." Margaret took Sophia's hand and led her through the crowd. "I grow most of my roses in pots, except for the Clementina Carbonieri, and a Belle sans Flatterie. Most of the potted roses are still outside. We'll bring them in a few weeks. Last fall was so warm—until the middle of November."

The greenhouse looked Nordic, because of its modern wooden frame. Its relative emptiness made the six pots of roses look more striking.

"These are my David Austins," Margaret cooed. "They need a lot of loving care but they're worth it."

"What are their names?" Sophia asked.

"Queen Nefertiti, Falstaff, Abraham Darby, Winchester Cathedral, Teasing Georgia, and Gertrude Jekyll. The names are eighty-percent of the fun."

Sophia nodded. That was something she might have said.

"Do you grow any roses?" Margaret asked.

"No. I don't know anything about them."

"What a shame. I was going to ask you if it were possible to grow hybrid teas organically."

"I'm not sure, but off the top of my head, I think you'd probably have better luck with old heirloom varieties."

Margaret sighed. "That's what I thought you'd say. Ooooh don't look over there." "I didn't," Sophia lied. Margaret's shelves were stocked with Miracle-Gro, fungicides, black spot and iron sprays. Through the panes of the greenhouse, Sophia saw the roses she'd seen on Danny's bedside table.

"What are those called?" she asked, pointing. "The yellow ones with the scarlet edges?"

"Those are called Double Delights."

Something about that name disconcerted Sophia.

"My two favorite ladies have found each other!" Danny exclaimed as he entered the greenhouse. His cheeks were bright red, his wine glass slanted.

"Don't knock anything over in here," Margaret warned.

Danny tottered to Margaret. "Are you friends already? Maybe Sophia can make you a compost pile."

Margaret's previously rosy complexion blanched. "Compost? Here?" She wrinkled her nose.

"If you do it right, it smells good, like fresh soil," Danny said. "Right, Sophe? You could show her how. It would be a bonding experience." He winked at Margaret.

"I'm too busy to do that for her," Sophia snapped. "Don't volunteer my time without asking me first." Especially since the lawsuit, or rather, worrying about the lawsuit, had consumed so much of the time she usually reserved for the chores she needed to do around Cally's home to justify her low rent.

"Look, I'll just email you a link to some composting directions," Sophia told Margaret.

"I'll have to think *haaard* about whether I'm ready for compost," Margaret said, too breathily to seem capable of thought. "I'm not sure I'm comfortable going au naturale."

"Liar," Danny said.

Where the heck was Ben? Sophia wondered. You could have cut Margaret and Danny's sexual tension with a knife. Or pruning shears.

"I don't want you to think I can't appreciate the great outdoors," Margaret said for Sophia's benefit. "I jog six miles a day, sometimes along the C & O Canal. That towpath is so pretty, with the overhang of the trees, and the little duck families paddling along. And the…aroma of the water."

"You mean the rotten egg smell?" Sophia clarified.

126

"I...guess that's what I mean," Margaret's glance at Danny was apologetic. "It's...earthy, isn't it?"

"It's sewage. From vents along the Potomac Interceptor line. Whoever is in charge should fix it. The residents near that part of the canal are furious about it."

"Bummer," Danny said.

"Yucky," Margaret agreed. "I'll have to go back to my treadmill. I'm addicted to working out," she admitted, with a conspiratorial bob of the shoulders.

"Sorry. Didn't mean to spoil the canal for you," Sophia said. But she had. Margaret's beauty, coupled with that babyish voice, triggered Sophia's inner sadist.

"Au contraire. I'm glad you told me about the sewage," Margaret assured her. "I like grossing Ben out. Ben, honey, come here. Want to hear a disgusting bit of trivia?"

"Not really." So this was Ben. Finally.

Ben was a few inches taller than Danny, with a lanky build and nondescript glasses.

He looked straight as an arrow to Sophia, who assumed all gay men worldwide would have selected more fashionable eyeglass frames. She took note that Margaret had referred to him as "honey."

"Hi," Ben said, holding out his hand to shake Sophia's. "Ben Campbell."

"Sophia's one of my pro bono clients," Danny said before she could reply. "I just saved her charter school a bundle."

"He's too modest," Ben told Sophia. "Are you a teacher?"

"She's a curriculum designer," Danny corrected. "Which is like a cruise director. Like Julie McCoy from 'Love Boat,' except that Sophia promotes environmental stewardship and grows organic fruits and vegetables with inner city children."

"What a saint," Margaret said.

"I work with saints but I'm not saintly," Sophia replied.

"Don't demur, especially not in front of Danny," Margaret scolded. "He tires quickly of women who are falsely modest."

Sophia felt offended. "Nothing false about me," she said with a purposely obvious glance at Margaret's breasts. They seemed too full for her tiny waist. Or maybe expensive pantsuits were super flattering.

"I just read an article on organic fertilizer," Ben told Sophia. "What do you think of liquid seaweed? I may try it to extend our growing season."

"It's a good idea. But it reeks," she added, for Margaret's benefit.

"I'll try anything once," Margaret said, meeting Danny's eyes. Her smirk was as breezy and chill as a Washington winter. "Help me in the kitchen, Ben?"

A few minutes later, a redheaded white woman in a sari flitted through the crowd, stage-whispering, "Two minutes to cake! Everyone gather in the dining room!"

Sophia looked around for Danny, but didn't see him, so she followed the crowd. Three bells rang, and then Margaret emerged through a side door, wheeling in a chocolate version of a wedding cake. The top was crowned by a gold "36," instead of by a pair of a creepily waxen newlyweds.

"Happy birthday to you, Happy birthday to you," Margaret began breathily. Sophia watched her botoxic red lips, waiting to see if Margaret would say "Mr. President" instead of Danny. Margaret wasn't nearly as attractive as Marilyn Monroe. Her face was too long, but her sexy voice and body made up for this, and her hair fell around her shoulders in a shiny brown curtain.

"Where are the candles?" Danny cried, perfectly timing his mock-protest to conclude the song and the applause.

"We didn't want to set off the fire alarm," Ben called out from the back of the room.

Margaret put her hand to Danny's right shoulder, and whispered something long and involved in his ear. Sophia watched his arm curl around Margaret's waist.

In Sophia's opinion, most fancy-looking cakes were too mousse-like, but Danny's birthday cake had the chewy light suspension of a Krispy Crème doughnut, and was generously swirled with raspberry jam. Ben used a similar cart to Margaret's to bring in silver punchbowls of vanilla ice cream, caramel fudge, and crumbled-up Heath bars. Sophia decorated her cake with all the trimmings and sought out a chair. She couldn't find a single empty one, or even a quiet space to stand. Several people accosted her.

"Margaret told me the news. I never realized the canal was so polluted," a serious-looking woman said, without bothering to introduce herself.

"Never going back there again," proclaimed a guy in a seersucker jacket.

"Thanks for spreading the word," said a man who introduced himself solely as "Elizabeth Carrington's husband."

"So I heard you were sewage," said a tall blonde.

"What?"

"I heard you were sued. Margaret said you'd been sued. I work down the hall from her at FDA." Why was this woman fishing for gossip that she clearly knew already? And Sophia didn't like it when people referred to government agencies as "FDA" instead of "the FDA." It was an inside-the-Beltway affectation.

"I only met Margaret tonight," Sophia informed the woman, "and I don't know you. Neither of you should have been discussing the lawsuit. It's none of your business."

Sophia extricated herself, only to have someone else approach her to complain about the sewer line.

"The canal's been part of my baby's daily routine," wailed the woman, as though Sophia had forbidden its usage. "I take Millicent out there in the jog stroller all the time. For fresh air. Only it never smelled so fresh."

"Better call your pediatrician," advised an eavesdropping stiff with a comb-over and bifocals. "About those fumes. Everything causes asthma nowadays."

Sophia winced at the realization that she had just discouraged a roomful of people from enjoying an urban green space.

Chapter 13: Would Your Relationship Make the Cut?

"Objections to eggplant?" Sophia asked.

Seven out of seven kids' right hands shot up.

"You can't blame us for trying," Maggie said. "How about mushrooms instead? For the vegetarian chili."

"We get to do both a meat chili and a vegetarian chili for the Luscious LoCal cookoff?" a sixth grader named Candace asked. She was wearing a fuchsia sweatshirt emblazoned with "Teen Diva" in gold lightening script.

"You space cadet. They said already that we would make two kinds," Kira said.

"How many reporters will be there?" Victor asked.

Maggie shrugged. "Three or four, maybe?"

"With cameras?"

"If it's a slow news day. And weekends are usually pretty slow."

"Good. Then I'll be wearing my exploding cauliflower suit. Get some publicity for it, so it will come to the right people's attention, and the next thing you know, I got my own action figure, and a movie deal." He swept a cupped hand across an imaginary marquee: "'Cauliflower Man—Exploder of Brains'."

"You can't dress up like a cauliflower for this," Malikah Cooper, an eighth grader, said. "Please Miz Lewis. Don't let him. Everyone will think we put cauliflower in the chili."

"What's wrong with that ingredient?" Maggie asked.

"I mean, cauliflower's okay and all, but not in chili. It wouldn't even look right," Rashid explained.

"I don't like cauliflower," Bernard said, glancing nervously at Victor.

"Me neither," said Tamika.

"That's what you think," Maggie countered. Most of Carver's students had been won over by the multicolored varieties of "challenging" vegetables, but not Maggie's own kids. They rebelled. So she snuck pureed cauliflower and squash into most of what she made at home.

Rashid elbowed Bernard, and probably would have whispered something if Maggie and Sophia hadn't been sitting right across from him. He ate at Bernard's all the time, so Sophia wondered if he knew Maggie's secret.

"If I can't wear my suit, I want first dibs on the name," Victor told the group.

"The name of our team?" Kira asked.

"Naming recipes," Victor said, without looking at her. "How about we make them like movie names, like Lava One and Lava Two? The vegetarian one can be the sequel because sequels are never as fun. I could make us a papier mache model of a volcano."

"I love that idea," Sophia said. She wanted to give Victor a hug, for being so creative, but she knew she would embarrass him and every other child at the table if she did so.

"No lava. We need appetizing names," Malikah said.

"Victor, we won't have room to set up a volcano," Maggie said gently.

"How 'bout two little volcanoes?" Victor asked. He certainly had a thing for explosions. Sophia made a mental note to discuss chemistry experiments with Tariq.

"I think we should get back to the ingredients," said Maggie. "The flavor's more important than the name."

Everyone looked back down at their food lists. The 11" by 17" pages were divided into three categories: SCHOOL GARDEN—the shortest list, because there'd be so little fresh produce available by January, a much longer PANTRY/FREEZER list, and a few LOCAL SUPPLIERS, headed by grass-fed, organic beef from Groff's Content Farm in Rocky Ridge, Maryland.

None of the kids said or did anything for a minute. There were so many choices.

"Are you guys overwhelmed?" Sophia asked.

"No," Kira said too quickly.

"If you'd like to, you could circle the foods you like best, and cross out the ones you don't think we should include," Sophia suggested.

Pencils immediately went to paper. Later, Sophia and Maggie made shorter lists of the most popular items, and used these to come up with twelve variations so that all six classes in the school could test one recipe with meat and one without.

Every year on the Saturday evening before Thanksgiving break, Carver's students prepared a feast that they usually based on the garden's last fall harvest. Sophia looked forward to visiting with everyone under one roof, especially since all the parents she had run into over the past few weeks had been discreet about the lawsuit. She knew from Barbara that the news had filtered down to them, but no one brought it up with her, even squeaky wheels like Mr. Simpson. Since none of the kids were looking at her funny, she was sure they hadn't been told. She wished she could send Harold Tompkins a note, to thank him for not talking about it with his friends. So many students from his new school, Shaw, knew kids from Carver.

A few days before the feast, Maggie made an announcement that disappointed Sophia. With the Luscious LoCal cookoff just two weeks away, she had decided to cancel the school's traditional Thanksgiving feast and replace it with an in-house cookoff, so the entire school community could taste and vote on the twelve chili recipes. Before this fall, Sophia loved any kind of chili, but now she was sick of it, and she longed for the variety and tradition of a real Thanksgiving meal.

"You'll get to eat those foods next Thursday," Maggie said curtly, when Sophia gave in to her irresistible urge to suggest a few side dishes.

"I know." Sophia sighed from mixed feelings. Her father and Connie's husband Bo would make deep fried turkey, apple pie with apples from the Harmonious Pears orchard, green bean casserole made with pole beans from Connie's garden, and spoon bread dressing from locally milled cornmeal. But Connie, who hadn't seen Sophia in months, would scan her goddaughter to see if she looked the same or heavier. Connie would check out her plate to see how much Sophia was eating.

"Why don't you invite Danny to our chili taste-testing?" Maggie suggested later, in the faculty room. Sophia had just told Maggie and Nadia that she and Danny had begun dating after the settlement papers were signed. She was comfortable making their relationship known to her friends because she trusted Danny more now as boyfriend material. Though she couldn't fully admit this to herself, she had been relieved when Danny insisted Margaret apologize to Sophia for gossiping about the lawsuit with her friend. And afterward, Danny told Sophia privately that Margaret was a needy person.

"I'm a little worried about Dawn's reaction," Sophia told Maggie and Nadia, "even though I waited until the lawsuit settled."

"Dawn won't dwell on it. She's involved in her own romantic intrigue right now," Nadia said with a smile.

Sophia and Maggie exchanged glances. "She has been hanging out with Tariq a lot," Sophia mused.

"No way!" Maggie squealed. "She's way too cautious to get involved with a teacher."

"I know," Nadia said, "I think she wouldn't get involved with him if this weren't serious."

And then Dawn walked in.

"What were you gals just talking about?" she asked them. "You look gossipy."

"We were gossiping about me," Sophia admitted. "I'm dating Danny."

Dawn sighed and put down the folders of papers she had been holding. "I knew this would happen," she said. "But I bet it will be over soon so I'm not going to stress about it."

"Thanks for your vote of confidence," Sophia said with light sarcasm. "And how about what you're doing?"

"What I'm doing is knowing what I'm doing," Dawn told the three of them. "And right now I know I'm making some photocopies. What is it, winter break already? Don't y'all have work to do?"

As soon as Sophia returned to her office she saw this email from Danny:

Turns out I'm busy the night of the chili tasting. May I housesit for you while you're away for Thanksgiving? My parents will be staying at my place and I don't want to sleep on the couch. They won't let me in the kitchen anyway while they're getting everything ready because I overseason everything. That's why I like you. You're spicy enough.
I can do some gardening chores for you while you're out of town. Just show me what you want me to do for you.

She wrote back:

Thanks, but most of the chores are too hard to explain. You could water my plants though, and my landlord's plants, if you don't mind. That would help me out.

Driving home from work, Sophia got a call from Danny. She pulled over to take the call.

"I've got a ton of work to do for a client but I want to blow it off," he said. "Do you want to grab some dinner? I know we're doing dinner on Friday night but I can't wait until then to see you."

"Sounds good."

After their conversation, Sophia didn't pull back into traffic right away. She was feeling some kind of emotion that caused a catch in her throat and would have made it hard to drive properly. This happiness and excitement was more intense than surprised pleasure over Danny's spontaneity.

Danny was very careful about some things, and deliciously lax about others. At the height of the lawsuit, he had told Sophia she didn't need to mention several of their conversations to Dawn. How liberating, to be told by a professional that you didn't need to be as conscientious as you thought you did. How generous he was, to join her when she'd felt so alone, at the wrong end of a continuum between reasonable and imprudent conduct. Danny was as sharp and clear as a broken wine glass. Maybe not as clear, she thought on second thought.

When Sophia got home, she grabbed a spiral notebook that she had intended to use for lesson planning. She knew she wanted to start a new journal. She wanted to write about Danny. She was embarrassed to be so excited about a player. She had never ever wanted to be one of the zillion women who got bamboozled this way. Players and their prey were a dime a dozen.

She opened the spiral journal to its beautifully fresh, clean first page. She picked up one of her favorite pens, a blue ball point with a medium tip that always had plenty of ink without being smeary.

No. This notebook is just for lesson plans, she wrote. *But I guess I won't need a whole new notebook for lesson plans now that I'm a part-time curriculum designer.*

Sophia's heart sank at the sight of the phrase "part-time curriculum designer." She would put off telling her parents about the demotion and never wanted Connie to know.

Sophia's thoughts fled to a nicer topic—Danny's handsomeness. Maybe it wouldn't really be journal-writing if she just made a list about him, and didn't use his name, even.

The numbered list Sophia composed about Danny was the closest she had ever come to writing a love letter.

1. Quick-witted
2. Affectionate
3. Relaxed

4. Decisive
5. The Lawsuit's Knight in Shining Armor
6. My Knight in Shining Armor?

She flicked the pen across the room. *Shoot*, she thought, just before the pen hit the wall. She shouldn't have done that since the walls were Cally's. But the pen didn't leave a mark.

Sophia read over what she had written, and couldn't stand the fact that she had written it down. No, that wasn't it. What she couldn't stand was the restlessness and self-pity she felt knowing that her journal was her only confidant. She couldn't bear to think this restless feeling was loneliness.

She resolved to interpret the itchy feeling as a specific, temporary problem. She had strong feelings for one person, and she wanted to talk strongly about him with one other person, who would not remember that Sophia was making herself vulnerable. If only she had a friend who was an amnesiac, or who had smoked weed for so long that their memory would be Swiss cheese. But no, all of Sophia's friends and acquaintances were solid citizens. Most were married or in such serious relationships that they might as well have been married. They might think her feelings for Danny were sweet. A type of infatuation that they remembered from their immature past lives.

What was Danny's romantic past like? Margaret came to mind. But surely a man and a woman could be longtime friends…even flirtatious friends, without hooking up. Danny had said Margaret got on his nerves sometimes. Sophia wished, for the jillionth time, that she could find out whether Margaret and Danny had ever dated in college or in law school. She kept wishing one of their old friends would mention something definitive in one of the comments attached to old photos of them on their respective Facebook walls. Sophia imagined a montage of all the drunken nights they must have shared. She was projecting her own college experience onto theirs.

The thought of Facebook made her think of pithy status updates. That was it, she would only write pithy status updates in her journal. Except these updates would be forever kept private. She would hide this new journal in a box marked "TAX RECORDS: 1995 to 2005." No one would ever look for it there.

Sophia's herbs missed her while she was away for Thanksgiving. After she'd unpacked, she strolled into the kitchen and saw that the mint had wilted, the stevia had shed an alarming number of leaves, and some of the rosemary branches had turned beige. The antique green glass bottles she'd paired with each plant (because they reflected sunlight and watering cans wouldn't), were almost as full as they had been on the day she had filled them up. Just a little evaporation, she realized. Danny had not watered the plants.

Sophia's adrenalin surged. She grabbed one of the bottles, and poured with too heavy a hand. Globules of soily water overran their containers, filling the clear plastic trays that protected the wooden table underneath. Sophia got a dishtowel, to dab excess water from the herbs' bottom leaves so they wouldn't develop black spot or mildew.

At first, she wondered if Danny had misplaced her key. Maybe he had never been able to get in the house, and maybe he didn't email or call her to let her know because he didn't want to interrupt her family time in Ithaca. She went into the bedroom and saw he had left the bed unmade, so he must have been able to get in after all. She thought of another explanation for his oversight. Maybe he wasn't sure he would water the plants correctly, so he figured it was better to leave them alone. But why wouldn't he have just emailed to ask? Would he have been more careful if she had spelled out the instructions for him by providing a numbered list?

She remembered emphasizing the heartiness of the herbs. "They grow like weeds, especially the mint." She hadn't said much more than that, and it must have been because she didn't want him to tease her. He'd called her a schoolmarm a few days after his birthday party, and she'd responded with a short "hmm" of amusement to hide her sensitivity. Now she wished she had explained why preventative care was important. Organic gardeners couldn't zap away problems with chemicals, and really, even conventional gardeners couldn't do so very well. Chemical "treatments" merely replaced one ailment with another. All they offered were short-term fixes, in exchange for long-term costs.

Sophia had been thinking about the negative pairing of short-term fixes and long-term costs since two days earlier while she was still in Ithaca. She picked fruit with Connie in the Harmonious Pears orchard.

"Sophia, darling. I hope you didn't feel depressed at the Thanksgiving table, being the only person there who wasn't married with children?"

"No, I never want to get married or multiply," Sophia replied. "There are too many starving children in the world already for me to feel comfortable having my own child. I'd adopt a poor, starving child in a heartbeat if I could afford to, but now I'm hardly going to be able to afford to since my hours were...uh...you know the economy might collapse again."

"Were you about to say your hours had been cut back?" Connie asked hawkishly.

"Yes. Carver's donors have less money to give us now."

140

"This is the perfect time for you to finish that PhD," Connie sniffed. "You could do it on a part-time basis. That's what Ryan did. He went to night school while holding down two jobs during the day and—"

"I forgot about Ryan," Sophia interrupted. "So sad that he never comes home to spend Thanksgiving with you. Too busy improving the nation's math curricula, I guess."

Sophia felt ashamed when Connie burst into tears.

"That was a low blow," Connie said. "Mentioning Ryan. You know he can't stand me and I'm not so confident that I don't feel pained by it. You've been especially aggressive with me since August. What's up?"

This would have been a great opportunity, Sophia thought later, to resolve her problems with Connie. Instead she said, "Nothing" like she was a child. If Sophia told Connie what she was thinking, Connie would initiate a long touchy-feely conversation. Then they would hug, and Sophia would have to spend more time with Connie (and write more substantive emails once she got back to DC) than if she just gritted her teeth for another forty-five minutes.

Sophia chose the short-term fix of shutting Connie out, but an hour later, she wasn't really free of Connie, because Connie occupied her thoughts for the rest of the weekend.

Now, as Sophia watered her dehydrated plants, and then Cally's dehydrated plants, she couldn't get Connie out of her mind.

She received an email from Connie the next morning.

Am coming to DC next week as part of my book tour for the paperback version of Noah's Ark: Would Your Relationship Make the Cut? *I would have mentioned it when I saw you but you seemed so out of sorts. You really do need a new boyfriend, Sophia. Jack left for Indonesia ages ago and ever since then you've been crabbier. Will you pick me up from the airport? And can you have lunch with me while I'm in town? Maybe Sunday brunch, just before I take the train to my Baltimore book signing.*

Sophia wrote back: *I am seeing a great guy right now and will introduce you.*

Connie wrote back: *I look forward to meeting your latest if the two of you are still together by then.*

Chapter 14: What Would the Six Words Be?

"You forgot to water my plants," Sophia told Danny as soon as she got to the restaurant where they were going to have dinner.

"Sorry," Danny said, standing up to give her a hello hug and kiss. "I knew I forgot to do something. I was with Margaret over the past few days. She's having some issues at work and needed a lot of advice."

"Does Ben help her with that too?"

"No. She needs me when these things come up."

"Do they come up a lot?"

"Yes. I read over a lot of her memos. She sometimes has trouble with details because she has such a quick mind. So are your plants fatally dehydrated?"

"No. But when you decide to quit law and become a plant-waterer, I'm not giving you a good reference." She wished Danny hadn't offered to help with the plants in the first place. She would have done what she always did when she left town for a few days—filled the plastic trays with water so the herbs could soak up what they needed through the holes she'd drilled at the bottom of her containers.

"Is there anything I can do to make up for this grievous negligence?" Danny asked.

"Yes. Will you have Sunday brunch with me and my evil godmother? She's coming into town and she's been bitching and moaning about the fact that I'm not in a relationship."

"Aren't we in a relationship yet?"

"Sure," Sophia replied. "But please don't tell Connie you're a lawyer. Are you ethically comfortable telling her you're a big success in any career other than law? She will immediately tell my dad I'm dating a lawyer, and he will freak."

"But at some point won't you tell your dad about me? I have no problem telling him I do something else, but how long can you keep up a façade?"

"I will tell him, maybe over Christmas, but I'd like to put it off until then."

"That's fine. It's a little known secret that many corporate lawyers would rather be architects. That's a cooler career than law."

"Perfect."

"This will be fun," Danny said. "I've never had brunch with a New Age guru before."

"Will you be sure to call her a New Age guru at some point? It bruises her ego when people use that phrase to describe her. Also, please use the word 'self-help' to describe her work. She tries to spread the phrase "enumerative guidance' but that's never caught on because it's too much of a mouthful for anyone other than diehard Countess Connie fans, including Connie herself."

"Consider it done. From all you wrote about her in your journal, I'll enjoy annoying her,"

Danny squeezed Sophia's hand. "I'm glad we're officially together now."

Sophia chose a Sunday brunch place where she knew the chef used locally-grown produce and dairy products from Loudoun Creamery.

"So what do you do?" Connie asked Danny in the same tone that another woman might have asked a man about his favorite sexual position. "I can tell by your clothes that you've done something right."

"I'm an architect, Countess Connie. Mostly working in Italy, around the Lake Como area. Have you heard of George Clooney? We're going to tear down his current property there and start from scratch."

Sophia winced. She remembered that Connie secretly read glossy magazines and might find out this wasn't true.

"George Clooney? Oh yes. *Up in the Air* was a brilliant film. I don't keep up with popular culture, however. On a related note, please don't call me 'Countess Connie.'" She gave Danny a penetrating look. "Sophia, this man of yours looks a bit like George Clooney, if George Clooney were handsome. Are you Italian, Danny?"

"Yes ma'am."

"I love the Italians. So lively."

"Have your bestsellers been translated into Italian?" Danny asked. "I know you write a lot of self-help and New Agey books. Are they as popular in Italy as they are in the U.S.?"

Connie straightened up in her chair, and gave Danny the lecture she gave to interviewers whenever they used those phrases to oversimplify her.

Sophia could barely restrain her laughter, but sobered up quickly once she forced herself to think thoughts of global warming. Whenever a kid at Carver said something unintentionally funny, Sophia thought about global environmental destruction to keep from hurting the child's feelings by giggling.

"So how long have you two been dating?" Connie asked, eyes narrowed.

"Since the lawsuit ended," Danny said.

Sophia froze.

"What lawsuit?" Connie asked, now widening her eyes.

"Uh, well, we met at a party through mutual friends, but I was so busy working on a lawsuit that we couldn't spend time together until about a month ago."

"What do you mean when you say you were working on a lawsuit?" Connie asked. "I thought you said you were an architect. Did one of your clients sue you?"

"Oh no, no, absolutely not," Danny said. Sophia had never seen him startled before. "I'm an experienced architect. I do everything uh, according to code. And because of that, I'm frequently asked to be an expert witness in lawsuits that happen to careless architects."

"I see," Connie said. "Well, I'm glad to hear Sophia's finally met someone professionally successful."

"All my boyfriends have been professionally successful," Sophia snapped. "As activists and as educators."

"I'm sorry, you're right." Connie made it clear from her tone that she had decided to humor her goddaughter. "But those bleeding-heart liberals didn't have two dimes to rub together. Poor you, Sophia darling. When I was your age, I could get any man I wanted just by saying six words."

"What were the six words?" Sophia and Danny asked at the same time.

"I will never tell," Connie said. "And I need to be going now. Busy, busy book tour."

"Nice to meet you, Connie," Danny said after Connie instructed him to pay the bill. "You're quite the cougar."

Connie's expression darkened. "You are as tactless as my goddaughter. But I hope you will let her keep you. Come along, Sophia. Time to drive me to the train station and you know what a tentative driver you can be."

That evening at Danny's house, Sophia said, "So what do you think the six words are?"

"Huh?" Danny asked.

"Don't tell me you've forgotten what Connie said, about subduing any man with six words." *Why six?* Sophia wondered. Was it just a coincidence that Sophia had mentioned her and Lucy's interest in six-word sentences?

"I hadn't forgotten that Connie had bragged about that," Danny said, "but I think she was just saying it to needle you and to make you curious. There's no such thing as a magic spell, and from what you've said, and what I read in your journal, Connie's full of bullshit."

"I know, and a few months ago I told her I was into six-word quotes, so she might be lying, but if she could think up a specific six-word sentence, I wonder what it would be. She does think well in numbers."

"Right. She told me she was an enumerative guide while you were trying not to bust your gut laughing."

The phone rang. It was Margaret.

"Calm down, Magpie," Danny said into the receiver. "What happened?"

Sophia watched Danny's face and posture shift with concern and alertness.

"No, I'm sure it wasn't your fault. She's just jealous of you because you're so beautiful and smart." He walked toward the bedroom, saying "Now tell me everything that happened. From the beginning."

Why didn't Margaret ever go to Ben for support? They were living together. Shouldn't Margaret discuss her problems with him, since he seemed to be her boyfriend?

When Sophia had met Ben at Danny's birthday party, she had been impressed by Ben's friendliness and great sense of humor. He had a better personality than Margaret, who was a drama queen. That's it, Sophia thought. Ben was sick of hearing Margaret's melodramas. She had to call Danny. They were best friends, after all. Men and women could be great friends. Connie didn't believe that, but just because Connie didn't believe that didn't mean Sophia had to adopt whatever Connie thought.

Sophia pondered Connie's six-word boast until Danny returned from the bedroom, half an hour later.

"I wonder why Connie said six words instead of two words. She thinks two is the most powerful number of all," Sophia told him.

"You've got to stop talking about this and thinking about it," Danny said.

"Dude, you just spent half an hour on the phone with Margaret helping her chew over something."

"Don't be jealous."

"I'm not jealous. I've never been jealous in a relationship."

"I've got two words for you," Danny said, changing the subject.

"What?"

"Kiss me."

Five hours later, Sophia couldn't fall asleep because her thoughts were looping over and over the question: *If Connie came up with a powerful six-word sentence, even if she did so just to goad me for my brevity mission, what would her six words be?*

Chapter 15: Two Is Company, Three's A Crowd

The next morning, Danny and Sophia rushed off to their respective workplaces. Later that day, he called to ask her if she wanted to have dinner that Friday night with Margaret, Ben, and Ben's boyfriend.

"Ben has a boyfriend?" Sophia asked. "I thought he and Margaret were in item."

"No. Ben's immune from her charms. I can't believe I forgot to tell you that. He's gay, and his boyfriend John is an investment banker. But, when you meet John, don't ask about his work. he got laid off last year."

Crap, Sophia thought, not because she wanted to ask this guy John about investment banking. She wished Margaret could be safely paired up with a boyfriend who would distract her from calling on Danny all the time and keeping Danny on a tight leash. Or rather, Danny let himself be kept there.

That Friday night as Sophia came outside to Danny's car, she realized she wasn't dressed warmly enough.

"Hang on, I'm just going to get a jacket," she told him.

"Jeez, Sophia. It's December. Didn't you know you'd need a coat? I don't want to be late for Margaret—," slight pause, "and Ben."

Before Thanksgiving break, Sophia remembered, Danny had alternated between playing the seducer and the old-fashioned suitor. The first time he opened the passenger-side door for Sophia he said "I hope I don't seem sexist."

"That's gilding the lily," she had told him. "You really got game."

He didn't reply, just handed her the swath of her flowing skirt, so it wouldn't get caught in the door.

On this night, Danny didn't get the door for her. He didn't even see her come up to the car because his eyes and thumbs were focused on his smartphone. The door was locked so she tapped on the glass. Without making eye contact, he unclicked the lock on his arm rest and she settled into her seat as gracefully as her short skirt would allow.

He glanced critically at her legs. "That's why you're cold. You're not dressed properly for the weather."

"Don't talk to me like I'm a child," Sophia replied. "Connie always used to lecture me on—"

"Can we not talk about Connie tonight? No offense, but after meeting her in person, I cannot understand why you think she's such a force to be reckoned with."

"I don't think that."

"You're obsessed with her, and people don't become obsessed with people unless they think that person has some power over them. Connie's a joke. Get over it."

"She was a second mother to me," Sophia protested. "People aren't rational about their mothers. I've got a ton of past baggage with her."

"I'd appreciate hearing less about her."

Sophia felt stung. She hid her pique and disappointment, then steeled herself inside. Clearly, she should figure out when a good time would be to break up with him. The right time would be after she had enjoyed sleeping with him for a few more weeks or even months.

"I'm glad we're going to Pastorale," she said. "I've read about the chef. She buys from local farmers."

Danny drove more erratically than usual, but Sophia didn't notice the pattern until they were half a block from the restaurant's valet stand. He must have had some drinks before picking her up. She would insist they take a cab home.

As soon as the waiter at Pastorale handed them menus, Margaret turned to Sophia. "You're not a vegetarian, are you?"

"No," replied Sophia.

"Thank God," Margaret said. "But didn't you say she was something?" she asked Danny.

"She's something else," Danny said. "And so are you."

"No really. It's a word that rhymes with carnivore."

Sophia attempted a chuckle. "Locavore?"

"That's it," Margaret said. "I knew you had some trendy sort of dietary predilection."

"The sustainable food movement isn't a fad," Sophia said. "And locavorism is only part of the solution. If everyone ate red meat sparingly, as a condiment rather than...." Danny put his hand over hers to cut her off.

"What is this, the Gong Show?" she protested.

He patted her hand. "You're just jealous."

Was it obvious that Sophia envied Margaret for having Danny under her thumb? And because Margaret had known Danny so much longer, the passage of time had made her bond much more powerful than Sophia's attempt at control.

Sophia, however, had misunderstood the meaning behind Danny's comment. He was setting up a labored local-food joke. "Sophia thinks international air travel shouldn't be wasted on salad vegetables and fancy nuts."

"Yeah, that's it," Sophia replied. His face was redder than it should have been, especially his nose. He definitely drank some cocktails before picking her up to go out to dinner.

"You poor thing," Margaret cooed to Sophia. "Teachers' salaries are so low. You can't afford to fly anywhere. I know you're too proud to admit it but you are noble to be doing what you're doing. What grade do you teach?"

"Actually, she's a curriculum designer, remember?" Ben said.

"I don't think you know me as well as you think you do, Margaret," Sophia said. "I can afford the plane tickets I need to buy."

"What is the age range of the students you work with most?" John asked politely.

"Middle schoolers," Sophia replied gratefully.

"Yuck!" Margaret exclaimed this as though a line of bedbugs had scurried across the tablecloth. "I could not stand to do what you do for a living because middle schoolers are dreadfully hormonal. I was insufferable from 6th through 12th grade." She turned to Danny. "I'm so glad you didn't meet me until college,"

"You must have been bad in high school 'cause you were a handful in college," he murmured back.

"What? I was not," Margaret exclaimed. She leaned toward him, delighted. She propped her chin on the edge of her fist. Audrey Hepburn's image appeared on the security camera video in Sophia's head.

Danny was happy to oblige Margaret's desire to hear more about what a badass she was.

"You were mischief itself. Remember the dental floss test?" he asked.

"Can we not talk about this?" John asked.

"Yeah, I cannot sit through the dental floss story again," Ben agreed.

"Dental floss?" Sophia asked. "That sounds tame."

"Taming," Danny corrected. "Margaret used the dental floss test to tame boyfriends. Whenever she started dating someone, she'd test their devotion by asking them to run out in the middle of the night to the twenty-four-hour drug store to buy her dental floss."

"It wasn't a test, Danny," Margaret said. "I can't sleep if I feel like there's something stuck between my teeth."

"You wound up with more packs of dental floss than a Johnson and Johnson warehouse, my dear."

"They get lost so easily. Like lipsticks and pens."

"That's true," Ben said. "We never have enough pens. The roses eat them while we're at work."

"No one ever said 'no' to you in college or law school," Danny said, staring at Margaret fixedly.

Margaret sighed.

"And you broke everyone's heart," he added.

Ooosh. Sophia put the last bit of her popover back on her bread plate.

"Whose heart did I break?" Margaret asked as though she were reciting lines she had said before. Sophia wondered if Margaret studied soap operas for behavioral tips.

"Too many guys to name in one evening," Danny began, "but among our closest friends I'd have to say Joshua, Andy, Chip Rogers, and Chip Rogers's dad...."

"Now hold it right there. I never let Chip Rogers's dad seduce me. I swear," Margaret interrupted. She looked annoyed but Sophia was pretty damn sure this was because she was trying to look annoyed. "Mr. Rogers was a train wreck."

A woman from the table next to theirs turned to look at Margaret, who noticed her immediately and said, "Not the Mr. Rogers from TV. Jesus!"

"Ooh," Danny said. "Do you kiss your mother with that mouth?"

"Shut up, Danny. Bitterness doesn't become you."

"I don't think Danny has a bitter bone in his body," Ben said mildly.

"That's okay, Benji," Danny said, patting his arm. "You don't have to protect me. Though Magpie did scrape me up pretty well, back in the day by flirting with my fraternity brothers. That was brutal."

Sophia wished she hadn't ordered such a big dinner. The appetizers hadn't shown up yet, and already she felt too queasy for the chicken gnocchi and mushrooms she had looked forward to tasting after reading about the chef.

"You know I was flirting for your sake," Margaret was telling Danny. Margaret's big, round brown eyes reminded Sophia of Danny's. Had their similar coloring attracted them to each other in the first place?

"That makes no sense. How could you have done that for my sake?" Danny reached for his wine glass. "I was so competitive with Joshua."

"Ooh, they're finally entering new territory," John said sarcastically.

"Excuse me, ma'am," the waiter said to Sophia. She turned to look up, and the waiter set down her appetizer. The man or woman who'd prepared these greens had drizzled them with ingredients Sophia usually loved to see and smell and taste: pale green olive oil and glistering black tapenade. Stuck in the middle of Danny and Margaret's verbal lambada, however, Sophia could no sooner have begun to eat than if the shrimp had been alive and writhing.

Margaret was enjoying herself. "You were always complaining about how girls clung once they'd slept with you, Danny. As soon as we became friends with benefits, I flirted because I knew it would make things more fun for us both. I prolonged your thrill of the chase." Margaret said this last sentence slowly, as though she were referring to Tantric sex.

Sophia jumped up from the table. This move knocked back her heavy, padded chair, which in turn knocked into the back of the man who was sitting behind her. He gave her a flamingly shaming frown and because of it, she didn't acknowledge or apologize for the bump.

Danny grabbed Sophia's wrist, but she pulled away, storming toward a corridor she hoped would lead to the bathroom. She went the wrong way, almost smacking into a waitress who *wasn't* holding a tray, thank goodness, and who swiftly redirected her toward the proper corridor.

Sophia splashed water on her face. She banged her shoulder into the paper towel dispenser as her body slumped, and a woman came out of one of the three stalls to ask if she needed help.

"I'm fine, thanks," Sophia replied, though this was a ridiculous claim, given the evidence. Her tears were immediately stanched by the pressure to calm down so as not to freak out and inconvenience this nice woman. She didn't want to ruin anyone else's expensive meal.

"Sophia?" It was Margaret, wide-eyed and dewy. Sophia didn't know Ben or John well, but she knew she would much rather have one of them come to her aid.

"What's wrong?" Margaret asked. "Was it something about the food not being local enough?"

"No," Sophia groaned, reaching for a paper towel.

"I just know you're very sensitive about your dietary regimen."

Sophia moved to walk out.

"Please don't go yet," Margaret asked more quietly. "Did my conversation with Danny upset you?"

"No," Sophia protested.

"There's something I should tell you about Danny."

"I don't think that's necessary—"

"Hear me out. Danny carries a lot of resentment against me. He thinks I scarred him romantically in college, so he sometimes tries to make me jealous while uh, embroiling me in his current relationships."

"Embroiling?" Sophia was about to ask what Margaret meant by embroiling, but Margaret wouldn't let her get a word in.

She put her hand on Sophia's shoulder. "I have something else to tell you. I think Danny might be more serious about you than he's been about other girls. Because usually he just dates girls who look like supermodels."

"Gee thanks," Sophia said. She remembered Danny's Facebook friend list, which could have been a modeling agency's headshot collection.

"From now on, " Margaret continued, "I don't want you to let it get to you when Danny and I get lost in our own world. I promise it will only happen whenever we talk about our past, and…."

157

Sophia had already compared Margaret and Danny's decade of romantic intrigue to her own nomadic history. Sophia's contact with ex-boyfriends was superficial: work-related emails, names and holiday cards.

"....your relationship with Danny is fine with me. I'm not threatened by you," Margaret said, rubbing the restaurant's lotion into her manicured hands. "in fact, I sometimes enjoy an unconventional bond with Danny's girlfriends, which, I have to admit sometimes deteriorates into threesomes or blossoms into threesomes, depending on your perspective—"

"I would rather eat factory farmed meat at McDonald's *and* drive a Hummer than hook up with you," Sophia said. She walked back to their table.

Danny and Ben stopped talking. "Are you all right?" Danny asked her. "I'm so sorry. I was at a bar crawl this afternoon, of all the stupid things to do, and I'm not myself tonight."

"You are always yourself," Sophia disagreed. "Tonight more so." She found her wallet at the bottom of her purse, pulled out three twenty-dollar bills. They were as crisp as hotel bedding from that afternoon's ATM machine. "This should cover my share."

"What is your problem? I always pay."

Ben and John slipped away from the table and out of the corner of her eye, Sophia saw them intercept Margaret. Ben steered her, via elbow, toward the bar area.

"I never thought you'd be the type to make a scene," Danny hissed.

"I'm not going to make a scene. She got her coat from the attendant, slipped a dollar in the attendant's fishbowl, and left without a backward glance.

158

Wind blasted her face as soon as she got outside. Danny was behind her at first and then beside her, taking her arm her slow her down.

"We need to talk about how jealous Margaret makes you feel. I don't think you're in touch with your jealous side," he said.

"I'm not jealous."

"You're too proud to admit it. You've teased me about being a player, but your game is that you act more in control than you really are. I realize that now about you. This dynamic has happened to me before but I thought you'd be strong enough to.... You two reminded me of each other, and I have been curious to see how you would react to each other."

"Yeah, Margaret mentioned the threesome thing you've done with other women. Which would never happen with me. But I would be less ashamed of doing that than I am of even getting involved a man like you." Nothing good was going to come out of further conversation. She broke away, and he followed her again. She sped up to make his words inaudible, wishing there were a Metro stop near her house. She'd have to take a cab, and since she had given Danny $60, she didn't think she had enough money left to get all the way home.

There was a Hilton Hotel on the corner. She headed for its revolving door, so she could pull out her wallet and count her cash in the privacy of their women's bathroom.

"Wait," Danny said once they were in the lobby. She looked around for the women's room. Danny couldn't follow her there. Was the closest bathroom down that corridor to the right of the reception desk, or on the other side, up the wide bank of carpeted stairs? She scanned the walls for signs when Danny grabbed her arm again, not with painful force, but she still said, "Let go, you're hurting me."

He followed her into the bathroom. The staleness and air freshener reek worsened her breathlessness. Another woman walked into the bathroom, saw Danny and Sophia there, and walked out again.

"We're done," Sophia told Danny.

"Don't break up with me over an awkward moment at dinner."

"It's more than that and you know it. I'm not interested in being part of a threesome, and I'm not interested in dating a guy who calls another woman 'Magpie' unless that woman's name really is 'Magpie.' Leave, because I don't want to be in here any longer than I have to be."

"Can we at least be friends?" Danny asked.

Sophia was miffed that he so quickly accepted the breakup.

"Of course we can be friends," Sophia agreed, remembering he had helped Carver, and wishing she had taken the time to break up with him the next day, gently and judiciously.

"I will give you a ride home," Danny said. "Come on, let's get out of the ladies room before my balls shrink."

"No thanks, I have enough money for a cab and I'd like to be alone."

When Danny left, Sophia checked her wallet and saw she didn't have enough money, so she took a cab part of the way and walked the rest through frigid air. Her high-heeled boots hurt so much that she bought a pair of drugstore flip flops. She used a credit card, breaking a promise to herself. In the wake of her demotion, she had vowed to stop buying things on credit except in cases of dire emergency involving fire or blood loss.

When she got home she saw that Danny had emailed her already. She scanned it before reading it, scared the content would upset her almost as much as the legalese had on the day she found out about the lawsuit.

...I'm bad at relationships, but you can trust me as a friend and as Carver's pro bono attorney.

Sophia heard her father's voice in her head. "Yeah right, buddy. Can't trust a lawyer further than you can throw 'im."

Chapter 16: Sophia Feels Like Cupid's Nonstick Skillet

For the first week of her unease with the breakup, Sophia couldn't sleep. Persephone recommended a good cry.

"I didn't think you liked him that much, sweetheart, but now I think he got under your skin enough that your heart is broken."

Sophia hesitated before confiding, "I would never admit this to anyone else, but you may be right. I was more physically attracted to him than I have been to other boyfriends, and his worry-free attitude, even if it's just a façade, was intoxicated. And I hoped it would be contagious. He certainly got me through the lawsuit smoothly. And I feel like if he could get me through that, he would be able to get me through anything, and not only that, but he'd be able to get me through anything with some humor. You know, I think I am more heartbroken over the fact that I don't have some enduring person in my life, the way he and Margaret have each other."

"You wouldn't want a relationship like theirs," Persephone pointed out.

"But maybe I do want to settle down with someone, not legally, with a white dress and caterers, but I want to be with the same person for a long, long time. Don't tell Connie."

"I won't," Persephone said gently. "But in *Noah's Ark*, she writes about how to use heartache to motivate oneself toward a better relationship. Maybe you should read that part."

"I will," Sophia agreed. They got off the phone, and she drank the rest of a bottle of wine.

The next night, after finishing another bottle of wine, Sophia tried to bring on healing tears by thinking about how much she envied Margaret and Danny's rich past. Her eyes stayed dry. She thought about the contrariness of certain physical urges. When she didn't want someone to know they had hurt her feelings, tears threatened to overflow, but now when she did want to weep in the privacy of her living room, tears were nowhere in sight.

Sophia remembered how hard it had been to sit through college lectures, because she learned best from actively working on projects. She would feel herself nodding off to the sound of her professor's voice. She would think that if only she could lie down on the floor of the lecture hall, she would enjoy the most delectably deep sleep ever. So delectable that it would be a shame she wouldn't be conscious enough to experience every second of it. The consequence of her professor's annoyance and her fellow student's scrutiny would be a small price to pay for bliss, so the only thing that kept her from sinking down to the floor was the knowledge that a busybody would poke her in the back or grab her by the arm on her way down. The shocked reactions of her classmates and professor would be too noisy to sleep through. Whenever Sophia returned to her dorm room after class for a nap, she would no longer be tired enough to nap.

This memory from college was a solitary memory, unlike Danny and Margaret's. Sophia now regretted the string of boyfriends who had liked her more than she liked them.

She got out her journal and wrote a six-word, private status update: *I feel like Cupid's nonstick skillet.*

After a week of drought in the "good cry" department, Sophia grudgingly turned to Connie's *Noah's Ark* regimen to subdue heartache.

The number-one problem that the lovelorn have is that the object of their love doesn't love them as much, or worse yet, loves someone else. Severing this inappropriate bond is easy.
Inoculate yourself from this day forward by recognizing heartache's two constituent parts:

one part humiliation, one part loss.

Looks like a simple recipe, doesn't it? Because it is.

Any obstacle can be understood and surmounted once you identify its Two Opposing Forces. This Enumerative Law is never wrong.

So in the case of heartache, remind yourself that heartache is just the unpleasant emotional pairing of humiliation and loss. The man or woman you lost is unnecessary to your present and future happiness. You are stuck on a pair of unpleasant feelings, you are not stuck on him or her. Distract yourself every time you feel these two heartache-inducing feelings.

Make a copy of this list so you can carry it around all day:

HOW TO GET OVER HIM/HER IN FOUR STEPS

1) Identify the hurt pride—better yet, say "hurt pride" out loud or write it down.

2) Identify the loss—better yet, say "loss" out loud or write it down.

3) Divert self from #1 and #2 with reading, hobbies, helping others, taking a walk, taking a cruise, etcetera, etcetera, etcetera.

4) Repeat #3 as needed until the problem is solved.

For maximum effectiveness and convenience, tuck this list into your bra (you may have to do some rearranging if you're wearing a lowcut top—in which case you're either on the road to recovery or on the rebound). Keeping this list in your bra will be uncomfortably itchy, but not as rough as heartache.

Sophia challenged herself in her journal to revise and improve upon Connie's longwindedness. She opened one of her 12 Step books and reread Dr. Bob's succinct prescription:

1. Trust God.
2. Clean house.
3. Help others.

She worked on adapting this, and came up with:

1) Accept loss.
2) Divert self.
3) Prioritize others.

Then she cheered herself up with another list that liberated her from her journal-writing limit of six-word updates:

NOW THAT I'M SINGLE I CAN:

1) Avoid lawyers and lawsuits.
2) Appreciate undivided access to bedcovers.
3) Drink more coffee until sleep graces me with her presence.

Sophia remembered Danny's wimpiness toward caffeine. He banned her sludgy, cheap octane from his Italian specialty coffeemaker. That machine must have cost as much as a Ferrari.

4) Eat more homemade bread and Loudoun Creamery cheese.
5) Read more post-apocalyptic fiction and inspirational DIY when not burying self in work.

By Inspirational DIY, Sophia meant the highbrow, smart subgenre of self-help: books and articles by Buddhists, yogis, and neuroscientists who studied mindfulness meditation. Also spiritual memoirs by practitioners of Western and Eastern faiths, and books about the spiritual aspect of creative and physical exercises. Authors who helped their readers find relief from and transcend ego. Connie envied and copied badly this respected subgenre.

Connie introduced Sophia to books by the Dalai Lama, Thich Nhat Han, Pema Chodron, M. Scott Peck, Erich Fromm, Jon Kabat-Zinn, and Judith Viorst. She had given Sophia a copy of the yoga sutras of Patanjali, and Stephen Cope's interpretations of them. Sophia received the gifts gratefully. Connie never hid her interest in these authors from Sophia, the way she hid self-help books like *Women Who Love Too Much* and *I'm Okay, You're Okay.*

When Sophia was home in August, she had overheard Connie on the phone with a talk show booker—probably from an NPR talk show like Diane Rehm's, or Leonard Lopate's:

"I'm not like those New Age quacks who claim cancerous tumors grow or shrink depending on one's self-esteem," Connie protested. "I am a crossover talent, bridging the gap between Walmart shoppers and upmarket audiences, the same way Oprah does. In fact, I promoted the same ideas that Oprah promotes now. You know, before she gave up the junky format of interviewing bigamists, and people who were addicted to dental surgery, and men who loved sheep and the women who loved them. I can talk compassion and mindfulness better than Eckhart Tolle AND get your couch potato listeners in shape for bikini season."

Connie invited Danny to Christmas in Ithaca, and specifically to dinner at the Harmonious Pears orchard "since you and Danny seem like a harmonious pair." Sophia emailed that she had broken up with him because she had decided it was inappropriate to date anyone who worked at Carver or had done work for Carver.

Connie asked why Danny had done work for Carver. Surely Carver couldn't afford the services of a high-end architect? Or was he helping them pro bono?

Sophia regretted her slip. She pounded out a quick answer. Yes, Danny did a blueprint pro bono, and now he would be in Italy indefinitely to help out George Clooney in Lake Cuomo.

Connie's reply was full of unsolicited advice, including the heartbreak antidote from *Noah's Ark*.

Sophia wrote back:

I'm fine, busy collecting six-word quotes with Lucy Dell, our English teacher. This time she's asked for motiviational six-word quote collection. The students are going to write up New Years resolutions.

If you write yourself some resolutions, may I suggest "Write more succinctly." That's my resolution. When we had brunch with Danny, you said that you used to be able to dazzle any guy in just six words. Isn't that a coincidence that you told me that after I'd already told you about Lucy Dell's six-word concept?

Your Noah's Ark heartache antidote is 283 words long. Here's my six-word revision:

1) Accept loss.
2) Divert self.
3) Prioritize others.

If you begin writing concisely, especially in this age of status updates and sound bites, you would have a competitive advantage within your realm of self-help.

Connie's reply was nine words long:

"Prioritize others" is your third priority???

The next afternoon, while stuffing Carver holiday card envelopes with Dawn and Maggie, Dawn talked about Tariq a lot.

"He's making paint with the kids from one of George Washington Carver's own recipes." She wiped the sponge pen over the edge of an envelope. "And I think the kids will love his Christmas tree farm idea. Have you written up the scavenger hunt for it yet?"

Sophia nodded, and pulled a copy of it out of her Science folder.

CHRISTMAS TREE FARM HUNT

1) Name and location for farm

2) Year-long calendar of business tasks

3) List of the types of evergreens we will grow, and why we've chosen them

4) Year-long calendar of evergreen gardening tasks

5 Summary of the conventional evergreen industry's eco-risks.

6) Summary of the methods that make our farm organic and sustainable.

Dawn frowned as she read. "For this last one, I know Tariq wants the kids to focus on soil and integrated pest management. Do you think you should add those in, parenthetically?"

"I could," Sophia said, making her tone cheerful, "but I think it's better to wait and see if the kids draw that conclusion from their research. If they don't identify them as priorities, we can always guide them there during wrap-up."

Dawn had never questioned a scavenger hunt to this degree of detail. She must want Sophia to defer to Tariq's opinion.

Dawn and Tariq were in the honeymoon phase, Sophia figured, though she was certain their courtship was chaste. Then Sophia remembered something that made her feel bad. At the horrible L'Eco Bistro lunch with Stephen, Stephen had mentioned that Tariq needed more academic control. Well, now that Sophia was part-time, he was going to move into what had been her territory.

"I've got to get going," Maggie said, "since my darling husband takes the kids' word for it when they say they've done their homework." She picked up one of the cake boxes they'd been using to store the cards and envelopes.

"You don't have to take the whole thing," Sophia said. "I can finish them up. You're so much busier this time of year than I am."

"Don't worry," Maggie said. "Bernard and Tamika will sass me at some point and I will just hand these over."

As soon as Maggie left, Dawn told Sophia that she seemed sad. Was it because of the breakup with Danny?

"Yes."

"You're better off putting him behind you."

"My ego can't put it behind me."

Dawn just nodded, but her gaze crowded Sophia.

"I'll be okay," Sophia continued. "I'm reading highbrow self-help."

"The ones you get quotes from?" Dawn asked, grinning.

"Yes, and Lucy lent me some post-apocalyptic novels because I don't want to get too optimistic. The balanced reading plan is part of a list I made to bolster myself. Because there's no buzz like the buzz of a new regimen."

Dawn hesitated, then said. "I know you will be with your family for Christmas, but I don't like the idea of your spending the rest of winter break reading alone, no matter how curious you are about what you're reading. I'm going to check my calendar for some times that we might get together."

Dawn invited Sophia for dinner on New Year's Eve. Sophia brought a pot roast made with beef from Groff's Content Farm, and two bottles of organic Virginia sparkling wine.

"Want me to bring that into the kitchen?" Dawn's sister Janet asked.

"No, I've got it." Sophia saw Tariq, who held up a green can of ginger ale to greet her. She was nervous when she first saw him, but that friendly gesture pleased her.

Sophia's enthusiasm over Tariq's warmth didn't last. As soon as they sat down to eat Dawn's macaroni and cheese, Tariq's salad, and Sophia's pot roast, Dawn made an announcement that made Sophia jealous enough to lose her appetite.

"Tariq thinks we ought to replace our current science plan with the Coalition of Science Teachers' Entrepreneurs & Engineers curriculum."

"It's got a more vocational orientation," Tariq said, "in addition to providing as many school garden-based experiments as we're already doing."

"And I know Stephen will love it," Dawn pointed out. "Like 'Math is Everywhere', it's a national curriculum from a well-established source. It would help us generate positive press." She must have seen from Sophia's expression that Sophia was upset. "Sophia, it's in keeping with what you once described as the George Washington Carver approach: 'New Frames for Time-Tested Methods.'"

Dawn turned to her sister to explain, "Sophia links most of her amazing scavenger hunts back to George Washington Carver's philosophies, and she's got a slogan for everything!"

"Like Maoist China," Sophia agreed.

"Isn't she self-deprecating?" Dawn murmured to her sister. "Sophia, Tariq and I hope you will help us present this E & E curriculum proposal to Stephen. And now that you're um, helping us out with substitute teaching, it's a good idea for us to outsource the science curriculum."

Sophia took a large sip of Janet's sangria. The apples had softened to the perfect consistency. She would want a refill in a minute, but then she remembered that she shouldn't drink another glass in front of Dawn and Tariq.

Dawn was drifting away from Sophia, not so much because of Tariq, but ever since the lawsuit and Sophia's decision to date Danny. A year earlier, Dawn would have privately told Sophia about the E & E curriculum. Sophia would have said no, and Dawn would have dropped the matter like yesterday's newspaper.

Because she couldn't drink more sangria, Sophia heaped more macaroni and cheese onto her plate. She remembered making macaroni and cheese for a dinner with Danny. The crust was chewy and bread-crumbed and perfectly browned, except where it was orange or golden from the Mornay sauce.

Danny said, "We both saved the crust for last."

"Everyone does."

"It's too bad you can't save the best for last in a relationship," Danny said evenly. "The thrill of the chase ends too soon."

"Is that a hint?" Sophia asked, raising an eyebrow.

"No." He had looked amused, too.

Sophia watched Tariq moon over Dawn. Neither of them would risk a romance if they weren't positive they wanted to be with each other forever. She knew nothing about American Muslim courtship and wondered what its rules and debates were.

Instead of asking this, Sophia cleared her throat and said, "Dawn told me you're on the board of trustees at your mosque. Does your congregation do anything special to celebrate in the new year?'

"No," Tariq replied. "Maal hijra's not a big holiday for us. Not like Nowruz, the Persian New Year that Carver celebrates in March." Tariq looked at Dawn to make sure this was true and she nodded. "But there's a community service aspect to Hijra, and since it coincides this year with Carver's Martin Luther King Work Day, Dawn has asked Nadia and me to do a panel on Islam and prejudice. I want to find out if our students and their parents think it's easier to be black in the 21st century than it was at the end of the 20th. Especially in the wake of 9/11, when Muslims everywhere were scapegoated."

"Sophia," Dawn said. "Why don't you, Nadia, and Tariq come up with a scavenger hunt about the basic tenets of Islam for the kids to do on the Thursday or Friday before?"

"Sure," Sophia said, and she meant it. She wanted to learn more about Islam.

173

Tariq was saying "…and I can bring in a video from the library at my mosque of Muslims from all different racial and ethnic backgrounds reciting the Shahadah."

"Is that the prayer that people say to become Muslim?" Janet asked.

"Yes," Tariq said. "The Shahadah is one sentence: 'There is no god but Allah and Muhammad is His Messenger.' You're supposed to meet seven conditions before you can say it meaningfully, and it isn't a one-time thing. We say it five times a day, in Arabic, as part of our daily prayers. It's the first of the Five Pillars of Islam." He took a bite of Janet's pecan pie, the last bite left on anyone's plate. "You know why they translate them as the Five Pillars in English, instead of the Five Principles?"

"Why?" Sophia asked.

"Because it's too easy to misspell principle. Isn't that right, Principal Jordan?" He winked at Dawn, then rose and began clearing the table.

"Don't," she said, jumping up.

Tariq wouldn't be dissuaded. "Please let me do it so you get more time to visit with your sister."

When Tariq was out of earshot, Janet said, "He looks like a player but he's absolutely sweet and devoted to you."

Dawn blushed.

"I'll help him clean up," Sophia offered.

When Sophia and Tariq returned to the dining room, Janet and Dawn were arguing.

"There won't be anywhere to park, and I don't want to be on the road on New Year's Eve," Dawn was saying.

"It's just a few blocks away," Janet protested.

"Don't tell me you can walk up that big hill in those heels," Dawn said.

"I wouldn't wear them if I couldn't." She stood up. "C'mon Dawn. I'm only in town a few days and I miss DC nightlife."

Dawn rolled her eyes.

"Where do you want to go?" Tariq asked Janet.

"A new club I want to check out, Barbary Coste. Just up the street."

"I saw their sign," Dawn said, looking at Sophia. "They misspelled 'Coast.'"

"No they didn't," Janet said. "The owner's last name is Coste, and I know her older brother so I'll be able to get us in for free."

"When have I heard that before?" Dawn said under her breath.

"Well, if they say no, I will treat the three of you."

"You don't have to pay for me," Tariq said. "How about it, Dawn?"

"But you won't be comfortable there," Dawn said to Tariq.

"I don't mind seeing how the other half lives."

"I agree with Tariq, let's go," Sophia said. She didn't like bars because the drinks were overpriced, but she expected to pick up a cute, uncomplicated guy once the other three went home.

Chapter 17: I Can Control Any Guy With...

The wait staff at Barbary Coste dressed like pirates. Yellow lanterns penetrated the darkness. Just enough light to find her wallet, Sophia thought as she reluctantly paid for an expensive Briney Martini, the house specialty. She drank it too fast, while marveling at a graceful waitress's ability to navigate a tray of beer bottles through the crowd.

"Hey, you didn't get one of these maps," a male voice said, close to her ear.

"Brendan! What are you doing here?"

"I'm here with some suits from Luscious LoCal." She saw that the paper he was holding was a treasure map. "They were handing these maps out at the door."

"I didn't get one," Sophia said. "I guess they only give them to people who paid the cover charge. Where does the map lead?"

"The bars in each room," he replied.

"Can I buy you a drink?" Sophia asked. "I'm about to order myself another one."

"I can't drink tonight." Brendan complained. "My stomach's in knots from all the holiday catering orders."

"It couldn't be that bad if they let you out for New Year's Eve." Oops, she thought when Brendan frowned.

He said something she couldn't hear, and then, "I'm just a means to an end for you."

"No you're not. Will I see you at the chili cookoff next week?" she asked.

"No, but I've been sweating bullets to insure we'll have enough ingredients for all the amateurs to stock up on. I can't believe they scheduled this thing for January. As though December wasn't busy enough. 'Warm-up food,' they're calling it on the posters. When they're not saying 'Chill out with chili.' So asinine."

"Maybe I should write some slogans for you."

"No. The situation's not that desperate."

She grinned. "Well, we're looking forward to it."

"Who's we?"

"Carver."

"Carver? Is that your boyfriend's name?"

"No. It's the George Washington Carver Public Charter School, where I work. We've got a team of students who've prepared great recipes. Using locally-produced foods, of course. The vegetables are from our school garden. We freeze...."

"I should have guessed you were a teacher."

"Curriculum designer," Sophia corrected.

"Well la di da."

"I didn't mean it that way."

"Brendan!" A tall, stocky man approached them. In the dim light, his thick beard looked blue. He put his beefy hand on Brendan's shoulder. "Would you excuse us?" he asked Sophia. "Let me take you back to the kitchen so I can show you the menus. It's too dark out here."

"My work is never done," Brendan told Sophia, instead of saying goodbye.

A bar stool opened up, and Sophia sat down. She ordered another martini and as soon as the bartender gave it to her, she swiveled around so she could locate Tariq and Dawn. They were talking intently. Sophia tried to eavesdrop by reading their lips but couldn't. So much for Dawn getting to hang out with her sister. Janet was talking to one of the waiters.

Sophia noticed her glass was empty again, but just as she was about to turn back around to the bartender, two tall men appeared to fill the narrow space to the right of her perch.

"I found you," the louder of the two men announced in the bartender's general direction. The bartender didn't seem to hear, so the loud man said "Yoo hoo," and waved the Barbary Coste treasure map. "I've tracked you down."

'"The bartender's easy to find when you're walking in a straight line," his friend said, winking at Sophia. "Hi, I'm Michael."

Michael was taller than his loud friend, with bushy hair that looked beer-colored. Maybe it was the same shade as Sophia's, though the lighting was so dim she wasn't sure.

"Did Tim bang into you?" Michael asked Sophia, who shook her head.

"Two pots of gold, barkeep," Tim was calling, holding up his map. "They'll be free cuz I found you on my map."

"What's your name?" Michael asked pleasantly.

Sophia introduced herself to both men, and then Michael asked if he could buy her next martini.

"I'm sort of Michael's brother but not really his brother," Tim said slushily. "We have the same last name, Sherman, but Michael's more of a sure man than me tonight because I'm having trouble seeing straight. Hey, can I borrow your eye

178

patch?" he asked the graceful waitress, trailing after her and her preternaturally stable drink tray.

Tim was back a moment later, wearing the eye patch.

He beamed at Michael and Sophia like a proud child. "I. Have. A. Secret. From. You."

"You can see through the patch, right?" Michael said, handing Sophia one of two Briney Martinis.

"How did you know it's see-through?" Tim said it so loudly that he attracted several amused looks from nearby women.

"I asked one of the waiters when we came in," Michael said. "I couldn't figure out how they kept their balance."

"I was wondering the same thing," Sophia exclaimed.

"Can you imagine the collisions they would have?" Michael said.

"You would think of collisions," Tim scoffed. "You ambulance chaser. Watch out for this guy," he told Sophia. "He's a loiyer."

It took a second for Sophia to figure out what the word "Loiyur" meant. She knew "Magyar" was the Hungarian name for "Hungarian," so she thought a Loiyur might be from some region that had been dominated by the Soviet Union. Maybe their homeland was somewhere between Central Europe and Central Asia. Her geography was rusty.

But then Michael said, "I'm not that type of lawyer," and she realized that "Loiyur" was "Lawyer" in the emphatic language of Tim's drunkeness.

Sophia slouched as much as her stool would allow. "Lawyers don't intimidate me."

"That's nice," Michael replied. He looked at Sophia sidelong, as though he thought she were weird.

"Mikey's not such a bad lawyer," Tim said. "He doesn't talk about laws with me."

"That's because I know you're sick of it," Michael said.

"I am sick of it," Tim agreed, and for Sophia's benefit, he explained that he had to work with lawyers all day long. She was about to ask him what he did for a living, when he said, "Lawyers never shut up."

Sophia laughed. "That's because they need to say a lot to twist the truth around."

"Huh?" Michael frowned. "That insult doesn't even make sense. I think you're as drunk as Tim."

"No, I am completely in charge of my faculty. I mean, my faculties," she joked.

But Michael was right. She'd had too much to drink. "Tim's drunkenness is contagious," she complained.

"So sue me," Tim joked, elbowing Michael.

"Ow." Michael flinched. "I told you, I'm not that kind of lawyer."

Sophia flinched too. The word "sue" stung like a bee in a bull's ears. "All lawyers are alike," she said, more to the last gulp of her drink than to Michael or Tim.

"Amen to that, sister," Tim said. "I'm buying two martinis, another for you and another for me."

"I think you've both had enough," Michael said, putting down Tim's waving arm.

"No, Mikey, no! Me no likey!"

"That's enough, Tim."

"Control freak." Tim snorted and began looking around him. He smiled at one of the women he'd amused earlier. She turned back to her friends.

Tim turned to Sophia. "You want to hear a riddle?"

"Sure."

"What makes lawyers such control freaks?"

Sophia hesitated. "Their hidden agendas?"

180

"Don't pick on lawyers," Michael protested. "It's unoriginal."

Sophia remembered Connie saying that during Martin's tirades.

Tim challenged Sophia to come up with a riddle.

"Not if it's about lawyers," Michael said. "Come on, Tim. I want to get out of here."

"The eve is still young, Mike," Tim said. "Make it a good riddle, Sophie."

"Give me a minute." She decided that whatever she came up with, the target couldn't be lawyers, because even though she wanted nothing to do with a lawyer, especially a cute lawyer, she didn't want Michael to walk away.

"How do you control a control freak?" she asked them both. She didn't have an answer for it, but figured she would tweak something from Tim or Michael's reply.

"You can't control a control freak." Michael replied.

"Yeah you can." Had Sophia been sober, she might have waxed psychological over this point. Control freaks were brittle, anxious, easily tizzied. She knew this because she was a control freak. Connie's control freakishness had been contagious.

"I can .... control a control freak," Sophia said, heart quickening. She felt like an actress who had forgotten a line from a script.

"How can you a control a control freak?" Michael echoed.

"I don't have to tell you," she snapped.

"Because you don't have an answer."

"Oh yeah, I do." Sophia searched her addled brain for something concrete, but it was hard to explain yourself when you had no clue what you were talking about.

"I can control any guy with…six words."

Chapter 18: The New Year Starts Off Badly

Picky Ricky's Diner was crowded when Sophia arrived to have her first meal of 2010 with Nadia.

"I just got here," Nadia said, getting up from her booth to hug Sophia hello.

Ricky came over to take their order, and Sophia admired the slogan on his t-shirt: "WHINERS LOVE DINERS, RICKY LOVES WHINERS."

"Do you like my new shirt? Brand new year. I had to come up with a fresh slogan," he told Sophia and Nadia. "Sophe, would you like your usual drink?"

"No thanks," she said, though she wanted a Bloody Mary or two.

"From now on, I'm going to be as sober as a turkey sandwich and potato chips," she told Nadia as soon as she had ordered both. "Sobriety is my only New Year's resolution."

A man and a woman were holding hands at the table nearest their booth. Too near the booth, Sophia thought. Why did they have to hold hands? *Get a room*, she thought grouchily.

"Did you get drunk last night?" Nadia asked. "I thought you were going over to Dawn's for dinner. She has such civilized dinner parties, and since she's dating Tariq now, I'm surprised she served alcohol."

"Dawn's sister took us to a new bar," Sophia admitted.

"Dawn went to a bar?"

"Tariq was there."

"Do not tell me Tariq went to a bar?" Nadia's voice was so loud that the hand-holding couple looked over. Sophia frowned to discourage the hand-holding woman's curious expression.

"Tariq convinced Dawn to go. So she could spend more time with her sister. He didn't drink. He is smitten."

"So is Dawn," Nadia murmured.

Sophia gave the happy hand-holding couple a sidelong glance. They were making each other laugh. She flushed with self-pity.

"So you had a good time at the bar?" Nadia asked this sweetly, but Sophia bristled. She decided not to tell Nadia about her boast. Such a stupid boast. Michael was a lawyer, but he was also cute and nice, and they might have exchanged phone numbers if she hadn't blown it with that corny one-liner, "I can control any guy with six words." That was worse than "Do you come here often?" or "Haven't I seen you somewhere before?" She was like a pathetic guy with a comb-over, hitting on women at a singles bar. And then she remembered that at Dawn's dinner party, Tariq had mentioned the Shahadah, which enabled a person to convert to Islam by saying one sentence.

"Sophia? Your hangover is making you very distracted. I do not think you have heard a word that I have been saying," Nadia protested.

Sophia startled. She felt caught in the act of comparing Islam's most sacred declaration to her fallacious pick-up line.

Could Nadia tell from Sophia's anxious facial expression that Sophia's stream of consciousness had been both lame and culturally offensive?

Later, when Sophia got home from breakfast, she looked up the wording of the Shahadah:

La ilaha illa Allah wa-Muhammad rasul Allah.

There is no god but God and Muhammad is the prophet of God.

She picked up her pen and opened her journal. She didn't want to write about the night before, or maybe she did want to write about it, but she wasn't comfortable doing so. Instead she decided to free-write as a way of beginning her work on the scavenger hunt about Islam. Knowing she was going to let herself loose in her journal, even through she was free-writing, for a lesson plan, felt like popping open a bottle of wine at the end of a tough or dreamy day. Not that she would ever drink again.

SHAHADAH:

My first impressions:
profession of faith,
majestic and lyrical
An unbroken circle, an unbroken ritual

Ask Tariq and Nadia how to define this for the kids, is there a children's book about it?

184

I read that the word Islam is defined in English as "submission." I can see how some Westerners might frame "submission" negatively. But I think Islam, like Buddhist mindfulness (and the philosophy of yoga, and the Twelve-Step belief in a Higher Power) offers its practitioners relief and freedom from egoism and destructive distraction.

At this point, Sophia stopped writing about the the scavenger hunt and started writing about the night before. Her hand darted back and forth on the pages as automatically as if she were sleep-writing. Her unconscious rattled and spilled:

... made that six-word boast because I'd had too much to drink, and I'll probably never run into that guy Michael ever again. But I feel as egoistic and absurd as Connie. And I copycatted Connie's dumbest claim ever. Maybe I shouldn't feel so embarrassed, but if Connie ever found out about this, through ESP or a psychic dream or whatever superpower she's into right now, I would die. Or maybe I would go find her son Ryan and camp out on his floor. Because wherever Ryan hides is always the furthest away from Connie that one can get. And he is cute so it would be fun to be on his floor. I couldn't boast to him though.

On the first day back at Carver after Winter break, Sophia was in her office, feeling uncharacteristically uncreative, when a knock at the door saved her. It was Nadia.

"I forgot to give you your Christmas gift at the diner the other day."

"You don't need to give me a present. Give it to someone else. I mean, that's so nice of you to think of me. But I didn't get you anything."

"Not to worry." Nadia smiled. "You know I don't celebrate Christmas."

Sophia decided to make Nadia a gift. She could give it to her in March, for Nowruz, the Persian New Year. Maybe a photo collage, using photographs of Carver students from last year's Nowruz celebration.

"Open it," Nadia urged.

The wrapped gift was the shape of a small paperback, but when Sophia picked it up, it didn't yield the way a paperback would have. The edges were ridged. A picture frame.

Nadia had gotten her a Persian miniature like the ones that lined Nadia's front hall. Sophia admired them when she babysat Nadia's son. This miniature depicted a beautiful woman veiled in gauzy yellow, and a fat man reclining under a tree. The woman was looking over his shoulder at the tree, as if to read it.

"The woman is Scheherezade," Nadia explained. "Have you heard of her story?"

"I think so," Sophia replied. "She had to keep telling stories, right? To save her life?"

"Yes, she kept a king so curious for a thousand and one nights, that in the end he spared her and all the women of his kingdom."

Sophia sighed. "It's a beautiful present.. Thank you."

"Scheherezade reminds me of you. Because you are so creative. And because you come up with a startling number of lessons that capture the students' curiosity."

Sophia squeezed Nadia's hand to thank her, and forced a smile. She remembered Dawn giving her a southpaw compliment during the lawsuit: "Your creativity is your saving grace."

Where would Sophia be without her creativity? She bet she was about to find out.

Chapter 19: Lawyers Are Like Human Tape Recorders

The students on Carver's chili cookoff team were dismayed by how little space each team had in Luscious LoCal's vast produce department.

"Where we gonna put up all our signs?" Victor asked Maggie, who shrugged and said they'd have to choose the two they liked best.

Bernard, Tamika, and Candace voted for "Made in DC" and "Eat Local." Victor argued for his "No jet fuel in our chili," slogan, and Kira backed him up, but Malikah said, "That's not appetizing," and Maggie agreed that they should use the simplest slogan. "We should have the kids donate these signs to the store," Sophia told Maggie after Kira had fastened the signs to the table front.

Sophia didn't hear Maggie's reply because her attention had been diverted by the sight of a preppy man who looked familiar. She searched her memory for the places she had gone most recently. He was too young and too white to be a Carver parent. He was dressed too expensively to have been at a community meeting. Was he a friend of Danny's whom she might have met at Danny's birthday party? No, she wouldn't remember back that far. She saw a mural in her mind, the mural of roiling waves at Barbary Coste and then she realized she had met this man on New Year's Eve. It was Michael Sherman. Her boast jostled its boorish way into the forefront of her mind. How stupid to say all men could be subdued by the same thing, let alone by six words. Of course, Michael Sherman would know she couldn't really do that. She knew she couldn't do that.

"Earth to Sophia." A man's voice. Brendan's.

"Hi," she said, surprised to see him standing still. She remembered how much he enjoyed portraying himself as a harried martyr. So instead of asking, "How are you?" she said, "Poor Brendan. You must be so busy today."

He moaned. "I am sooo busy. You have no idea how hard my life is." He caught her looking away. "Sophia? Do you know that guy who you're staring at while I'm trying to have a conversation with you?"

"Hmm?" She raised her eyebrows innocently.

"That guy is Michael Sherman," Brendan said.

She turned back to look at the apple section, where Michael had been, but he wasn't there any longer.

"I wasn't staring at him," she lied. "But he did look familiar. I think I saw him at Barbary Coste on New Year's Eve."

"That makes sense. A whole posse of us were there from Luscious LoCal. Michael is our new in-house counsel. It was interesting to run into you that night."

"This store has its own in-house counsel?"

"No, he handles the whole grocery chain from DC."

"Ah." Sophia made a mental note to begin grocery-shopping elsewhere. Even now, in the dead of winter, when her beloved farmers markets had sparse offerings. She would resort to buying the fruits of industrial agriculture, and florescent yellow processed cheese foods.

"I should get back to our table, and let you get on with your busy work. I mean, I don't mean busy work. I mean, I should let you get back to your work because I know you are busy." Sophia spoke distractedly because she was checking out Michael again.

"Sophia? He's not right for you."

"Who?"

"Michael Sherman. He spends most of his time with lobbyists."

"I don't care. I'm not interested in him. I don't date lawyers."

"Do you date grocery store buyers?"

"No, I'm afraid not," Sophia said, trying to look disappointed.

Brendan looked downcast.

"I'm surprised you would want to date me anyway. I always talk your ear off about local food producers."

"I know, you drive me insane," Brendan said. "But you've grown on me. I used to think you were like a mosquito, but now I think you're like a mosquito bite that I can't stop itching. It might be fun to go out for coffee together some time. I have acted impatient with you not because I hate to hear about the local producers, but because you never ask me how I'm doing. Personally."

That's because you always volunteer your self-pity, Sophia thought, but she said, "I'm sorry you feel that way." She looked at his face longer than she ever had. No spark. "I just got out of a relationship. I'm not even ready to have coffee with a guy. Maybe I'm not even ready to purchase coffee from a male barista."

"Doesn't sound promising," Brendan said. "Come say hi next time you're shopping here. But just say hi. Don't pitch a local producer."

"I will see you soon," Sophia said, expecting they would meet again when Hell froze over. No one from Luscious LoCal would ever see her again after this cookoff. She had to avoid reencountering Michael not only because she was embarrassed about what he would think of her, but because the mere sight of him reminded her she had copycatted Connie.

Moments after Sophia returned to the Carver table, the blasting tune of a bugle startled everyone, channeling their attention to the makeshift podium in front of the produce department. A tall middle-aged man strode up, patted the bugler on the shoulder and assumed his place at the microphone. He wore a Luscious LoCal t-shirt over his dress shirt, so the shirt was taut against the rectangle of his torso.

"Good afternoon! I'm Ken Burnett, and on behalf of my entire Luscious LoCal team, I want to offer a warm welcome — no, make that a hot and spicy welcome, heh heh, to all our chili makers and chili fans! This is our first chili cookoff ever." He nodded proudly. "Samples are just 25 cents each, and 50 percent of the proceeds will be donated to REGROW, a non-profit that supports farmers in drought-affected regions worldwide."

"They should've chosen a charity for local farmers," Bernard whispered to Maggie. "REGROW sounds like they're going to donate the money to guys with bald heads who can't afford Rogaine."

"Son, what do you know about Rogaine?" Maggie asked Bernard.

"I watch a lot of TV commercials. I mean, only after finishing my homework and chores, and only when you say I can. And even then I just watch PBS."

"They don't show Rogaine commercials on PBS," Maggie

190

said.

"Now that explains a lot," Bernard said, stroking his chin like a sage.

Sophia turned to Victor. "Since you like math so much, why don't you and Kira handle the money."

"That would be fantastic!" Kira said with an un-Kira-like outburst of enthusiasm. "Yeah, Victor and I could totally work together on that!"

"Teacher's pet," Victor grumbled. Kira looked at Sophia for a reaction, and Sophia winked at her. Kira looked away immediately, back to the customers, but her lips pursed as she repressed her smile.

Soon, the chili was gone and the kids were comparing notes with each other about the compliments they had received. Theirs had been the most popular table. Sophia scanned the crowd, wondering who the judges were, until Tamika noticed Luscious LoCal's CEO, Ken Burnett, approaching the podium. Tamika said, "I hope they're not going to toot that horn for him again."

"I'd like to introduce our celebrity judge," Burnett told the audience. "She's the author of *Around the World In Chili Days*, Vivian Racklin!"

Like Ken Burnett, the woman who stepped up to the podium was wearing a noticeably tight t-shirt. The shirt was a blue and tan map of the world—more like two globes than one thanks to her huge breasts. The applause, half-hearted for Ken Burnett, now swelled for Vivian Racklin. Burnett put his hand on Vivian's shoulder and then removed it. Sophia wondered if he had done this out of self-consciousness, realizing he looked like a letch.

Vivian Racklin announced the vegetarian chili award winners first. A group called the Vegan Vixens won first place, and the three of them jogged up to the podium. Had they planned this vivacious approach? To show you didn't need to eat meat to fuel yourself?

"It was the cashew butter that did it!" one of the women said as she accepted her kidney bean-shaped trophy and oversized Luscious LoCal gift certificate. As soon as the women had jogged back to their table, Vivian said, "And now it's time for chili con carnivorous!" Ken Burnett guffawed like a laugh track.

As Racklin read through honorable mention, third place, and second place, Bernard gave an excited little hop with each name, and Kira clutched Victor's arm. What was with Kira today? Sophia wondered if, perhaps, serious Kira had a crush on Victor. Victor couldn't be serious for thirty seconds.

"Opposites attract" was a cliché Sophia had never experienced until she let down her guard with Danny.

"And the winner is the George Washington Carver Public Charter School Garden chili!" Vivian Racklin proclaimed.

It was a long title for a type of chili, Sophia thought. Eight words long. she counted.

As the team made its way forward, Sophia hoped the thunderous applause was sincere. From the security camera in her mind, Countess Connie appeared as a cynical anchor woman:

"I hope that nice audience doesn't think Luscious LoCal rigged this contest so an inner-city school with eco-savvy children could win."

Sophia felt a hand on her back, and it was Stephen's.

"You are out of the doghouse," Stephen said. "Congratulations."

"Thank you," she replied, glancing to see if Tamika, who had been standing right next to her, had overheard. But Tamika was focused on beating Victor to the microphone next to Ken Burnett. Sophia loved that girl's assertiveness.

Tamika launched into the speech she'd practiced for weeks. Sophia pictured its outline, written in Tamika's bubbly cursive: Part 1's explanation of why organically grown produce was more nutritious. Part 2 about how local food tasted better because it was fresher. Part 3, about the grass-fed, free-range meat. Sophia had practically memorized Tamika's conclusion: *Carver's chili tastes best because when we grow vegetables in our school garden, we baby them like our little sisters and brothers.*

Sophia looked for Tamika's little brother Bernard's reaction to this cannabalistic metaphor. He was still smiling. Now Tamika was thanking Luscious LoCal, and Vivian "Rockin" and "everyone from Carver who worked on the bake sale that raised money for us to do this."

"Don't forget to thank your mom," Victor called out, and Tamika turned to scowl at him, instead of immediately taking his advice. This brief moment, when her head was turned away from the microphone, was all Bernard needed to grab the mike.

"We also want to thank our beautiful, patient mom , Maggie Lewis, for teaching us how to cook and helping us come up with the recipe and—"

"Okay, Bernard. They got it. Now hold up everybody." Tamika held up a Luscious LoCal customer comment card, and Sophia held her breath because she hoped Bernard or Victor would not interrupt what she knew Tamika was going to say.

"If y'all want to encourage sustainable food production, just fill out these customer survey cards asking Luscious LoCal to begin labeling foods so you know where your food's coming from."

"Did you put her up to that?" Stephen whispered to Sophia.

"Isn't she brave?" Sophia replied.

"Did you tell her to say that?"

"No," Sophia said, because she hadn't *told* Tamika to say it, she had merely suggested Tamika say it.

Now Ken Burnett was saying, "Tameesha, thank you for that. I think you've got a future in politics—" Something, or someone, caught his eye. "Hey, Michael Sherman! Don't go anywhere, Michael. Ladies and gentleman, that man trying to slink off toward the bakery is the man I would like us all to thank for inspiring this cookoff. Michael, come on up here, and that's an order, not a request. Heh heh."

Sophia wished the members of the Carver chili team were taller so she could hide behind them.

"Michael's a local boy," Ken said. "Born in Baltimore, raised on a farm in southern Maryland, got his BA from Georgetown, his law degree from George Washington and then worked at...."

Sophia recalled the image of Danny wearing his rumpled grey GW t-shirt. Did Michael know Danny? She would have to consult Danny's Facebook friend list as soon as she got home.

"Michael loves chili. Buys all his ingredients here in the store on Friday afternoons, makes a week's worth every weekend, and brings it to lunch most days..."

Sophia also prepared most of her main dishes on the weekends. It helped optimize her work week. She viewed this habit as a pleasing ritual instead of as a chore.

She looked at Michael, and saw he was staring at her. She was glad for an instant, until she remembered her boast. Was he staring at her because he remembered her dumb pickup line? His gaze was neither admiring nor flirtatious. It was the look of someone who knows you well.

Sophia felt dizzy, like a shell caught in a wave. And then

194

she felt an arm come round her shoulders. It was Maggie, shepherding her back to Carver's table because the event was over. Sophia began packing up like Noah before the flood. She couldn't wait to get back to the van. You had to slam the driver's side door to close it properly. The slam would feel good.

"Sophia, may we talk to you a moment?" Stephen said as he walked over to the table with Ken Burnett. "I just gave Ken a copy of your seasonal produce scavenger hunt."

"Great," she lied.

"Can I give this to our newsletter editor?" Ken asked her, giving her the admiring smile that most people gave her, especially when they knew about Carver's mission.

Michael Sherman joined them.

Sophia's stomach flipped. Ken began reading Michael the scavenger hunt.

"I'm glad our judges had that double anonymity policy," Ken told Sophia, Michael, and Stephen when he looked up from the page. "If I'd known about this hunt ahead of time, none of the other contestants would have had a chance."

"Carver's a very special place," Stephen told him. "Sophia's our curriculum designer, and in addition to making sure we meet or exceed the DCPS's standards, she converts all our teachers' major lessons into scavenger hunts."

Sophia hoped Stephen's praise meant he would ask Dawn to restore her to full-time status.

"…and the hunts are never more than eight steps long, so the children don't get overwhelmed."

"No more than eight steps?" Michael echoed, smiling.

"That's right," Stephen replied. "Because George Washington Carver wrote a credo for his students to follow that was made up of just eight steps."

"Sounds like your scavenger hunts are to-do lists in

disguise," Michael said to Sophia. She flushed. Sophia depended upon her scavenger hunt framing device to feel creative, to distinguish herself from her godbrother Ryan's math curriculum, and to distinguish herself from Connie. Hunts represented the best aspect of Connie's influence: numbered lists.

"Do you two know each other?" Stephen asked Michael before turning his gaze on Sophia. "You seem to know each other."

"No," she said.

"Yes," Michael said. "I mean, we don't know each other, but we met on New Year's Eve."

Sophia winced. "Met" sounded proper but "New Year's Eve" didn't. "New Year's Eve" implied booze, sloppy kissing, and drunkards playing Auld Lang Syne on kazoos. Only "we met in rehab" would have been worse. Why couldn't she have met Michael on a sedate holiday? Arbor Day, perhaps. Or the Persian spring festival of Nowruz?

"You look uncomfortable," Michael said.

Sophia was horrified at the prospect that Stephen and Ken might have heard him say this, with that tone of we-just-hooked-up familiarity. Mercifully, Stephen and Ken were walking away together, toward the false sunset of one of Luscious LoCal's many murals.

"Are you uncomfortable?" Michael asked again.

"I heard you the first time," Sophia muttered. "I feel nauseous. Probably ate too much chili. I need to find the bathroom." *Ha!* She thought. That vulgar comment will get rid of him.

But it didn't. He teased her: "'I need to find the bathroom.' That's a six-word sentence. Are those your magic six words?"

"Congratulations on your counting ability," she murmured sarcastically.

"The women's room is over there." He pointed near a bank of cashiers.

"Thanks," Sophia said, remembering that Danny referred to women's rooms as ladies' rooms. When Sophia was in college, she and her friends glowered when they encountered the word "Ladies" instead of "Women" because it sounded patronizing and sexist. Since that time, Sophia had always preferred men who said "women" instead of "ladies."

"I'll see you on February 13th," she heard Michael say.

"What?" She turned around.

"Stephen invited Ken and me to Carver's Hearts Night potluck. Ken can't go, but I said I would."

Hearts Night was the party Carver hosted for the school and its neighbors on the eve of Valentine's Day. They served healthful food, while nurses gave free blood pressure tests to any grownup who wanted one.

"Great. I'll look forward to seeing you there," she said.

"Wait. Will you share the secret six-word message with me before you go? No pun intended. Get it? Before you *go*? To the bathroom, I mean."

"Eew. No." She replied. "I wouldn't bother to use the six words on you. I never date lawyers."

Right after she said those words, she regretted them.

What a presumptuous, conceited thing to say, Sophia thought as she drove the van back to Carver. Especially since Michael Sherman hadn't been flirting with her or asking her out on a date. In fact, he had done the opposite. He had poked fun at her for her drunken boast. He made a gross bathroom joke as though he were talking to one of his guy friends. He would not have made that joke if his curiosity about her had been romantic.

Instead of saying "I don't date lawyers," Sophia now wished she had said, "I don't hang out with lawyers." That would have been cooler. Then she realized, with searing regret, that "I don't hang out with lawyers," would have been a perfectly dismissive, smooth, relevant six-word sentence. A sentence that might have spared her from having to dream up a better sentence, which she probably should do, right now, just in case. She tried to dismiss this thought. Why should she have to come up with something. She would avoid him at Hearts Night. Connie's voice came to mind: "You hide behind your students."

What had Michael just said about hiding? About a disguise? And then she remembered with a pang that he'd said her scavenger hunts were to-do lists in disguise. That made her feel sneaky and dictatorial.

She wished she did have a magic six-word sentence that would glue his mouth shut. Lawyers were like human tape recorders. And his ability to count fast was an unfortunate coincidence.

Sophia needed to distract herself. She tried to think about that meeting with Lucy Dell on Monday, the one she wasn't prepared for. She would tell a white lie, use the cookoff as an excuse.

She stopped at a red light next to a bus stop. An old woman stood waiting in the cold afternoon air without a coat. Her oversized sweatshirt featured a list of words in five lines:

Being
In
Total
Control of
Herself

The woman's eyes met Sophia's. Then someone's honk behind Sophia let her know the light had turned green. She drove home through Kalorama, taking Danny's street for the first time since the breakup. She slowed enough to notice the shuttered windows and white, shallow staircase. She had never seen anyone on those stairs, and there was no one there now, but her heart fluttered into an ache.

Until her short, brutish experience with Danny, Sophia believed Connie's claim that heartache was as easy to avoid as telemarketers (who immediately betray their identity by mispronouncing your name).

That night after Sophia printed out the coming week's substitute teaching schedule, she tried to read a novel but found herself counting the words in sentences. Then she stared out the window awhile, more staring *at* it than out of it. On winter nights, windowpanes became dark mirrors. She heard the click of number cubes from an old clock of Connie's that she had hated and then inherited.

Connie's old clock reminded Sophia of the time Connie had volunteered to substitute for Sophia's pregnant English teacher. On Connie's first day in the classroom, she marked her temporary territory by taping up a four-word sign, under the classroom clock:

Time passes, will you?

Sophia shrank from her godmother's unprovoked harshness, though her classmates didn't seem to mind, and several thought Connie's wordplay was clever.

Now Connie's number-cube clock clicked again. The sound brought Sophia back to the present time, which was 10:34. Because Sophia had just relived an unpleasant Connie memory, the fact that Sophia had missed her ironclad bedtime felt like a slap. Sophia heard Connie's voice from years earlier, "If you

199

don't get to bed right now you will have a rotten day tomorrow, and you will only have yourself to blame."

Sophia remembered that she had no new scavenger hunt for Lucy's English class, just a white lie at the ready. She had felt creatively blocked since New Year's Eve. This whole school year had been horrible. The lawsuit, then Danny, then the six-word boast. All of it made Sophia feel defensive and out of control.

Chapter 20: Mottos Offer Helpful or Annoying Advice

At Carver, Sophia slipped out of Assembly early to photocopy the previous year's February scavenger hunt for Lucy. She had meant to do it before the first bell, but she had hit the snooze button instead of getting out of bed when she was supposed to.

The faculty room's prehistoric copy machine didn't jam as often as it usually jammed. When Sophia got back to her office, she saw she had ten minutes left before the meeting with Lucy. Not enough time enough to update the scavenger hunt. She tapped her pen. Any second now, the hallway would crawl with kids spilling out from the auditorium.

Sophia looked up at Nadia's picture of Scheherazade and regretted hanging it there. The jewel tones and the garish gold frame were out of place, and it was dwarfed by her quote-covered bulletin board. She reread an old Countess Connie quote from *Live Like Your Days Are Numbered*:

"A numbered list subdues any problem."

Sophia counted the words. It happened to be a six-word sentence. Was this a positive or negative omen? Perhaps the only way to answer that question was to hunt for six-word sentences on her board. Maybe she could find a six-word sentence that was compelling enough to make an honest assertion of her boast. Then she would feel wittier than Connie.

Sophia reviewed a slogan she had composed as a New Year's resolution for the students to consider adopting:

Creative and kind, just for today.

She had discovered the "just for today" clause in Alcoholics Anonymous's 12-Step literature. She also admired the brevity of AA's five-word slogan "One Day at a Time." It was three things at once:

a motto
a regimen
a limit

Another six-word sentence Sophia found encapsulated mindfulness:

This Moment is the Perfect Teacher.

It was the title of a book by Buddhist nun Pema Chodron. How Connie envied Pema Chodron. From now on, Sophia decided, she would conclude all her emails to Connie with that quote pasted under her name as a signature line. With that quote, Sophia would be able to control Connie's stream of consciousness for just one moment. Sophia wanted to subliminally remind her godmother that reporters and critics didn't make fun of Pema Chodron the way they mocked

Countess Connie.

Sophia looked back to the board, continuing her hunt for six words. She found two six-word sentences from Dorothy Parker:

The cure for boredom is curiosity. There is no cure for curiosity.

This witticism had inspired Sophia's "Curiosity is Fuel" Carver motto. When Sophia spoke to her Carver students about curiosity, she spoke of it as a virtue. Connie, in contrast, warned her readers, and Sophia, that boundless curiosity was as dangerous as substance abuse, and even the cause of addictions.

In *Live Like Your Days Are Numbered*, Connie admonished her readers for their addiction to motivational books.

Don't read about life, live life! Break the compulsive reading habit by limiting the life guidance you seek to my enumerative guidance. I can just see you, standing in a bookstore, thinking, Countess Connie gave me good advice but maybe these next books will give me even more. You become like an addict.

Drug addicts ask, if I could just do one more hit, would it be as good as the hit I'm craving? Will another pill make me forget? Will it knock me out so I don't have to lie here waiting desperately to fall asleep? Will this high be the one I've been looking for—an experience so satisfying that the memory of it will render future drugs unnecessary?

Sophia remembered spying on Connie, who privately binged on self-help books and magazines.

If Sophia saw Michael Sherman at Hearts Night, and if he

asked her about the six words, she decided to use Dorothy Parker's "There is no cure for curiosity" as if it were her own composition. Michael probably wasn't literary enough to have heard of Dorothy Parker. He was a lawyer, after all. Therefore, Sophia wouldn't get caught passing off a wittier woman's words as her own.

Lucy Dell knocked on Sophia's office door.

"Perfect timing," Sophia said, deciding, in a split second, that she'd better not try to channel Dorothy Parker's words. The appearance of an English teacher was the perfect antidote to quell plagiaristic impulse.

Sophia and Lucy began by going over the scavenger hunt, which focused on guessing the definition and function of anatomical vocabulary words. In February, with the ground frozen in the garden and Hearts Night prep dominating the first two weeks of the month, lesson plans across the curriculum were focused on human biology and preventative health.

"Doesn't look like you made any changes to last year's hunt," Lucy commented.

"I'm creatively blocked," Sophia admitted impulsively. Then her defensive side kicked in. "But only because I haven't slept very well the past few nights. I fought off a cold and feel better this morning."

"I didn't mean to imply that you needed to make changes. It's a great hunt," Lucy said too quickly. She looked at the Persian miniature. "What a lovely picture. Is it new?"

Sophia couldn't tell if Lucy was trying to change the subject or if she felt genuinely interested. "Nadia gave it to me for Christmas. It's Scheherazade."

"I thought so. The world's most famous storyteller."

"Do you want to borrow it, to show the kids?" Sophia asked hopefully, taking the picture down so fast that the nail shot out of the wall.

"Yes please," Lucy said. "The garden around her is lush." Lucy made a note on her clipboard. "I think I will introduce this image to the children with this metaphoric description: 'Imagine Scheherazade as a gardener of story seeds.'"

Creative minds work so fast, Sophia thought with a pang. "You can have the picture for your classroom."

"No. Nadia gave it to you as a gift."

"Scheherazade creeps me out," Sophia explained, and regretted it as soon as those words had flown out of her mouth.

"How could you think she was creepy? She was a heroine."

"She was under intense pressure to be creative."

"Well sure, that's what makes her story dramatic. That's why her story has been passed on from generation to generation, and why—"

Sophia shrank from Lucy's liveliness. Now she had two colleagues to envy—Tariq and Lucy. The envy and sadness must have shown, because all of a sudden, Lucy asked quietly, "Sophia, may I ask you a personal question?"

"Sure," Sophia said, switching on a smile.

"Do you feel intense pressure to be creative?" Lucy asked.

"Oh no. Not me. Never. But I worry a little about the kids."

"Why?" Lucy looked confused.

"I mean, it's great that we give the students opportunities for creative input, but maybe we're pressuring them."

"I'm astonished to hear you say that," Lucy said. "The kids want to collaborate on the hunts. At conventional schools, students are lectured to death and the teachers have to teach to the test. Not to mention the mediocrity of worksheets and state-mandated textbooks." Lucy shook her head. "Your scavenger hunting reminds me of Tom Sawyer, coaxing his friend Ben to whitewash the fence for him. You disguise the facts and skills the kids need to learn by fueling their curiosity and their creativity. Curiosity and creativity go hand in hand. I never knew that before I encountered your scavenger hunt format."

Sophia remembered Michael saying her scavenger hunts were to-do lists in disguise. She felt like a con artist.

Just before school ended that day, Sophia met with Tariq in the science lab to give him last year's scavenger hunt about digestion. "Chasing Chocolate" was vile and popular with kids like Victor. "Chasing" tracked the route that Valentine's Day candy journeyed from one's mouth down the alimentary canal.

"Can I make a suggestion?" Tariq asked after reading over the hunt.

"Sure."

"I want to focus more on the enteric nervous system."

"Interic?" She had never heard that word before.

"Maybe you've heard it called the gut brain?" Tariq asked. "Have you heard of neurogastroenterology?"

Sophia shook her head and pursed her lips to keep from giggling. Could such a long word exist? Those crazy doctors. They had a Latin fetish.

"Let me show you," Tariq said, and she followed him over to the anatomical manikin whom Chalis, the former science teacher, had named "George W. Bush." That name made the kids laugh. They liked dismembering the "George W." manikin as they learned the names of body parts.

Tariq pointed to George W.'s sheathed stomach muscles. "Over the past few years, researchers have discovered that the tissues running from the esophagus, through the abdomen, and down to the colon have more neurons than the spinal cord. The gut brain doesn't have to depend on the brain in our head for digestion. The central nervous system and the enteric nervous system constantly communicate, which is why we feel all our emotional reactions in our torso."

"We feel all our emotional reactions in our torso?" She put her hand over her mouth, confused by the power of her excitement about this fascinating idea.

"What?" Tariq asked, curious and smiling.

All of a sudden, Sophia liked him. "It's neat to learn that the phrase 'gut feelings' is biologically accurate since I always thought of it as a pop-psych term. When the kids learn about the enteric system from you, I think they will understand more about the body-mind connection than 99.9% of all grownups. I doubt most adults they encounter have the insight to educate them about the relationship between their physical and emotional sensations."

Tariq smiled. "Valentine's Day is the perfect holiday for telling the kids about the enteric system. Not only because we focus on human biology in February, but because the gut brain gives kids butterflies in their stomach, and makes them lose their appetite when they've got a crush on someone."

"The 'Chasing Chocolates' hunt was gross in a good way though," Sophia said wanly of her old Valentine's Day hunt. "At least, it enabled kids to recycle empty chocolate candy samplers."

"You're right. But I think that lesson will inspire a lot of poop jokes, and I just don't feel like going down that road," Tariq said.

"Can't argue with that," Sophia told him.

As she drove home that evening, Sophia felt relieved to have had a pleasant, enlightening exchange with Tariq. Jealousy, resentment, and physical attraction dissipated.

She marveled over the idea that people have two brains—one

upstairs with a birds' eye view, and one to make butterflies. She would have to ask her landlord Cally if neurologists referred to two brains in conversation. "Two brains" sounded ghoulish. Something Victor would contemplate. She knew all the kids would find Tariq's lesson illuminating—he would shed light on the feelings they'd probably attributed to their hearts. In a non-embarrassing framework. And maybe she could use what she had learned from Tariq to manage the vulnerability she couldn't repress this school year.

When she got home, she wrote in her journal:

Just as it is good to know where food comes from, if I remember that aversive feelings have a biological location, I can manage them more constructively. Like a suit of armor to protect my heart.
Does Connie know about the enteric system?

Sophia emailed her godmother about what Tariq had told her. To jab Connie and echo the gut theme, Sophia concluded the message with:

Brevity makes information digestible.

Connie wrote back:

Thank you for informing me about the enteric system. I didn't know you knew anything about human biology. I will now pitch an article about 'ab flab feelings' to a fitness magazine.

On a related note, I want to give you some fitness advice because you looked heavier at Christmas. (I hope you're not

overeating over Danny.)
Stop whatever you happen to be doing every time you feel a
pang in your gut about the breakup and do sit ups.

Put this motto on your refrigerator: "Make queasiness a
reminder to exercise!"

Chapter 21: Roses are Red, Violets Are Blue

Sheryl Stuyvesant, the math teacher, poked her head into the faculty room where Sophia, Nadia, and Dawn were soaking up quiet.

"One hour until Hearts Night," Sheryl said. "The eighth graders and Maggie's kids are almost done with the buffet preparations, and the sixth and seventh graders already decorated the cafeteria with Barbara."

"Kira Hughes needs some TLC tonight," Sheryl told them.

"Why?" Sophia asked.

"She gave someone a valentine and he ignored it."

"Who does she have a crush on?" Dawn asked.

"Cauliflower Boy," Sheryl replied. All of the teachers called Victor Jones "Cauliflower Boy" since he obsessed about the similarity between cauliflowers and brains. Tariq had encouraged Victor to begin researching cauliflower's structure for his science fair project.

"Kira is so serious and guarded," Sophia said. "I sensed at the chili cookoff that she liked Victor, but I can't imagine her taking a romantic risk."

"She slipped the card into his backpack. It was an anonymous Valentine. Sort of."

"Then why was she upset that he didn't respond?" Nadia asked.

"She wrote 'Roses are red, violets are blue. I like sitting next to you.' I assigned them to sit together in my class because they are equally good at math. Kira figured he would immediately get the hint."

"She doesn't know how clueless adolescent boys are," Nadia said.

"True. But Victor isn't clueless about math. Kira and he are my smartest seventh graders this year. Kira has begun to confide in me."

Dawn shook her head. "Isn't that fitting? That one of our brightest kids would choose a math teacher as a confidant?"

"That's sad," Sophia mused aloud. "No offense, Sherri. I just mean, I wonder if Kira is lonely." She changed the subject back to the neglected Valentine. "Maybe Victor didn't discover the card in his bag yet. Maybe his bag is messy."

"That's what I told her to comfort her," Sheryl said. "I attribute this uptick in her crush to a superstition. She was playing a fortune-telling game in which you recite the alphabet while twisting an apple stem until it breaks. Her apple stem broke on V."

"I didn't realize kids still twisted apples like that," Sophia grinned.

"I used to do it," Sheryl admitted. "Until my freshman year of college, when I learned Littlewood's Law of Miracles."

"What's that?" Sophia said, perking up. It would be a miracle if she could come up with six words to trounce Michael, or better yet Connie, in one elegant sentence.

"Someone who's last name was Littlewood said that the

average person experiences about a million events each month if she only sleeps about eight hours per 24 hours. We don't recognize the numerousness of our daily lives, so we lose our rational minds when coincidences happen. But coincidences are statistically likely to happen, since we experience a million things a month. If a coincidence seems meaningful, we mistakenly interpret it as a miracle."

"I don't know whether to feel jaded by that or to look forward to a miracle a month," Sophia said.

"All I'm saying is that lovesick people shouldn't read too much into an apple stems," Sheryl replied.

"You should mention that to Kira's class on Monday. I think it's a great antidote for the perils of romantic coincidence. And so is something Tariq told me about gut feelings." Sophia told them about the enteric system.

Sheryl asked Sophia to create a scavenger hunt about the folly of fortune-telling. "Your creative engine runs faster than mine. I bet you'll think up something by the end of Hearts Night."

"Don't count on that prediction coming true." Sophia swallowed. "I mean, in keeping with the message behind the hunt."

"Some people in Iran still use books of Hafez's poetry as divining tools," Nadia told them. "You open up to a verse, and use your analysis of its meaning to untangle your mind, so you can find the pathway to a solution."

When Nadia said Hafez was a Sufi, Sheryl asked about their beliefs. "I can never remember the difference between Sikhs and Sufis," Sheryl admitted as though admitting she couldn't remember how to find the square root of a number."

"Sufism is the mystical arm of Islam," Nadia told them. "Its concepts and practices are similar to Buddhism's and yoga's emphasis on transcending separation and duality. Sufi imams dominated the faith from the 11th to 19th centuries, through religious orders called Tariqah."

"Is that where Tariq's name comes from?" Sophia asked.

"Tariq's?" Nadia laughed. "No, Tariqah's etymology is from Sanskrit. Tariq's name is Arabic. It means messenger or finder, the one who knocks at the door at the end of a long night. Its Koranic meaning is 'morning star.' He is a Sunni Muslim, as most African American Muslims are. My family is Shiite, which is the religious majority in Iran. A few million people there practice Sufism, and like most Persians. In Iran right now, a few million people consider themselves to be Sufis. Some people associate Sufism with Persian culture, since three of the most prominent Sufi poets came from Iran: Hafez, who, legends say, gained that pen name by memorizing the Koran, and Rumi, and Attar, who influenced Rumi. In fact, Rumi said something beautiful to pay tribute to him: 'Attar roamed the seven cities of love—We are still just in one alley.'"

"Where were the seven cities?" Sophia asked breathlessly.

"Nowhere you can bike or fly to," Nadia said, sighing. "There were seven stages in the route to enlightenment that Attar described in his poetic journey, *The Conference of the Birds*. A teacher bird and 29 other birds try to find a legendary bird called a Simorgh. I don't remember all seven stages they go through, just four of them: love, detachment, bewilderment, and the transcendence of ego. In the end, it turns out that they themselves, the bird pilgrims, as a community, are as magical and powerful as the legendary Simorgh. The word Simorgh in Persian means '30 birds.' The surprise ending relies upon a play on words. And the moral of the story, as I was taught it, is 'strength in numbers.'"

Sophia, who was quickly growing adept at counting words,

realized that 'strength in numbers' was a three-word slogan. It summed up Countess Connie's Enumerative Guidance.

"Sophia, you and Lucy might want to read up on the Sufis," Nadia said, grinning. "You can get a lot of good quotes from their poets."

"I'm surprised you didn't tell me about the Sufis when we were working on the scavenger hunt about Islam with Tariq."

"Oh please," Nadia groaned. "I didn't want to confuse the students further. I'm still not sure they know the difference between Persians and Arabs, and the difference between the terms "Persian" and "Iranian", and the differences between Iran and the Arab countries."

"Only one of our Muslim students wears a headscarf," Sheryl observed.

"Yes, Sharifa. She says her aunt wears a different color hijab for every day of the week."

"Barbara knows a textile artist who hand-dyes them," Nadia said.

"I learned a lot from Tariq's presentation," Sheryl said. "I hadn't heard the concepts of submission and jihad defined in terms of every person's struggle for self-control."

"Yes," Sophia agreed. "That's something any regimen-hungry soul can relate to. And I was drawn to the idea of practicing the Salat prayer five times a day. As a way to reconnect to one's best self and get back on track."

Sophia thought each observance of Salat must be a comfort and a guidepost. Like a good quote. Sophia remembered that Tariq had gently rejected two quotes from the Prophet Mohammed that she had suggested he prominently display on the science lab's bulletin board:

214

Listen to the words of the scientist and instill unto others the lessons of science.

and

An hour's study of nature is better than a year's prayer.

"I like the way these quotes dovetail with advocacy of environmental stewardship," she had told Tariq carefully.

He hesitated. "Nadia and I are already having the kids research and write mini-biographies of Muslim scientific and mathematic contributions. I prefer to follow that approach. Your quotes are good, but I don't like the idea of plastering these two sentences on the wall. We don't need to try to prove, via quotes, that Mohammed was an enlightened thinker, and by extension, that Muslims are pro-science." Tariq smiled at her gently. "That seems defensive to me."

"Understood," Sophia had said, feeling almost as defensive as she felt about the possibility of seeing Michael at Hearts Night.

She checked her watch. The four teachers had gotten so caught up in faculty room conversation that they were going to be late.

Colorful posters lined the cafeteria walls like patchwork quilt blocks. Sophia admired the students' depictions of fruits, vegetables, and hearts—both the anatomical kind and the Valentine kind—in every shade of red, maroon, and pink. None of the posters acknowledged the fact that this was Friday the 13th and there were no images of exploding cauliflowers. Victor must not have had a chance to make a poster.

Kira's imageless poster read: "Don't compost commercially-produced roses. They are dipped in chemicals." Sophia cringed. She resented the way environmentally-savvy children were forced to focus on gloomy realities by the rest of the world's unsustainable wastefulness, thoughtlessness, or poverty.

Standing before Kira's maudlin poster, Sophia considered biking over to Margaret's greenhouse—after all, who locked a greenhouse, even in DC? She imagined stealing a few of Margaret and Ben's best roses for Kira.

"This sign is depressing," said a male voice.

"I was just thinking the same thing." She turned around and saw Michael Sherman. She felt electric, and he was holding a tray of fragrant cookies.

"Would you like to try one?" he asked. "I baked this batch, and asked our bakery department to make two hundred more for tonight."

She chose the biggest chocolate-chip cookie that wouldn't require jostling. It tasted as good as it looked, due to a perfect pairing of salty with sweet.

"I also brought some people from a dairy called Loudoun Creamery to serve rBGH-free milk with these cookies," he said. "Now though, I think I should have brought whole grain crackers instead of cookies out of respect for the health theme."

"No worries, I'm glad to find out you know of Loudoun Creamery. We used to take the kids out there for field trips, and I've been trying to get Brendan, your buyer, to give Mimi some shelf space."

"You must not have been in the store recently."

"What? How do you know that?" Oops. She sounded defensive.

"We've had Loudoun Creamery's milks and cheeses for two

216

or three weeks now. I use their light cream to make custard. And not to brag, but I make crème brulee really well."

A pause gave her time to count his words. "*I make crème brulee really well"* was a seductive six-word sentence.

"...favorite thing to make is chili," Michael continued. "Though it isn't as sustainable as the chili you made with the kids. I use ingredients from all over the world. You'd be horrified if I had you over to dinner. My pantry is as geographically diverse as the United Nations."

She tried to ignore the fact that she liked Michael's sense of humor. It made him a kindred spirit. She offset this thought by schoolmarming him: "You ought to challenge yourself to use local ingredients. You could make a game of it."

The sentence "*You could make a game of it"* rang in her ears. Was it six words, or seven? She tried to count, but the distraction of Michael's presence made that impossible. With Michael here, and amidst the happy, purposeful crowd, Sophia felt like a sneak surrounded by saints.

"Have you gotten your dinner yet?" Michael asked. "I don't have to hand out the rest of these cookies and I'd love to eat with you. I don't know anyone here."

"Oh, I can't eat with you, because, um, unfortunately, I just ate. The kids made yellow spaghetti squash instead of spaghetti because the squash is higher in fiber. Which reminds me, uh, would you excuse me? I promised the nurses that I'd stop by their tables to get my blood pressure checked. Not that I have any problems with my blood pressure, but uh, in case they need to calibrate their machines they might need, um, a tester to come by their tables."

"Don't let me keep you," Michael said, again with the smile.

For the next two hours, Sophia did everything she could to stay away from Michael. This required her to keep checking out where he was. For much of the time, he talked to Tariq. Tariq was helping students at the buffet, dishing out an endless supply of his surprisingly popular cauliflower gratin. Victor had inspired the recipe.

Dawn tapped her on the shoulder. "We should talk."

They wandered over to a relatively studentless, parentless corner.

"A weird thing just happened," Dawn began.

"Weird bad or weird good?"

"I don't want to presume."

Uh oh. Formal speech was a bad sign.

"Remember how you said you'd never date another lawyer?"

"Yes." Oh for crying out loud. Dawn's concern was going to have something to do with Michael Sherman.

"Well, over the past two months, I've had some legal questions."

"About the lawsuit?" Sophia felt cold.

"No, no. Nothing that serious, by any means. But there have been enough little questions here and there that I don't feel comfortable phoning Peter Resnick each time, but I can't call Danny Giordano either because…" She didn't finish her sentence.

"Don't avoid him on my account. You don't have to protect me in any way."

"I know I don't. It's just that, well, after you and Danny broke up, he said he wanted to keep helping Carver pro bono, but then called me to say he'd be out of the country a lot this coming year and that he'd be unable to help us further."

"That's flaky and slick." She remembered telling Connie that Danny was off to Lake Cuomo indefinitely.

"I knew you'd interpret it that way," Dawn said. "But he

218

sounded sincere."

"Lawyers get paid to sound sincere."

They exchanged a smile.

"Is that what you wanted to tell me?" Sophia asked as pleasantly as she could.

"No. I wanted to give you that background because Michael Sherman, Luscious LoCal's in-house counsel, just offered to be our new pro bono attorney. Stephen had told his boss, Ken Burnett, that we were looking for someone."

"Oh, okay." Sophia mentally rummaged through her kitchen cupboards. If she had any Jack Daniels left she would have a shot as soon as she got home.

"I am telling you this privately because I overheard him ask Maggie a weird question about you. Moments before he made the offer."

"What did he say?" The cold feeling came on again.

"He asked her about her work-life balance. How she balanced her roles as a parent with the long hours at Carver, and then he asked if other Carver teachers had kids. He asked if you were 'married with children' with just that emphasis, to be sort of funny. But I got the feeling, and Maggie got the feeling, that he was on a fishing expedition."

"How do you know she had that feeling?"

"Um."

"Were you talking about my business behind my back? Yes you were. Don't sweat it, I'm teasing you." Sophia lightened this exchange to hide her defensiveness.

Dawn continued. "Maggie told me that Bernard poked his head in on the conversation, once he heard Michael asking about your personal life, and Bernard said—Well. I don't know exactly what he said. I wasn't there."

"What did Maggie tell you he said?"

Dawn smiled sheepishly. "I don't know. I can't remember. Ask her. Or Bernard. No, don't ask him."

"Of course I wouldn't." Sophia scowled. "I know better than to ask a kid something like that."

"I needed to give you a heads-up about Michael," Dawn said. "Since I know you've sworn off lawyers." Dawn's voice lilted upward, making this more question than statement.

"I have, don't worry. I wouldn't want you to have to search for yet another pro bono attorney."

"I wouldn't mind," Dawn said, but her voice betrayed her relief. Sophia felt defensive. Clearly Dawn assumed that all of Sophia's relationships expired as speedily as milk.

"Stephen has recruited Luscious LoCal as a source of donations to replace the money we lost recently," Dawn said. "Their CEO, Ken Burnett, wants to use photos of the kids in our garden for free publicity. This might be a match made in heaven. As Stephen put it, uncertain times require flexibility and creativity."

After Dawn went to greet some parents, Sophia looked for Michael in the crowd. He was in the dessert section, standing between Tariq and an attractive woman from Loudoun Creamery whom Sophia did not recognize. She was talking to Michael while curling her hair over her ear in a way that revealed her interest in him. Michael's attention was on his dessert. Then he looked up, as though he knew Sophia was checking him out. He winked.

Michael Sherman stayed late to help clean up. Sophia watched uncomfortably as Tariq, Dawn, and Michael chatted as though they were old college friends. When she couldn't take it any more, she began hauling food scrap bags to the compost heap, and the smaller bags of non-recyclable, non-compostable garbage to the dumpster in the parking lot. She could handle three or four bags at a time, because nothing felt heavier than the worry in her chest. And, in contrast to the optimistic philosophizing she had done in her journal a few nights earlier, localizing that worry to her chest didn't lighten the emotional load.

Sophia and Tariq had just hurled the last of the trash bags into the parking lot dumpster when he asked a six-word question that shocked her.

"Do you have plans tomorrow night?"

Sophia's adrenalin level spiked, and her thoughts raced miles ahead. Tariq was a two-timing creep. How should Sophia tell Dawn that Tariq had hit on her?

But what Tariq said next made Sophia feel bad about assuming the worst. "Dawn and I were hoping you'd join us at a Luscious LoCal benefit that Michael Sherman invited us to. It's at a restaurant called Samsara, to support REGROW, that international farmers' organization."

Danny had taken Sophia to Samsara on their first date. She interpreted this as an ominous sign, despite Sheryl's explanation, via Littlewood's Law, about the frequency of coincidences.

"... Dawn and I thought it would be good for you to come with us to tell Michael about the Entrepreneurs & Engineers curriculum. We're hoping Luscious LoCal will help us implement it."

"What? Are we involving Michael Sherman in that, too? I thought Dawn said Michael was just going to help us with some pro bono legal work."

Sophia wondered why Dawn and Tariq weren't doing something on their own tomorrow night? It was going to be Valentine's Day.

I should have given you a heads-up first," Tariq said, "before asking Michael to involve Luscious LoCal in our E & E curriculum, but opportunity struck. He seemed to have such a good time tonight, with the kids. I told him I thought the students in the after school program should start a personal chef business, on a small-scale of course. That way, when their parents come to pick them up at six, they'd be able to pick up that night's entree as well. The after-school kids could make it in Maggie's kitchen."

"What about doing their homework?"

"They could do short shifts, since many hands make light work. Anyway, Michael got all excited and suggested we bring the kids to Luscious LoCal for two field trips. First to the business and marketing offices, then to catering and the prepared food department. At that point, I felt I shouldn't go further without your input."

"But we're not supposed to do any more field trips," Sophia stammered.

"Oh, right. Dawn said she'd make an exception, in my case. Anyway, I do hope you will join us tomorrow night."

"Thanks," she said. "I'll be there."

That night, Sophia lay awake for hours. She daydreamed, or rather, night-dreamed, that she had stolen twelve of Margaret's roses for Kira. She imagined forging Victor's signature, under a six-word verse:

"Roses are red, violets are blue…"

She could not come up with an answering rhyme.

Chapter 22: Find A Generalization That's Always True

At six-thirty the following evening, Sophia decided to take a long, long walk to Samsara. She would arrive fashionably late, and stay just long enough to hear whatever Tariq said about the E & E curriculum. She would be friendly to Michael, and then she would leave. A moonlit walk home afterward would soothe her. She missed the fatigue of accomplishment.

Sophia put on her sneakers, and tucked her black boots into her knapsack. She hadn't worn the sleek boots since New Year's Eve.

Twenty minutes away from the restaurant, Sophia heard a man yelling. She was breathless from the exertion of a long walk that was mostly uphill, and now felt her heart pound with fear. Where was he? Then she saw a very short, portly man standing in the middle of an apartment building driveway. He was too far away to have seen her, and he continued to yell into his cell phone. When she got close enough to distinguish his words, she bent down, pretending to retie a shoe, so she could find out what he was yelling about.

"Ask me if I *seen* it. *Not* if I *took* it. I didn't steal nothing from you." he shouted.

Sophia suspected the person on the phone with him had lost money. To keep eavesdropping, she bent down to pantomime more shoe-tying for an unrealistically long time. The man moved on, so she did too. She replayed the memory of the man's booming voice for several blocks. Considering how angry he'd been, he had defended himself with surprising precision. "Ask me if I *seen* it. *Not* if I *took* it."

"Sophia!" a man with a higher voice called from behind her. She recognized that voice immediately. Michael Sherman. The sensation from her heart was flutter-fear, not pounding fear. *Localize the flutter,* she told herself, to calm down from feeling stirred up.

"This is the second time you've snuck up on me in twenty-four hours," Sophia told him.

"I was sure it was you," Michael said when he caught up to her. "Nobody else has hair like yours."

Sophia brushed it behind her ears in a gesture she was sure Michael would misread as flirtatious. Was he making fun of her hair? Cold weather made it especially stringy.

"I hope you're on your way to the benefit dinner at Samsara?" he asked.

"Yes. Tariq invited me."

"The more people the better. Do you live around here?" Michael asked.

"No," she replied.

"I don't live around here either," he volunteered. "I'm downtown off 17th Street, in a building called the Cairo."

"I know that building." She envied him for having a hip Dupont Circle apartment. The Cairo had an Art Nouveau façade and a burlesque history. It was the tallest residential building in DC, and Congress passed the Heights of Buildings Act after it was built to prevent other architects from dwarfing the

Washington Monument.

"Why are you walking?" she asked. "Is your car in the shop?"

"I don't own a car right now. I don't need one. I bike to work or take the Metro. Or walk. I wanted to walk tonight."

"Me too," Sophia said. "I don't like to bike after dark."

"I bet people at Carver don't drive much."

"You're right. What with the kids being under sixteen and all."

"I meant Carver's teachers." He looked amused.

"We're fuel-efficient. Did you get to meet many kids last night?"

"No, but I had an interesting conversation about you with the kitchen director's son. What was his name? Benjamin?"

"Bernard." Her heart beat perceptibly, hopefully. She hadn't thought she would ever find out what Bernard had told Michael about her.

"And what's Bernard's mother's name?"

"Maggie. She's our kitchen director."

"Right. Maggie and I were discussing work/life balance. Bernard said you would never marry or have children because you were too much of a control freak."

"He said that about me?" Sophia's stomach hurt from the surprise. She had always thought Bernard thought she was cool.

"He didn't say it in a judgmental way," Michael clarified, more for accuracy's sake than to cushion the blow. "I think he wanted to say the word 'freak' to shock his mom. He also said you let Carver keep you too busy."

Sophia didn't like the sound of that either: "you let Carver keep you too busy." This reminded her of Connie's unflattering theory that Sophia hid behind Carver. But she didn't hide behind Carver, did she? The pairing of her personal life and professional life had been seamless before this school year.

Sophia thought of Danny. He was as charismatic as her godmother. If only Danny had been capable or willing to be her knight in shining armor after the lawsuit ended.

"What's on your mind?" Michael asked.

"Walking uphill," Sophia said.

"Are you winded? Full of hot air?" he joked.

"Takes one to know one, counselor."

"Oh yeah. You've got this thing about guys who are lawyers. Did a lawyer break your heart?"

"No," she stopped walking, then started again so he wouldn't notice he had shaken her. "I think female lawyers are separately-but-equally untrustworthy."

"How can you make fun of lawyers when what you do for a living alienates people too?"

"What do you mean?" Sophia asked, though she anticipated the answer.

"You're a do-gooder. You probably lecture everyone about environmental sins."

"No. I don't lecture," Sophia snapped. "That's what the scavenger hunts are for. They take me out of the equation. I couldn't stand my godmother's lectures when I was a kid—I mean, I couldn't stand being lectured by anyone when I was a kid, and I don't want to subject my students to long rants. Or alienate their parents with unsolicited advice."

Sophia remembered that she had had no problem lecturing people in college. That had ended badly. Would Michael Google her background the way Danny had? If Michael was going to, or if he already had, she wanted to defend herself ahead of time, so she did so, impulsively:

"In college my friends and I harangued other students to reduce waste, instead of promoting conservation in an engaging manner. We wrote longwinded letters to our college newspaper, and all the banners I made for protests had to be held up by two or three people because my slogans were so wordy that they required extra-long banners. We had great ideas, like trying to get everyone to substitute mugs for disposable coffee and beer cups, but we were so arrogant that when we tried to sell them, people ignored us. We denounced clutter, but wound up having to stuff our dorm rooms with cardboard boxes of unsold eco-mugs."

"Eco-mugs? That sounds like earmuffs."

She laughed, something she hadn't done in a few weeks.

"I like your laugh."

"Thank you." It had pleased her, the sound of its return. Like the audible equivalent of catching oneself in a mirror under flattering light.

"Kids laugh more than adults do," she mused. "Maybe it's got something to do with puberty." Half a block later, she realized, and said aloud, "There's no humor in my scavenger hunts. I mean, in the way I write them. But then some pretty funny stuff happens when the kids start going down the list of things to do. They always take the ideas a step further."

"You're nicer than I thought you were," Michael said. "When I first heard you did scavenger hunts with your students, I thought it sounded sinister. Like you were a Pied Piper, lording secret treasure over kids' heads."

"That's an awful analogy. The Pied Piper was a merciless guru."

"Well, you're the one who bragged about having some magically manipulative six words. I shouldn't have compared you to the Pied Piper, maybe. You might be more like the Wizard of Oz, or the con artist who sold Jack the magic beans."

The phrase "con artist" always made Sophia hear the sound

of Connie's moniker, "Countess Connie, Countess Connie, Countess Connie." Thinking it three times added up to six words and left her empty-headed.

"Let's change the subject. Have you eat at Samsara before? They have a good menu."

"How many guys have you told about your six words?"

She shook her head. "I lost count after a thousand."

"You must be aware that it is the goofiest pickup line."

"Not when I say it," Sophia said.

"It's a test of wits then. Since you're a scavenger huntress and an educator, I would think you can't help but play games to test a guy."

"Mmm hmm."

"It is a sexist claim. That all guys would respond to the same thing. You didn't mean it, right? You couldn't have. It's too stupid."

Stupid is the word I had in mind, Sophia thought.

"Tell me. Tell me just two of them at least. Four?" He had a persuasive grin.

Sophia swallowed hard. It would be simpler, but not easier, to admit she had been drunk. Michael didn't look like the type who would drink enough to lose control of his words. She bet he rarely embarrassed himself, and now he had entered her Carver orbit, so she had to keep her cards close to her chest.

Then without any noticeable effort on her part, her mind provided this irresistible way to elude Michael's investigation:

"Maybe I already said them to you."

That suits like a glove, she thought. She was done. How serendipitous that she didn't have to consciously come up with that line. She wondered if Scheherazade had unrolled her 1,001 life-saving stories consciously or unconsciously.

Michael was quiet. Maybe he was counting the words in her

sentence. She counted them, and realized that *"Maybe I already said them to you"* was not the perfect six words, because it was seven words. She should have left off the "maybe" qualifier. She wished she had found some way, just now, or at Hearts Night, to work in Dorothy Parker's *no cure for curiosity* line.

Sophia wanted to slip into a time machine and rewind. Enough to erase impulsive actions. Not far enough to ensnare her in childhood when Connie controlled her.

"I'll have to be on the lookout, when I run into you, for your subliminal trickery," Michael said.

"What?" Sophia asked.

"Well, if you really said the six words to me and I didn't notice them, than you're using some sort of subliminal programming."

The restaurant's awning was in sight. Sophia quickened her pace.

"Cat got your tongue?" He was poking at her like a bramble bush.

'I've never had anyone accuse me of subliminal programming," she said, trying to sound playful instead of defensive.

"Don't get me wrong," he said. "I don't think of you as like, uh, a dog whistle or something."

"You're comparing me to a dog whistle now? What an ego boost. Didn't your law school professors show you have to subdue people with flattery?"

"I promise not to tease you about your pickup line if you'll stop making lawyer jokes in my presence. Seriously, for a few years I've been searching for the right pro bono project. Carver touched my heart last night." He paused. "Pun intended."

She hadn't noticed the pun on "Hearts Night." His mind worked fast.

"How about a truce?" he asked.

"We're fine," she said, shaking the hand he offered. "I don't even know you."

"I hope we can become friends." He smiled as he held the door open for her.

"Of course," she said evenly, thinking "*I hope we can become friends*" was the six-word sentence that no one ever wanted to hear from an increasingly attractive person.

A wallpaper of electric blue chrysanthemums (the color of 1980s spandex) and saffron-colored tablecloths brightened the dimly lit main dining room at Samsara. Curry perfumed the air, the dishes tasted less flavorful than they smelled. Sophia ate slowly to avoid dripping peanut sauce down her shirtfront while Tariq and Dawn pitched Michael. Dawn said the personal chef enterprise would be a great way to integrate the students' academic lives with their responsibilities at home. Michael said he knew of a vendor who might donate several warming trays and some other equipment.

Sophia admired Tariq's smooth face and demeanor as he pitched. What would Tariq's six words be? His insight that all emotions are felt in the torso was succinct and indisputable. Sophia imagined scrawling a six-word sentence across an empty page in her journal: "Find a generalization that's always true." As though that task would be as easy to check off as numbered items on her to-do list.

"I've got to go," Sophia told Michael, Dawn, and Tariq. She was glad there was no bill to settle. They had all paid at the door, and the tickets were cheaper than she had anticipated.

"How will you get home?" Michael asked. Sophia saw Dawn and Tariq exchange glances.

"I'll walk for a bit and then catch the bus the rest of the

way."

"Are you kidding? It was freezing when we came in and the temperature's probably dropped by few degrees. Let me share a cab with you."

"That's okay," Sophia said. "This weather feels warm to me because I'm from upstate New York."

She walked all the way home. She kept intending to get a bus, but there were several people waiting at each stop, which made her think there must be some delay. Momentum propelled her, and the desire to tire herself out completely so she'd fall asleep faster. By the time she got home, it was 10:45, just 15 minutes past her school-night bedtime.

She decided to she didn't feel creative enough to compose a scavenger hunt for the six words. She would unwind by reading Louis Halle's *Spring in Washington*. She read *Spring in Washington* every year, starting in late January to commemorate the first day of his hunt for another spring half a century earlier.

Sophia reread a powerful line, *The spring shall make you free*. It was enviably six words long. She set the book aside and wished she hadn't had to cancel her cable subscription. She thought of the movie *You've Got Mail*, a romance between an idealistic, independent bookseller and a corporate shark. This reminded her of Danny teasing her, calling her a pinko with a pitchfork. She didn't miss him so much any more.

Brendan said Michael worked with lobbyists. Michael must be a Republican, in addition to being a smug lawyer. How had he wound up working for a grocery chain that promoted itself as being greener than its rivals? Sophia decided to assume the worst of him. Instead of seeking out the opportunity to work there because he wanted to be a force for change, he probably sought to limit reform. She imagined herself back at Samsara, with Dawn, Tariq, and Michael. Tariq was an experienced debater. What if the four of them had wound up arguing about some issue like hog-farm lagoons. Just that phrase, *hog-farm lagoon*, grossed out everyone at Carver other than Victor, but maybe Michael would roll his eyes over the use of the phrase the way a man who described himself as pro-life would object to being labeled anti-choice. Whenever she saw him again, she would lobby him relentlessly the way she lobbied Brendan. Then Michael would avoid her and he wouldn't grill her about the six-word sentence.

Sophia remembered Ken Burnett mentioning that Michael had grown up on a farm. Michael's background bothered her because farm-raised childhood made her jealous, and made her wonder if he knew as much about growing food as she did. Now she imagined how wonderful it would be to find out that Michael had grown up on a horrible factory farm. If he were an apologist for unsustainable agriculture she could dismiss him from her thoughts and wouldn't dwell upon him to the point of keeping herself up too late.

Chapter 23: Sophia and Michael Conceal Their Pasts

"Are you free Saturday night?"

"Sure," Sophia said when Michael called to invite her over for dinner.

"Can I bring anything?"

"How about the six words on a platter?" he suggested.

"I was thinking more along the lines of dessert."

"You could buy a grocery store sheet cake and have them write the six words in gluey red cursive."

"I don't buy no stinkin' sheet cake."

As soon as they got off the phone, Sophia picked up her journal to gripe:

Why didn't I say I had plans for Saturday night?
I should have suggested a weeknight. He said he hoped we could be friends. A weeknight would be friendlier.

She stopped writing, jolted by a cringe, then wrote this:

A femme fatale with six magic words would have dates or a long-term relationship for all Saturday nights. Michael already knows I was dateless for both nights of Valentine's Day weekend.
Dawn will think I'm hitting on every lawyer who passes Carver's way. What would Dad think?

She paused.

Why is Michael free on a weekend night?

Sophia put her journal aside to hunt for Michael's past. He wasn't on Facebook, so Sophia couldn't friend him, and anyway, she wouldn't friend him. She would want him to friend her.

She surfed the Internet for an embarrassingly long time, clicking pages and pages of links like a stalker. All she discovered was that anything juicy from Michael's past was undiscoverable. First, she had found endless numbers of Michael Shermans. Then she finally found links related to his time at George Washington University. He had written articles on regulatory agencies for their law review, and he clerked for a judge in Baltimore, which reminded her that Ken Burnett had said he was from Maryland. There were a few Luscious LoCal press releases, and someone named Michael Sherman worked for the USDA for a few years but maybe that was someone else with the same name. After trawling through impersonal citations, she gave up.

Then she remembered that drunk, voluble friend of Michael's. Was his name Tim or Jim? He said he was "sort of" Michael's brother. She didn't know what that meant, but surely Tim or Jim would know what made Michael tick, and especially, what sort of woman attracted him. It would be so much easier to

234

customize a six-word sentence if she could subtly debrief someone close to Michael. She had a feeling there weren't many people who met that description, and assumed Michael had found some lawyerly trick to hide written clues to his personal past.

The silver and black lobby of the Cairo was sleek and lined with mirrors that made corners look like alcoves. Michael's door was at the end of a hallway that smelled like marinara sauce, and she guessed correctly that he was the source of that fragrant warmth. The small living room had a dining table on the other side of the galley kitchen. The door that she guessed led to the bedroom was closed, with a framed photograph nailed to its center. She would have to check out that photograph. Books lined one wall, and on the other two walls, generous windows rose from two or three feet off the ground to the ceilings. Exposed brick drew Sophia's attention to the wall sections under those windows. There were two sliding doors along the entryway, one of which Michael opened to hang up her coat, and a long, shallow closet maximized storage space.

"That closet is well-organized. Did you ever live in New York City or Japan?" Sophia asked him as he carefully tucked a corduroy-padded hanger into the shoulders of her down jacket.

"No. I've got to live small until I pay off my student loans, and my mom has expenses that I help her out with."

"Like what?" Sophia asked. "Sorry, I don't mean to be intrusive. My mom has a lot of expenses too." Sophia hesitated, but not for long enough. "She's paralyzed from the waist down."

Sophia immediately regretted telling him. Now he would always think of it whenever he saw her. At least she hadn't admitted the accident was her fault, and she decided that she had better not tell him. She would monitor her wine flow.

"My mom is healthy," Michael said quietly. "I feel grateful for that. She started a campaign though, very impulsively, and now she wants seed money from me to pay back some of her loans." He paused. "I don't feel comfortable talking about this."

Sophia wondered if Michael's mother was a politician. "I don't feel comfortable talking about my mom either," she said. "Um. I like the exposed brick on your walls." Then she added, "I mean, who doesn't like exposed brick. That was a clichéd thing to say."

"Are your six words a clichéd phrase?" he asked.

"No. They are a magic spell." She was relieved to have answered his question with a six-word phrase. She wondered if he had noticed that she had used a placeholder. He didn't say anything.

She walked over to the bookshelves, hoping she wouldn't find out Michael liked to read for pleasure. Unfortunately, he had great taste. Nonfiction by Bill McKibben, M.F.K. Fisher, Wendell Berry, Barbara Kingsolver, Michael Pollan, Shelby Foote, and Joan Didion. That revered quartet of Kingsolver, Berry, Pollan, and McKibben was strong evidence that Michael was a good guy when it came to sustainable food advocacy. So much for her attempt to unearth proof that he was a shill for industrial agriculture.

Michael's shelves also held fiction by Roald Dahl, Alice Munro, Jack London, Josephine Tey, and Russell Banks. There were plays by Tennessee Williams and Marsha Norman. Sophia spotted the same bright yellow-orange edition of *D'Aulaires Book of Greek Myths* that her maternal grandmother gave her for her birthday one year. That was before Persephone's accident. Sophia had been captivated and frightened by When Hades consigned the Greek Persephone's to the underworld, allegedly for eating pomegranates, Sophia was captivated and frightened that the goddess-daughter had been geographically crippled. What frightened her most was not the sudden lack of freedom, but Persephone's lack of such important information. How unfair of Hades to punish her without telling her the rules in advance.

One of Sophia's mom's more discomfiting jokes came to mind: "If you ever find yourself in the underworld, don't eat local no matter how good the pomegranates look."

"I've got more books in my bedroom," Michael said, "but the best ones are out here. I'm going to check on the stuffed peppers."

Sophia read the spines of his cookbooks. She had never met a man who had such a great cookbook collection, filling two whole shelves. Why didn't men of her generation buy cookbooks? Many of her male peers cooked well, but perhaps they were reluctant to seek direction from cookbooks.

Sophia heard clanging coming from the kitchen, and figured Michael was occupied enough that she could snoop. The picture nailed to the bedroom door was a yellowed photograph of ten kids. Their arms were draped around one another and they each had the same bowl-cut hair. There was Michael, puppy-faced like Carver's sixth graders. All the boys and girls in the photo were white and their smiling mouths were open. Perhaps they were singing a funny song at the moment the photographer snapped the picture. The image was dappled with pale grainy spots, immortalizing a darkroom mistake.

"Can you tell which one is me?" Michael asked her.

She startled as though he had caught her looking through his underwear drawer. "This one?" she asked rhetorically.

"Yeah, and Tim's right next to me."

"Tim?"

"The drunk I was with New Year's Eve. Maybe you were

too far gone to remember him?"

"No, I remember." *Shoot*, she thought. She should have said she didn't remember that night at all. It would relieve pressure to come up with a witty-enough six-word sentence.

"Was this taken at a summer camp?" she asked.

"Yeah. Well, it was more of a year-round place."

"The farm you grew up on?"

He tensed. "How did you know I grew up on a farm?"

"Your boss mentioned it at the cook-off."

"Speaking of farms, most of the vegetables tonight are unseasonal, I'm afraid," Michael said. "Would you mind tasting the sauce? I may have overdone the garlic."

She looked over her shoulder at the photo. The kids looked less happy than at first glance. But very awake.

"I noticed you had the beef satay at Samsara, so I figured it would be okay to use beef," Michael told her as he lifted the lid off the pot.

She thought it strange that he remembered what she had eaten. "I eat grass-fed red meat occasionally. My favorite supplier is Groff's Content Farm in Rocky Ridge, Maryland. Might be something for Luscious LoCal to look into."

"You should tell our buyer about that. I'll write down his name for you." He pulled a square of blue paper from an old cracker tin.

"I know Brendan."

"Oh right, you mentioned that you knew him at Hearts Night."

"I mean, I don't know him personally. We have talked once or twice about local producers." She hoped Michael wouldn't ask Brendan about her. "Just enough of an acquaintance to make suggestions from time to time."

"Ah. You ever use the six words on him? To get him to buy

238

local?"

"Yeah right," she said, looking for something innocuous to comment upon. "I like your scratch paper stash. I have one of those in my kitchen, but I keep mine in a beat-up envelope. I like this cookie tin better." Why did Michael have to be organized, and a good cook, and frugal, and quietly good-looking, and a reader of books she loved?

"Did you happen to bring dessert?" Michael asked her. "If not, I have snickerdoodle cookies."

"Yes," she said with just half her mind on the question. Michael's great books didn't guarantee he shared her politics. Maybe a relative died and left him those books. Or maybe he was against sustainable food production and contorted arguments by Barbara Kingsolver and Wendell Berry so that he could build counterarguments. Maybe he didn't ever read for pleasure, or cook. Maybe he planted the cookbooks to seduce women.

"So where are you hiding it?" Michael asked her.

"Hmm?"

"Dessert?"

"Oh. I forgot to take them out of my backpack." She headed back to the hall.

"Them? Did you make more than one dessert?" He sounded hopeful.

"Gingerbread squares. Well, more like rectangles."

"I love gingerbread. We can warm them up before we eat them, and I've got Loudoun Creamery heavy cream, so we can make whipped cream."

"I brought whipped cream," Sophia said, pulling out a foil-wrapped Tupperware container of it.

"Is this from Loudoun?" he asked, as he slid it into his enviable/covetable Sub Zero refrigerator.

"Trickling Springs Creamery. They were at the Adams Morgan Farmers Market this morning."

"Are you a regular there?"

"Yes," she replied.

"Mm. I only shop at Luscious LoCal."

"I'm sure most women would find that impressive," Sophia joked flirtatiously before she remembered her friendship agenda.

"The minute they start making baking powder and spices in the greater Washington area, I promise to be the first to buy some, and I'll make sure Luscious LoCal carries it," Michael said as he wiped his hands with a cloth napkin. In the kitchen Sophia had seen a stack of colorful dishtowels. Unlike Danny, Michael was not—to use her student Nicole Furlani's phrase—a paper towel pig.

While they ate dinner, Michael asked her interesting questions about herself, and shared some anecdotes when something she said triggered his memory. She liked that give and take, which she experienced more frequently with women than with men. Michael monitored himself to ensure equal conversational time. She found this endearing, rather than awkward. He exaggerated his stories into hilarious crescendos. She was pleased that he didn't bring up law until they both heard her cell phone buzz.

"Do you want to answer that?" he asked.

"No. I forgot to turn it off earlier."

"A friend of mine is a litigator," Michael said. "He's got a case right now where an ad exec is suing a cell phone manufacturer for ruining his career. Apparently, the guy was making a presentation, and his cell phone was in 'vibrate' mode, which is almost as loud as the ringer when you're sitting in a conference room. When the phone buzzed, the company's CEO thought the ad exec had farted. The CEO was a germaphobe, and

I don't know that you can contract any illnesses through flatulence, but the ad exec lost the account and got fired. Now he's unemployable because he's known as the Farter of Madison Avenue."

When Sophia had stopped laughing, she said, "Is that true?"

"As true as your ability to control any guy with six words."

"Then it is a true story."

"That's another six-word sentence that isn't the right six-word sentence," Michael drummed his fingers on the table and then picked up the platter to serve himself a second block of gingerbread. "May I give you another piece? It's delicious."

"Sure," she said so she wouldn't appear to have lost her appetite. "You have wonderful taste in books."

"I love reading," Michael told her. "I rarely turn on my TV, just have it there in case there's some national emergency or something."

"I wish my students spent less time watching TV. My godmother—I mean, my parents—never let me watch TV."

She hoped he wouldn't ask about her godmother and he didn't.

"I wasn't allowed to watch TV either," Michael continued. "They didn't have one on the farm. I bought a DVD player a few years ago, along with all the Christmas and Halloween specials I missed growing up. It was so satisfying to find out what a Grinch looked like, and to hear Charlie Brown's voice, and the other Peanuts characters. The Peanuts are a new discovery for me as well. We didn't have any newspapers or..." He trailed off. "Mind if we call it a night? I've got to get back to Ken on some stuff before his bedtime Blackberry check." Michael checked his watch. "Thank goodness he goes to bed late."

This seemed like a cattle prod. Sophia got up from the table. He must not be physically attracted to her, she assumed.

241

"I'm going to wash my hands," she said.

Michael's bathroom smelled of man shampoo or aftershave, and was warmer than the rest of the apartment. There was no tub, just a shower stall, and Sophia opened the medicine cabinet to snoop, and also to distract herself from imagining Michael's naked body. She was embarrassed when the cabinet creaked, and turned the faucet on as though the sound of the running water could rewind time and cover up that creak. She looked back at the door, to reassure herself it was still closed. Maybe he hadn't heard the sound. She eyed the contents of the cabinet from top (bandages and other first aid supplies) to middle (over-the-counter cold medicines, including no less than three cough drop brands) to bottom shelf, where there were two bottles of Advil and one prescription pill bottle. *Zoloft, 100 mg.* She was pretty sure Zoloft was an antidepressant, but not positive, so she committed the name to memory. She would look it up when she got home. The water was still running as she closed the cabinet, but the precaution was unnecessary because the cabinet shut silently.

Michael was cleaning up in the kitchen when she emerged. "Find anything interesting in the medicine cabinet?"

Nothing like getting caught to make one's enteric system flutter.

"What do you mean?" she asked, feeling nauseous.

"Well, you ran so much water that I figured you were either taking a sponge bath or inventorying the medicine cabinet."

"I was looking for a Band-Aid."

"You cut yourself?"

"No, um. Yes. I thought I did. But it turned out I didn't." She felt like one of her students.

Where should she say she hurt herself if he requested evidence?

Michael dropped the interrogation. "I washed out your whipped cream container and put in some of the leftover stuffed cabbage." He handed it to her.

"How thoughtful." Through ESP transmission, she told him he would be perfect for a non-numerically boastful woman.

"Mind if I keep the rest of the gingerbread?" he asked.

"Please do."

"Is your recipe a secret?"

"No," Sophia said. "I got it from a book by Laurie Colwin and the recipe's all over the Internet. I'll send you a link."

"Thanks. Maybe I should give you a ride home? I have a bike rack on my car."

"You're kind to offer but I'm fine."

"Okay. Hey, you've got something on your forehead."

Sophia yanked her hand up to feel for it.

"Wait," Michael said, gently pulling her hand away and patting the center of her forehead with his index finger. Then he bent over and lightly kissed the spot. "Bike safely."

"Okay," Sophia said, and stumbled down the corridor to the elevator as though she'd just been hit by a truck.

Chapter 24: Scavenger Hunting for the Six Words

The next morning, Sophia ignored her chores for Cally and her schoolwork to study recipes for gingerbread. The Laurie Colwin recipe she had used the day before had twelve ingredients. Sophia had four other gingerbread recipes. She set to work in her journal, trying to distill all this tempting, gingerbread knowledge into a six-ingredient, six-step recipe that would be irresistible and foolproof. Connie said the way to a man's heart was through his stomach and through his eyes, which is why she nagged her readers to exercise a lot so they could flatten their own stomachs. Connie was a real sweetheart.

Sophia glanced at the "12" she'd written in the margin of the Colwin recipe, after she had counted its twelve ingredients. That number twelve, and the fact that Sophia had been trying to drink less made her think of Alcoholics Anonymous's twelve-step program. It struck her now that AA's twelve-step program could be framed as a twelve-step scavenger hunt. Perhaps the most compelling scavenger hunt of all time, since it was the only regimen that could wrench away the bottle from so many desperate people who had tried other methods and failed.

Sophia looked over her attempts at a six-step recipe, and then wrote:

What if the six steps weren't confined to a recipe? What if they were six steps of a scavenger hunt?
I need to bypass this creative block long enough to devise a scavenger hunt that will do three things for me:

1) Guide my hunt for six words.

2) Enable me to string Michael along. I refuse to admit that I ended last year and ushered in this year as a drunken dork. That is inauspicious and too embarrassing for words.

3) Enable me to feel creatively superior to Connie by coming up with something wittier than she could ever imagine, even if I never tell her about this, which I absolutely shouldn't and won't.

I'm a scavenger huntress and therefore more likely to construct a compelling six-step hunt than a six-word sentence.

Sophia wrote a six-word command in her journal:

Brainstorm six words. Quality via quantity.

How good it felt to create a regimen! Almost as good as creating lesson plans. This six-word command would do for her what the hunt framework did for her students. She now had a succinct goal that was simultaneously a route to the goal.

She gave her hunt a six-word title:

Scavenger Hunting for the Six Words

1) Every day, write lots of six-word sentences.
2) At least ten a day.

No, not ten. If ten were good, twenty sentences would be twice as effective. She revised step #2 to twenty a day., and thought of how Connie and DC yuppies did a fixed number of exercises per day. Discipline, she resolved, would restore her lost confidence and creativity. She would earn back her talents.

Fifteen minutes later, Sophia had learned that contracting "I will" into "I'll" was an easy way to lop off a seventh word as in:

1) I'll rob a bank for you.

2) I'll resolve your baggage from childhood.

3) I'll resolve the Israeli-Palestinian conflict.

4) I'll find a cure for cancer.

5) I'll make the chase worth it.

She rubbed her right hand, which ached as though she'd been writing through concrete instead of scrawling her uninspired and uninspiring ideas across a journal page.

Sentence #1 was just ridiculous. On New Year's Eve she

had claimed she could subdue *all* guys, not just some guys, but all guys. But "all guys," or at least, any guys she would be interested in, including Michael, would think she was a nutjob if she offered to rob banks.

Sentence #2, about the childhood baggage, was equally stupid. She imagined struggling through a long airport security line with Nadia's toddler in tow. Hardly the thing to make a guy pant, let alone all guys all over the world.

She then winced over sentence #3's reference to the Israeli-Palestinian conflict, and winced yet again over sentence #4 because she couldn't claim to cure cancer without a medical degree or an act of God.

The fifth sentence, *I'll make the chase worth it*, perpetuated the original boast.

"Chase," she said under her breath. This was a powerful word.

Now she wrote,

6) The chase never has to end.
7) You choose how long to chase.

Neither of those sentences would work because they were so obsequious that she would sound like a loser instead of chaseworthy. She wondered if the word chaste and chase were etymologically related, and got up to Google it, but then she remembered she had thirteen more sentences to compose. She sat back down and wrote another impossible promise:

8) Nothing will ever be boring again.

Again, that would just perpetuate the boast.

Instead of writing 12 more bad sentences, Sophia pep-talked herself by writing:

> *Don't be discouraged by how bad these sentences are. People always tell single women that they have to kiss a lot of frogs to find the prince. Lucy Dell says the world's best poets have written more bad poems than the worst poets, because great poets became great because they weren't afraid to practice.*

She sighed. Her ego was too bruised to churn out another lame sentence. Maybe she should take a break and study men's magazines. Mainstream ones--nothing pornographic because she didn't want to buy a pornographic magazine, or even look online for that sort of thing. Instead, she could look up Abraham Maslow's hierarchy of needs, something she had learned about in the developmental psychology course she took to get her Masters in Education. That would be a more highbrow research foray.

Or could she conjure a six-word spell from what she now knew about gut feelings? Could she use Sheryl's insight about miracles? Or Nadia's mention of opening a book of Hafez's poetry and finding some illuminating line?

No. Sophia felt exhausted by the prospect of researching all this stuff just so she could manipulate a guy and assuage her pride.

She decided to go for a walk to the drug store, to buy US Magazine or OK Magazine, so she could feel superior for being too frugal to spend 7,000 dollars on a purse.

Sophia walked past a rug shop, one of the many storefronts with permanent *Closing Soon* signs in their windows.

"Closing soon" was their tease, she thought. The rug store was playing hard to get with a groundless claim. They were trying to inspire the thrill of the chase in passersby.

We're all closing soon, she imagined writing in her journal, and a line from Blues Traveler came into her mind: "it won't mean a thing in a hundred years." Nothing would matter in a hundred years because she and everyone she knew would be as dead as the dusty pile of rugs in that shop window.

She pulled a piece of scrap paper and a pen out of her jacket pocket, and wrote down a clichéd quote so she wouldn't forget it: "Life is not a dress rehearsal." She had seen that line long ago on a coffee mug or a poster in a suburban mall. In addition to being true, the mawkish sentiment was six words long. Too bad it wasn't good enough to be the sentence she sought. Then she remembered the Buddhist concept of Samsara. Samsara was a life sentence. Suffering, endless suffering, desiring stupid things like dominance over all men, or a pretty purse that would scuff the first time you took it out on the town.

The Buddhist teachers Sophia had read about taught that happiness wasn't the best revenge, detachment was. Not a numb detachment, but the ability to see the world clearly and compassionately. The way the best teachers at Carver forgot about themselves in their enjoyment of the students, and the wonders of the school garden, and the importance of environmental stewardship.

If only Sophia could let go of the search for a shatteringly witty six-word sentence.

If only she could give up the desire to surpass Connie's claim.

She wrote again on the scrap paper:

By hunting for a way to subdue another person (whether it be Connie, or a man), I'm wasting time, and doing something trashy, and condemning myself to a life sentence.

When Sophia got home, she half-wanted to make sense this stream of consciousness in her journal, but felt more compelled to do something Nadia had told her about. Like a Persian seeker opening a book of Hafez's poetry to a random passage, Sophia put her finger on a random page in one of Connie's books, *My Spiritual Quest: Revising Buddhism's Four Noble Truths and the Eightfold Path.*

The page that fell open jolted Sophia like electricity, because Connie had covered the same terrain that Sophia had just thought about on her walk.

Joseph Campbell proved are grail quests, and I add that all stories, all myths, are also illustrations of the Buddhist equation of Desire = Suffering.

Jay Gatsby suffered because he wanted Daisy Buchanan. Pandora caused suffering because she wanted to open the mysterious box. Hades wanted Persephone's brightness, so he caused suffering by restricting the goddess-daughter's movement. He caused himself suffering as well, because he had to live without Persephone for half the year.

In the first act of the Hollywood blockbuster Crimson Tide, Denzel Washington movingly says goodbye to his adorable child and pet dog. Then he kisses his wife goodbye, and though the kiss is discreet, you sense they have a great sex life. The filmmakers are letting the audience know he has a lot to lose, but he's a hero, so he virtuously seeks the greater good. He doesn't cling to personal desire. Detachment is the heroic solution to the problem of desire. Desire is always unquenchable and craving is its cost.

Reflecting upon the power of detachment gave Sophia her compelling six-word sentence. It was the line she had used to break up with all her ex-boyfriends:

I just want to be friends.

That line had led to drunken phone calls from men who begged her to take them back. That line harnessed the power of detachment, even though it was the type of cliché that boys in baseball caps relied upon.

Sophia would use this cliché on Michael when the time was right. "I just want to be friends" didn't promise anything that she couldn't deliver. It was the opposite of a promise or an offer. Because it was so hackneyed, it would imply that she was too nonchalant to waste time or energy on an original sentiment.

Sophia then made a list of pros and cons. The first con she wrote down was "Sounds too immature." The second con she wrote down was "It is too immature." She put down her pen, remembering that throughout her twenties, Connie had criticized her for being immature.

Sophia felt flooded by resentment. She isolated the flooded feeling to her torso, but that technique didn't help. Then she remembered some pithy wisdom from an Al Anon article she had read when she was trying to find six-word motivational quotes: *What makes you hysterical is historical.*

Sophia didn't sleep much that night because she kept waking up to write in her journal. She wasn't brainstorming six-word sentences, she was writing about Connie, but in a different way than she ever had before.

The next night, she slept a little more, dreaming that she was working in the orchard with Connie, and that they were having a harmonious time together.

She opened her journal at the breakfast table to write a new regimen. She would give Connie a clean slate every time they communicated, not for Connie's sake, but for her own sake. This wasn't a six-word sentence, but it did strike Sophia as magical because her pleasant dream inspired it. She felt she had successfully eavesdropped on her subconscious. She was also cheered by the knowledge the next two weeks at Carver would be completely absorbing, thanks to Nowruz, the celebration of the Persian New Year and the spring equinox. Carver's students would celebrate mostly through Nadia's social studies unit, but also with science, math, English and artistic tie-ins. Sophia would celebrate Nowruz by treating Connie and herself to a clean slate.

In her office at school, Sophia reviewed the Nowruz scavenger hunt. Nadia and Sophia had written the Nowruz lesson plans together, two years earlier, and since the rituals of Nowruz hadn't changed much in 3000 years, Sophia saw no need to alter this year's plans. There was one thing she would need to do before sending the document to the Parent-Teacher Oversight Committee: she had to replace the opening evening's bonfire with a yellow and red ribbon dance. She suspected the committee would think the bonfire was too dangerous, especially in light of The Harold Incident.

Later that day, she emailed the parents committee what she thought was the revised Nowruz document.

The next morning, Sophia and Dawn received an email

message from the curmudgeonly John Simpson, on behalf of the committee. The email was cc:ed to Stephen.

> *Dear Miss Green and Miss Jordan,*
> *We have just reviewed with dismay the Nowruz plan. Is bonfire building wise? With children? In light of the school's recent litagory history? And how religious will this Nowruz observance be?*
> *Respectfully submitted,*
> *John Simpson,*
> *Concerned Parent and Committee Secretary*

The following afternoon, Sophia was in Dawn's office, and Dawn was dialing John Simpson's number so they could talk to him over the speaker. Sophia had already emailed him, cc:ing Dawn, to let him know there wouldn't be a bonfire. She had apologized for sending the old version of the hunt, and attached the revision. He still insisted on a conference call with Dawn, Sophia, and Stephen. Dawn was able to convince him that Stephen didn't need to be on the call.

"I'm going to feel like we're on *Charlie's Angels,* talking to him this way," Dawn muttered.

"I'm sorry," Sophia said, feeling like she was saying it for the millionth time this school year.

"You've been preoccupied lately," Dawn said. "Is it because of the demotion?"

Simpson's voice, booming static, broke in: "Thank you, ladies, for phoning me to   discuss this urgent and pressing matter."

Dawn pressed several times on the volume button by the telephone's receiver so she could lower Simpson's voice without asking him to lower his voice.

"I need to officially inform you I am recording this phone call," Simpson said pompously. "I see from the revised plan Miss Green sent me that the bonfire won't happen, but how religious will this be?"

"Our version's not religious," Sophia said. "We're not trying to get the kids to adopt any religious beliefs. Our Nowruz is a regional celebration, to expand the kids' appreciation of the Middle East. All they see these days are negative news reports about Iraq and the Israeli-Palestinian conflict and terrorism and...."

"You don't need to tell me there is trouble in the Middle East," Mr. Simpson said, "I thoroughly skim a news magazine once a month."

Sophia continued. "...the Nowruz rituals—I mean, learning activities—lend themselves so well to seasonal topics we're covering in science, math, English and art. To make the event even more multicultural, we will replace dancing around a bonfire with Chinese ribbon dancing and costumes that we've borrowed from the Chinese Cultural Center."

"I can't imagine you would have enough for all the students," Simpson said.

Sophia hadn't thought of that. "The costumes are just oversized tunics. They're easy to put on and take off. The kids can take turns wearing them and twirling the ribbons."

Sophia wished this year's Charshanbeh Suri could encircle a real fire. She longed to burn the ripped-up pieces of her six-words brainstorming and the aggressive emails she had sent Connie.

"I like Charshanbeh Suri's emphasis on red and yellow," Sophia said. "Instead of associating negative traits with blackness and purity with whiteness."

She was hoping Mr. Simpson would compliment her for saying this, but the opposite happened. "Miss Green, I am not

254

interested in your philosophy about race relations. I just want to make sure you will always prioritize the safety of our schoolchildren."

Sophia swallowed hard. "Of course," she said. "Thank you for your support of the kids. We always appreciate hearing your concerns, and hope you'll never hesitate to touch base."

"Yes, thank you, Mr. Simpson." Dawn winked at Sophia.

Chapter 25: Perfect Dishes for Clean Slate Seekers

Despite the literal lack of spark, the students were as delighted by the Charshanbeh Suri celebration as they had been when open flames were involved. Even quiet kids like Maria ran around with the ribbons as fast as they could to "horizontalize" the ribbons. That was Tamika's word for it. Sophia had expected the students to mingle the red and yellow ribbons, but instead, they enacted the meaning of the Nowruzian "yellow-red" chant by dividing into groups of yellow and red. The yellows ran after the reds, shrieking, "Your red to me, my yellow to you!" The din of spoons hitting pots and pans drowned out Sophia's remorse about the past six months. She was grateful to the students for this high decibel peace, until she realized it was too noisy for her to *falgush,* or eavesdrop. Nowruz was the only holiday Sophia knew of which encouraged eavesdropping. According to Persian legend, whatever you heard could be used to predict the future for the next 12 months. Originally, women did this to find out their romantic fortunes, but Nadia has tweaked the tradition to neutralize it for the middle schoolers.

Sophia remembered the man she had eavesdropped upon the

night of the Samsara benefit: "Ask me if I *seen* it, not if I *took* it," he had said. She identified with him because he defensively reshaped words. As lawyers do, she now realized.

Nadia joined her. "It is as hot as if we'd lit a real fire right now, don't you think?" Nadia's coral red and sand-colored scarf was striped with gold threads. Sophia commented on Nadia's beautiful scarf, and Nadia said, "You know who looks beautiful? Kira. She looks so happy that she has forgotten to be self-conscious." Sophia made a wish on Kira's behalf. It would be great if Kira *falgush*ed and overheard Victor tell someone that he liked her. The chances were slim, but a girl could dream.

And then Sophia heard a boy's voice, shouting. She turned and saw, to her surprise, that it was Nelson Kobi. Nelson never shouted. Something must be wrong. But then she saw and heard other seventh grade boys shouting, and then eighth grade boys as well. She heard applause, and a boom box blasting go-go music. Go-go music was the only musical genre she knew of that had been born and bred locally. Her pulse quickened from the thrumming of a great Chuck Brown song, *Six Minutes*.

And then Sophia saw, to her horror, that the boom box was propped upon the shoulder of a man in blackface makeup and black overalls with a red shirt underneath. It was Tariq. He was dancing in a slightly tilted manner, due to the boom box.

Sophia couldn't take her eyes off him. The sight pained her as if her father had emerged in a bathing suit to get down and boogie.

She heard Nadia laughing beside her, and grabbed Nadia by the arm before Nadia could join the crowd radiating around Tariq.

"I thought we weren't *ever* going to let anyone play the Hajji Firuz character," she whispered. "It's inflammatory. If John Simpson sees this he's going to accuse us of racism."

"Oh Sophia, don't be so uptight and white." Nadia laughed. "Tariq wanted to play Haijji. He read all the materials I gave him about Nowruz and found out that Haijji Firuz represents a link to the holiday's Mesopotamian origins."

"I don't think the children should witness him acting like this. In that getup. He looks drunk. Or, well, no fear of Tariq getting drunk, I guess, but seeing him in blackface is more incendiary than a bonfire."

"At least something's flammable this evening," Nadia joked.

"He looks like a…a… "

"A minstrel?" Nadia said. "That's part of Hajji's function. I should have mentioned this to you earlier, but you weren't the only one who revised the Nowruz lesson plan. Some kids express wariness at first, when I showed them illustrations of Haijji Firuz. I put them into a slideshow presentation, next to the images of Amos and Andy, and of white people in Blackface. I explained that Haijji was an updated version of Domuzi, the Sumerian god of the underworld. Remember when you and Lucy included Domuzi in the mythology scavenger hunt?"

"I remember," Sophia replied.

Nadia smiled over a memory. "Jake called Domuzi the soil god, and it wasn't long before Victor got gory, with a tale that Domuzi had been a farmer who fell asleep in his field and got buried and had to scrabble his way back out of the earth, leaving his face covered with mud. You have to admit, that corresponds with the myth."

Sophia nodded.

"In any event," Nadia said. "Tariq's name alone makes him the perfect man to play Haijji. His name is often translated as 'morning star.' He's a beacon of spring, an auspicious herald."

Sophia sighed. "If trouble brews from this, please let Stephen and Grumpy Simpson know it wasn't my idea."

"Are you still feeling guilty about the lawsuit?" Nadia asked.

"No," Sophia said so sharply that the "no" admitted guilt. She watched Victor dancing around Tariq in circles and remembered how quickly Victor and Harold had bonded during Harold's brief stint in Carver's sixth grade. Now Victor was chanting something over and over again that ended with "ah ah ah ah."

"Can you make out what he's saying?" Sophia asked Nadia.

"He's saying 'Buried alive, buried alive,' to the tune of that old Bee Gees song, 'Staying Alive.'"

"Are you sure?"

"Yes. He did it on the way out of the class about Domuzi. I was so impressed he'd heard of the Bee Gees that I suggested Tariq play the song on his boom box but he insisted on playing go-go because go-go will die out if we don't share it with this generation."

Sophia watched the kids form a conga line behind Tariq. *He's the Pied Piper*, she thought, remembering how Michael had criticized her by calling her that. But Tariq was a wholesome Pied Piper.

Sophia smelled the bean and noodle soup that kids from the after school program had made with Maggie. It was called *aash-e reshteh*, and the children tied the noodles in knots before tossing them into the pot. The knots represented life's entanglements and the promise of unraveling them. The children had also prepared a snack mix called *ajil-e moshkel-gosha*, which was translated as "problem-solving nuts." Perfect dishes for clean slate seekers.

Sophia got to work late the next morning, an unlucky morning to be late because of the vernal equinox. The sun had crossed the equator eight hours ago, making today the first day of spring and the first day of the Persian New Year. Nadia explained that whatever happened during the thirteen days of Norwuz would predict what would happen over the course of the coming year. Nadia's favorite manifestation of this superstition was Shab-i Jom'e, a dinner eaten on the last Thursday before Norwuz. Whatever you ate that night would be what you ate regularly, even weekly, for the coming year. Nadia's mother used her children's belief in this ritual to reward good behavior. She let the most chore-willing child dictate the menu. In addition to their favorite rice dishes, Nadia and her brothers often requested the vegetables their siblings detested most in order to jinx them into a full year of those vegetables.

Sophia missed the morning's breakfast meeting. She was on her way to the faculty lounge when she ran into Nicole, or rather, Nicole ran into her.

"Oh Miz Green," Nicole reached out her hand as if she had been about to grab onto Sophia's, but she caught herself and now brushed back her hair with both hands. "Do you think Bernard's going to be suspended?"

"What?" The scene at Charshambeh Suri had been pretty wild. Maybe it had gotten wilder after she left. "What did he do?" she asked Nicole. And then she rephrased the question: "What was he accused of doing?"

"At dinner last night, Tony Young was falgushing, like we were allowed to do, and Tony overheard Bernard say something anti-Arabic. I mean, anti-Islamic, um ... something prejudiced. And now Bernard and Maggie are in Dawn's office, and the door's closed."

"Do you know what Bernard said? Or, what Tony said he said?" The legal term "hearsay" entered Sophia's mental courtroom.

"Well, in social studies, we had been researching the seven

260

things on the sofreh haft-sin table, and one of the ceremonial items is that book with the stories about the Persian kings."

"The Shahnameh."

"Right, that word starts with an S, and so does the prayer Muslims say to become Muslims. Is it the Shadamah?"

"Shahadah."

"Those words sound exactly alike to me. And Bernard must've got them confused too. He said he wanted to memorize the Shahadamah or whatever you call it. He said he thought all the Christians at Carver should memorize it, so if one of us were ever kidnapped by terrorists we could say that special sentence, and it would be like saying 'open sesame.' They'd let us go, because by just saying that one sentence, we would have converted to Islam right before their very eyes."

Sophia shuddered. She remembered her own mental desecration of the Shahadah when she had compared it to her six-word boast.

"The worst part, Miz Green, is that you know how Rashid and Bernard have been best friends since forever? Now Rashid is pissed—I mean, angry—because he says Bernard is prejudiced against him and his family. They're not going to be friends anymore. That's what Rashid said." Nicole was breathless and sweating.

"You should get a drink of water and then get to class," Sophia told her.

"What do you think is going to happen?" Nicole persisted.

"I don't know and none of us are going to know in the next few minutes, so you might as well head to class so you won't be late."

"Okay," Nicole said, eyes downcast.

"Thanks for letting me know about this." Sophia chastised herself for being so late to school that she missed the breakfast meeting.

"Don't thank me for telling you, Miz Green, I thought you were going to know more about it than me. I'm so curious to find out what Bernard's punishment will be." And with that honest reply, Nicole was off to the water fountain.

Sophia attended Bernard's disciplinary hearing even though she wasn't a member of the discipline committee. Dawn had asked her to come up with a scavenger hunt about racial and ethnic tolerance, and Sophia wanted to collect ideas at the hearing. She hoped to support Maggie with her presence, but wondered if Maggie would feel defensive instead to see a faculty member there who wasn't required to be there.

"I wish I could go back in time in a time machine," Bernard told Rashid and everyone else. He said he had forgotten all about falgush, that he didn't mean to be overheard. He just wanted to make Jake laugh. Another seventh grader, named Hassan, said he wished they could all go back in time.

"Everyone distrusts us," Hassan said. "Bernard might not have meant to hurt us, but non-Muslims don't know how much it sucks—I mean, how much it stinks—to have everyone be so distrustful of us all the time because they think our religion is violent."

"We ought to leave Carver and go to an Islamic school," Rashid told Hassan loudly enough for everyone to hear him clearly. No one spoke until Tariq broke the silence.

"You'd just be postponing conflict, Rashid. Being in a diverse community creates some painful situations but if you take on the problems while you're young in a school, you'll be better able to handle situations that come up once folks are supposedly grown up. Situations that restrict your freedom in more serious and demeaning ways."

Tariq suggested Bernard do community service at the

Islamic Community Center in lieu of suspension, and on Sophia's way out of the hearing, Tariq and some other teachers said they looked forward to seeing her reconciliatory scavenger hunt.

Sophia was so eager to do it that the hunt wrote itself:

RESPONDING TO PREJUDICE
1. Weekend Homework:
Find two or three newspaper or magazine articles about a hate crime. Preferably articles that include reactions and recommendations from local leaders.
Group A should find articles on hate crimes that occurred between 1970 and 1980
Group B's time range is 1980-1990
Group C's time range is 1990-2000
Group D's time range is from 2000 up to now.
2. Monday in-class writing: Write two paragraphs, the first summarizing the hate crime, the second summarizing local leaders' reactions and recommendations.
3. Monday homework: polish what you wrote for tomorrow's group work.
4. Tuesday group work: Review your teammates' articles and summaries of hate crimes. Vote on one to focus on as a group.
5. Tuesday homework: Pretend you are a local leader—write a draft of an op-ed in which you provide two opinions: what caused the crime, and how should the community respond?
6. Wednesday group work: Review these op-eds. Vote on the strongest points. These will become bullet points for your presentations in class Friday. By the end of the class, each team member should be assigned a presentation prep task.
7. Wednesday homework: Do your group-assigned

presentation prep.

8. Thursday in-class presentation prep: who will say what and when?

9. Thursday homework: Practice your part.

10. Presentations. Take notes as you listen to your classmates.

11. Weekend homework: Write up 4 critiques—for the other three teams and for your own. The first paragraph of each critique should offer a compliment and suggestion about the proposed source and solution to the hate crime. The second paragraph should offer a compliment and a suggestion with regard to the presentation itself. Did the group member speak clearly? What did you think about how they organized their points?

12. In class on Monday, read what your classmates said about your ideas, and the way you presented them.

Toward the end of class that Monday, the children would be given the surprise 13th step:

13. According to Nowruz tradition, the vernal equinox symbolizes a new year, and a clean slate for us. Try to forgive and feel forgiven, even if you don't feel capable of either. We will express this effort through the last Nowruz tradition: a Sizdah Bedar picnic.

Sophia realized this was the first scavenger hunt she had ever done that was longer than eight steps. She hoped thirteen steps wouldn't be bad luck. The number thirteen fit the theme of Sizdah Bedar, which marked the thirteenth and last day of Nowruz. On this day, celebrants brought themselves good luck for the coming year by escaping their usual indoor activities. Carver students and teachers would spend the whole day outdoors, working in the school garden, picnicking, and playing pranks, including "the lie of the thirteenth." Pranks were sanctioned by ritual on this day, an acknowledgement of cosmic chaos and a means of controlling chaos, just for one boisterous day.

Sophia thought, *it's okay to fib at Sizdah Bedar.* She wished she had a better sense of timing. She had picked the wrong new year's holiday for the whopper she had told Michael.

It was the first time she had thought of Michael and her boast for that whole day. Maybe this was the clean slate she had been looking for—a respite from self-recrimination and self-centeredness.

Sophia sent Connie a friendly email. She asked how Connie and Bo were doing, and asked about apple blossoms in the orchard. At the end of her email, she deleted the passive-aggressive part of the signature line she had been using in emails to Connie. Sophia regretted distorting the intent of Chodron's compassionate insight: *This moment is the perfect teacher.*

At the Sizdah Bedar picnic in the school garden, the students held flats of sabzeh grass they had grown with Tariq in the science lab. Growing sabzeh grass was another beautiful Nowruz tradition, but the grass flats looked scraggly now that they were two weeks old. Everyone who had grown the now-scraggly grass was supposed to throw it into the nearest body of running water. This ritual represented the casting off of past burdens.

Since Carver was river-less, the kids would throw their flats onto the compost heap. Sophia looked around for Bernard and was astonished when Tariq, Rashid, Khadijah, Hassan, and Sharifa lined up next to him.

"One, Two, Three, GO!" Khadijah called out, and the six of

them threw out the old sabzeh. Then they exchanged high-fives.

"You guys are friends again?" Sophia asked them.

"Yeah, Miz Green. Life's too short to hold grudges," Sharifa said.

"I agree," Sophia told them, and voiced what she assumed they might be thinking. "I guess you didn't need a white teacher's sensitivity training to work things out."

Hassan and Bernard smiled politely, nervously. She regretted making them feel awkward and hoped they weren't having to search their minds for something to say.

Sophia's cell phone rang. *Saved by the bell*, she thought.

Sophia was surprised to hear Michael's voice, because the morning after he had had her over for dinner, she had sent him a thank-you email with a vague offer to reciprocate at some point. He replied immediately and equally vaguely:

It's a date.

She hadn't followed up to suggest which date "it" would be.

Now she said, "How are you?" in the same friendly voice she used with her colleagues. Professional, affable, anything but vulnerable.

Chapter 26: Who Just Wants to Be Friends?

A few hours later, Sophia and Michael were drinking Briney Martinis back at Barbary Coste. Michael had suggested they meet there, and Sophia hoped to replace Michael's Barbary Coste memory of her at New Year's Eve with a new memory of her in empowered teacher mode, so she brought up Nowruz even though she was feeling a little Nowruzed out.

"It's a deep holiday. Nowruz's rituals reveal what inner adolescence longs for. We're all adolescents at heart, or rather, I am. Nowruz provides safe, playful outlets, and because it lasts two weeks, you can sink into it the way you can't on holidays that only last for a day. Nowruz is like a vacation. Okay, I've gone on about this long enough. What shall we talk about next?"

"I dunno," Michael said. They sat quietly, but the quiet wasn't awkward. "I feel like we've seen each other more than we have," Michael said. "I can't believe this is only our second date."

"Yes," she said, glad he used the word "date."

"I regret giving you the cold shoulder after you came over for dinner. I didn't want to talk about my mom," Michael said.

"I didn't think you gave me the cold shoulder," Sophia replied.

"I haven't been busy all this time. I've avoided getting in touch with you because I thought we would hook up and then become serious too soon. I've never dated a woman as smart as you before. You're weird enough to be unpredictable, and I can't tell if you are a player or not. Also, you'll wrench my past out of me and I don't want to talk about it. At least I have thought I didn't want to talk about it."

"You're not an ax murderer or a pedophile, are you?"

"No, nothing like that. But my mother isn't speaking to me right now, and most of my past, present, and future colleagues would disapprove of the way I was raised."

"Didn't you grow up on a farm?" she asked. "Were you forced to work at too young an age or something?" She felt too buzzed to resist the urge to pry. She hoped Michael was equally buzzed but he probably wasn't because he was nursing his first martini with the self-control she lacked.

"On second thought, I'm wrong to ask you to tell me since you don't want to," Sophia said.

Sophia longed for Michael to say she was so great that he wanted to confide in her. Instead he said, "You know, you and I are playing this silly game over your mysterious six words, and it makes me rethink the games I play to keep people from knowing about how I grew up." He looked away. "I, uh, grew up on a commune."

"And?" Sophia asked.

"That's it."

"That's it? What's so bad about that?" Sophia asked. "Most of my college friends who were interested in social justice grew up on communes. They were cooler than cool. I was jealous and impressed by their families. Their parents raised them as environmental stewards."

"I hung out with a conservative crowd in college," Michael said, "because I rebelled from everything that my mom, and environmentalists like you, thought was cool. The reason why I'm not a big drinker is because one night toward the end of my junior year, I got so shitfaced that I spilled the beans about my childhood. For the rest of college, I regretted telling my frat brothers. They teased me about it relentlessly, calling me Hanoi Jane and Granola Betty. Drove me crazy inside. You know how you were saying you were in close touch with your inner adolescent? I relate to that. I feel stupid admitting this, but I do mind when you make fun of lawyers. I must like you a lot to hang out with you."

Sophia grinned. "I can't believe your friends had never asked about your childhood before you told them. They must have noticed you were secretive about it. Weren't they curious?"

"Frat guys don't exactly grill each other on their childhoods, and I purposely chose to date moronic girls. They talked about themselves or bitched about their sorority sisters. Occasionally they asked, '*Do these jeans make my butt look big?* '"

"Sometimes I hear the girls at Carver ask that question of one another. It makes me sad."

Michael nodded.

"Did you stay close to those guys from your fraternity?" Sophia asked.

"Sure. They made me laugh my head off when I wasn't the target. The frat boy atmosphere was exotic and drove my mother crazy. The walls of our suite were plastered with models in bikinis. I mean, posters of models in bikinis." Michael blushed. "The only substantive person I let myself get close to in college was my college advisor, who was also my U.S. history professor. When he mentioned he was researching a book about the Sixties, I asked if I could be a research assistant and told him I had grown up on a commune. He hired me to do the research, but said I shouldn't mention my background when I applied to law school or in job interviews unless I was interested in public interest law."

"Why did he say that?" Sophia asked. "An unusual childhood would make you an asset in anything substantive."

"Professor Rooney considered himself to be an expert on 20th century counterculture. He said I'd be taken less seriously. Over the years I realized that he was wrong. Growing up on a commune wouldn't be a strike against me, but now it's been so many years that I feel like my friends and co-workers would be hurt to find out. They would wonder why I hadn't trusted them enough to let them know earlier. My friend Tim, who grew up with me on the farm, is my only link to my past."

Sophia nodded, pleased to understand why Tim had said he was "sort of brothers" with Michael.

"There are so many stereotypes about communes," Michael continued. "Orgies, gurus, brainwashing. I didn't suffer any of that. We took a bus every day to and from a good public school. We were exposed to great vegetables, the way your students are, but we weren't forced to live on cabbage and brown rice. My mom's really into evolutionary psychology, and she had a theory that most kids are pickier eaters than adults because that trait is a survival instinct."

"What do you mean?" Sophia asked, intrigued.

"Kids have smaller bodies than adults. If they eat something bitter or with too complex a taste, they might unconsciously associate it with something that could make their stomach hurt, or even poison them. So they like simpler, sweeter tastes because those seem safer to eat."

"I never heard that before," Sophia said, feeling a pang of

guilt about Harold throwing up from the pokeberries. "I'll tell our kitchen director and our science teacher about your mother's theory. Is she insightful in general?" No wonder Michael was smart, Sophia thought.

"Sure, except that she and the other adults were chain-smoking when they weren't eating brown rice and millet and vegetables. They rolled their own cigarettes and grew their own tobacco. I'm sure doing that encouraged them to smoke more. Luckily, my mom stopped smoking a few years ago. Said she was motivated by a new cause. She's launched a public awareness campaign. An oral history project that she's filming, with a website portal. She's collecting interviews with kids of my generation who grew up on communes and had positive experiences, to counteract the sensationalistic stereotypes. I said I'd help fund the project, but I refused to be interviewed for it. She takes my checks, but doesn't talk to me."

"That's terrible," Sophia said. "But why didn't you want to participate, now that you're established in your career?" Sophia asked. "I bet the professor you loved would be interested in participating also."

"He passed away a few years ago, unfortunately. I told my mom that my participation would threaten my career. She saw through that excuse." Michael caught the bartender's eye, tapped his glass to indicate he wanted another martini. "I can't bear to face skeptical people who will assume I was brainwashed as a child. I can't bear to read memoirs about abuse on communes, can't bear the anger I feel at sociopaths that try to control vulnerable groups of people. Whenever I see or hear a reference to the massacre at Jonestown I want to throw up."

"I know what you mean," Sophia agreed. "I avoid movies and TV shows that have rape scenes, especially if the directors and writers are men. I think they exploit the horror of rape to

271

make the story grittier. But a rape scene is like a castration scene. I don't want to be exposed to it, and I wish I had a dollar for every rape scene ever filmed. I would donate the money to a Rape Crisis Center."

"And similarly, no one thinks audiences would be riveted by tales of a peaceful commune," Michael said.

Sophia's thoughts raced. Should she admit what she wanted to admit about her own past? She didn't hesitate long enough to consider that question.

"You and I have past baggage in common," Sophia told Michael. "I'm not estranged from my mom, but the thought of her makes me uncomfortable, even though she is a loving person." Sophia told him how she blamed herself for her mother's near-fatal dash across the school parking lot. Then she found herself telling him about Harold's accident with the pokeberries. Connie had introduced her to pokeberries like Hades had introduced pomegranate seeds to Persephone in the Greek mother-daughter myth of Persephone and Demeter.

"I irrationally blame my godmother for the pokeberry accident. Why would she have suggested we do an ink project with poison berries when there are so many other great plant dyes?"

"That sounds innocuous to me. Is she a difficult person in other ways that make you to resent her?"

"She's sadistic and longwinded, especially when she heaps on the unsolicited advice." This description led Sophia to tell Michael the secret she had kept from her colleagues: that her godmother was Countess Connie.

Michael's reaction gratified her. "No offense, but I can't stand Countess Connie," he exclaimed. "New Agey gurus like her make intentional communities look bad."

"Is 'intentional community' the p.c. phrase for

'commune'?" Sophia asked him.

"Yes," Michael looked sheepish. "Does it sounds pretentious?"

"Not as pretentious as Connie's phrases. Oops, I forgot the decision I just made not to rant about her. Nowruz inspired me to give her a clean slate from now on, every time I communicate with her. For my own sanity. Also, there was an anti-Muslim incident that came up among the kids. I've always felt judgmental about Middle East conflicts. I thought, *why can't they get over it, it's hurting them all so much.* But I've been so petty about my past with Connie. I should just make peace with her. I've always liked the quote, '*Be the change you wish to see in the world.*'"

Sophia looked away, at the mural of waves. The waves swam before her eyes. She was teary not because she was sad or buzzed, but because she wasn't sure she should have told Michael all this deep stuff. It was like sleeping with someone too soon. She remembered her Inspirational DIY books. Discomfort was like a wave crashing to shore. Waves subsided. Then they came back again, but they would keep subsiding, and at low tide they would retreat for hours. No one feeling, no matter how strong, was too hard to handle if you could just remember that you wouldn't keep feeling as bad as you did in an uncomfortable moment.

Sophia concentrated on the waves of her breath—out and in, out and in. She swiped at her eyes, but instead of getting rid of the tears, the gesture made them more apparent.

By now, Michael had put his arm on her back. She shook her head but it didn't keep the tears from spilling down her face.

I'm not crying because I'm sad," she told him.

"I don't believe you."

"I think I'm crying because I've never voluntarily told

273

anyone about my connection to Countess Connie."

"Voluntarily?"

"During the lawsuit I had to hand over my journal. The lawyer learned everything about me. I bitched and moaned a lot about Connie in there."

"Given how you feel about lawyers, that must have been awful, to have him or her read your innermost thoughts."

"It was a him." She hoped that sentence didn't sound loaded.

"Do you feel relieved to have told me about this?" Michael asked.

"I don't know yet." A phrase came into Sophia's mind—an idea she would write down in her journal later if she remembered it: *Relief is a source of joy.*

She said it out loud.

"Relief is a source of joy," Michael repeated. "That's a six-word sentence."

He seemed to be waiting for her to shape the moment with meaning. She felt her pulse quicken. She cared too much about him now to say "I just want to be friends." She decided to stop looking for a six word-sentence that would amount to more than the sum of its words.

"Sophia, I would feel *both* relief and joy if you would tell me the six words already."

"But you're so substantive that the six words wouldn't count."

"But didn't you say you could control *any guy* with six words?" Michael was speaking in a different tone now. Not of skepticism, not of challenge. He sounded as though he were trying to lighten the mood. "My first impression of you was that you prided yourself on making guys your conquest."

"You're not a conquest," she said.

"No one should be. Now that we've had this touchy-feely conversation, I hope we're getting to be really close friends. Do you feel that way?"

"I do." Earlier in the evening Michael had called this their second date, now he was telling her he felt like they were better buddies than before.

The provocative waltz between trust and distrust was over. He had just neutered it. Sophia should have felt off the hook, but her heart felt the Titanic after it merged with the iceberg.

Chapter 27: Hubris, the Fancy Word for Pride

The April weather was June-like, so the students begged to plant the seedlings they were nurturing under solar-powered grow lights.

"Why do we have to wait until May?" Sophia heard Jake ask Tariq in the cafeteria line.

"You've got to be patient. There could still be another frost."

"That would thrill my mom," Jake muttered. "She forces me to wear sweaters whenever she feels cold. I wish global warming were more reliable."

This made Sophia laugh, and she immediately repeated it to Lucy, who was on cafeteria duty.

"How did Tariq respond?" Lucy asked.

"He said 'Give it a few more years.' And Jake said, 'But I won't be at Carver then.' So Tariq told him he could always come back to help with spring planting." Sophia adjusted the way she was holding her tray. It was getting heavy. She was about to head for the table where Kira was when Lucy replied, "Tariq is a gem. I hope you don't mind, but I revised the hubris story seed because of a suggestion he made."

"Just a moment." Sophia slid the tray onto the nearest counter she could find with an empty surface. She came back. "What was his suggestion?"

"Oh, it's so good." Lucy clapped her hands. Behind her, a whole table of kids mimed applause to make fun of her. Sophia didn't give them a dirty look because she was curious to hear what Lucy was going to say.

"Well, as you know, the kids are brainstorming ideas right now for the science fair scavenger hunts they're going to create for themselves."

"Right," Sophia agreed.

"And I'm having them brainstorm their hubris story seed, so Tariq suggested that they use their science fair topic to sow their hubris tale!"

"I don't get it," Sophia said. Lucy's gardening metaphors could be confusing.

"Well, for example, Victor's question for his science fair topic is—"

"Why are cauliflowers shaped like brains?" Sophia said. "He is brilliant to observe that cauliflowers are ridged and shaped like brains. I never in a million years would think to notice that cauliflower, or anything else, looks brain-like."

"Right. So Victor's hubris tale is about a mad scientist, intent on harvesting brains, who winds up with nothing more than a field full of regular old cauliflower. And thanks to that story idea, Victor is researching neuroscience for the science fair!" Before saying anything further, Lucy looked over her shoulder as if to make sure that none of the nearby kids would overhear. "But I'm a little worried that the final draft's goriness will drown out his research."

Sophia nodded. "I'm excited about this time of year. They

finally get to write their own scavenger hunts from scratch. And therein lies the end-of-the-year surprise for the sixth graders."

"Speaking of sixth graders, I better station myself nearer their tables. I am too lax for cafeteria duty," Lucy admitted.

"Why be good at something you don't want to do?" Sophia asked.

Lucy frowned slightly. "Personally I agree with you. Professionally, I need to do a better job of maintaining discipline at all times. It just makes my work in the classroom harder if I don't. What's that slogan you always tell the kids, something like 'Steer today to make tomorrow easier.'"

"I guess I do say that." *But my godmother said it first,* Sophia thought.

"See you Friday afternoon at the Read and Feed," Lucy said instead of goodbye.

"Thanks. I'll be there." Sophia felt grateful to Lucy for expressing the invitation as a statement rather than a question. It made her feel reliable.

Sophia attended all Lucy's Read and Feeds, and always came bearing treats as the scavenger hunt's surprise. This afternoon she had brought rectangles of angel food cake. The cake was from one of Maggie's stealthily healthful recipes, thanks to the inclusion of yogurt and apple butter.

"I thought angel food cake would be a good prize for this hunt about hubris," she explained to the class, "because it is hubristic for human bakers to presume they know how to make food fit for angels."

Kira asked if she could read her story first. Since a few weeks after her Valentine disappointment, Kira had become outgoing. Surviving vulnerability had strengthened her.

"This story is dedicated to Miss Green because her

scavenger hunts never lead us on a wild goose chase," Kira announced.

Everyone in the class clapped. "Oh, you guys are just being nice to me because I brought in cake as the surprise," Sophia joked, but she was touched.

Kira's story was about village elders, meeting to discuss how best to increase the yield of their bean crop:

"With the new magic bean seeds that I just bought at the mall, I can promise a four-out-of-four success rate," said the youngest village elder.

Lucy and Sophia chuckled appreciatively over "youngest village elder."

"I didn't mean for that to be funny," Kira told them. The thin gold frames of her eyeglasses bolstered her stern look.

"Sorry," Lucy said. She wrote something down on her notepad. Sophia guessed it was a note to herself to tell the kids what an oxymoron was sooner than she had intended to. Sophia made the same note on her pad, with an arrow symbol to remind her to also make a notation on the glossary checklist in her journal.

Kira continued:

The older elders scolded the young braggart. They followed an ancient rule when it came to bean planting: "One for the mouse, One for the crow, One to rot, One to grow."

"Hey, that's plagiarism!" Victor exclaimed.

"It is not, it's a proverb," Kira replied with admirable calm. "Miss Dell said we don't have to cite proverbs."

"Kira's right, especially since it's one of the gardening

proverbs that your class learned in sixth grade. It's common knowledge to everyone at Carver."

Kira resumed her reading:

"Don't shush me," shouted the braggart, whose name happened to be Jinx.

Sophia's attention fell from the story onto the word "jinx." It was strange, how when you didn't hear a word for a long time, you forgot about the concept behind it. She had jinxed herself on New Year's Eve and after. Her defensive refusal to admit she couldn't subdue Michael in the blink of a six-word sentence had subdued her real talent. No wonder she had been creatively constipated since January.

For the millionth time in her impulsive life, Sophia wished for a better sense of timing. When you lied on April's Fool's day, or Norwuz's Sizdah Bedar, you were being festive, playful, true to the spirit of the day. When you lied on New Year's Eve after downing sangria and martinis, and perpetuated your lie for pride's sake, you embarrassed yourself.

"He's leading us on a wild goose chase!" the second-to-oldest elder exclaimed.
"Goose? What's a goose got to do with this? I thought we were talking 'bout beans!' said the dumbest village elder.

Sophia's scavenger hunts had provided students with "short- and long-term prizes," as she had once put it in a speech to Carver's donors. She wished she had a short or long-term prize to offer Michael, so he would find her irresistibly powerful.

When the class's applause startled Sophia, she was sorry to see Kira sit down. What if Kira had tried unsuccessfully to make eye contact with her? Kira might think Sophia's preoccupation meant Sophia had been bored by the tale that Kira had dedicated to her. Sophia would have to ask Lucy for a copy of the story, so she could read it carefully that night. It was always important to Sophia that she compliment stories with specific feedback instead of saying "Great job."

Victor begged to read next, and the class cheered because he was a genuinely amusing class clown:

"Why that guy gotta be fronting with the bling?" Luther, a parking attendant, said about Dr. D, the Evil Harvester of Hubris. Dr. D was an evil neuroscientist, whose pearly white Lexus was detailed in the finest fourteen-carats—and not the kind Peter Rabbit stole from Farmer MacDaddy.

Sophia wondered if the kids really thought "bling" was powerful. Was bling their definition of treasure, the way a perfect six-word sentence had become her Holy Grail? How could anything calculated to manipulate other people be powerful? It couldn't. People who tried to impress others by saying a cool thing, or by dressing expensively, seemed pathetic to Sophia. In her confident past, she had always attracted men because she didn't try. The six-word sentence wasn't her Holy Grail, she decided. She just wanted her confidence back. Or even something richer: a deep-down peaceful confidence.

That evening, Sophia took home copies of all the hubris tales, so she could read them properly and write comments on them. She had made extra copies of Victor's story and of Kira's, because she wanted to give them to Cally. She hoped there might be some internship opportunity at NIH that her two favorite students could apply for—perhaps not as middle schoolers, but she wanted Cally to start hearing about them in case there were high school internships they could do a few years down the road. Sophia knew she couldn't control her romantic future with Michael, but she couldn't resist subtly trying to bring Victor and Kira together.

On the last day of the science fair, the gym swarmed with Carver teachers, students, parents and Stephen. Sophia headed straight for him.

"Stephen, it's so nice to see you," she began. "Have you had a chance to check out the sixth graders' tables yet?"

"No, but I shall."

"I am so proud—I mean, we are so proud of them not only because they covered their topics thoroughly, but because they created their own scavenger hunts to do so."

Stephen was looking over her shoulder, for greener pastures, no doubt.

"Would you excuse me, Sophia?"

No she wouldn't, not before she was done advocating upon her own behalf.

"At the school garden orientation this past September, I promised the sixth graders that by spring, they would have the experience of switching places with their parents and teachers. And this afternoon's slideshow will demonstrate the fulfillment of that promise. I've been documenting their work on these project for several weeks now."

"That's impressive, Sophia, but I do wish you hadn't told me that. I was so looking forward to being surprised by the contents of the slideshow. With my demanding schedule, it's the closest I get to enjoying a whodunit."

She forced a chuckle sound, though he didn't stick around for it. In the respite between his exit and the approach of a student, parent, or colleague, she looked across the room at her carefully-loaded slide projector. It was still there. She pulled a piece of scrap paper from her back pocket. She had read and reread it so many times over the past few days that it felt as soft as her jeans. Her favorite line was:

You kept your eyes on the prize, without shortchanging the process.

Harold had inspired the phrase "without shortchanging the process." Her memory had often returned to his voice, asking the question that initially irritated her but impressed her a year and a half later: "Why don't you call them treasure hunts, instead of scavenger hunts?"

Now she thought, *I call them scavenger hunts instead of treasure hunts because the process and the search matter more than the final step's reward.*

Kira tapped Sophia on the arm and asked her to come see her display. Kira's science fair question was "Do animals with feathers and scales undergo seasonal changes the way mammals do?" She had drawn diagrams of every animal that bore its own armor.

Sophia wondered where Victor was. After scanning the crowd, she saw him with his father. She couldn't remember why Victor's mother wasn't in the picture. Death or divorce? Or had Victor's father adopted him? No, they looked too much alike, except that Victor's father was frowning and Victor's face was lit up and he was talking about something that clearly delighted him.

"Mr. Jones." Sophia held out her hand. "It's so nice to see you again. I'm Sophia Green."

"Yes, Miss Green. I was hoping we'd get a chance to see you. Thank you for connecting us with Cally Douglas. She said NIH doesn't have internships for children as young as Victor, but she invited us to visit her research lab, and I understand that Kira Hughes was invited as well, so they will go on the same day."

"I want to do it, Miz Green," Victor said, then he went shooting off after Nelson Kobi and some other boys.

Sophia turned to Victor's project display as though she were seeing it for the first time. He had done two illustrations each of the cauliflower and of the brain, and had red lines radiating out from each illustration to label their parts. Below the illustrations were four pages, which explained the functions of each part, how its form served their function.

"Victor is a genius," she marveled to Mr. Jones. "He united two interesting objects of study that most people would never think to bring together."

"Could I have everyone's attention please?" The microphone fuzzied Tariq's voice. "We only have an hour left of the science fair. The eighth graders will now share some impressive numbers with you about our projects."

On cue, all the eighth graders in the room made their way over to him. Each student read a statistical fact of an index card.

Average length of time spent on the projects: Seventeen hours
Average percentage of recycled materials used in the displays: 50%.
80% of the students had drawn upon the school garden for a topic.
6% of those students studied fruits.
73% chose vegetables.

Sophia thought this made sense, since the majority of the plants in the school garden were vegetables.

21% investigated organic gardening techniques.
3 students studied the affect of aging and different storage techniques on seeds.
24 children conducted experiments with non-toxic herbicides, pesticides, and remedies derived from household staples like lemon juice, different kinds of vinegars, salts and spices.
17 made carbon footprint comparisons.

When the last eighth grader, a girl named Lois, finished reading her statistic, she turned expectantly to Sophia. "And now, without further ado," Lois paused and several kids laughed.

Sophia telepathically dared Lois to say the word "doodoo," and thought Lois's friends were probably doing the same thing. She imagined Lois introducing her as "…speaking of shit, here's Countess Connie's Princess of Bullshit. Connie taught her everything she does and doesn't know." *Oops,* Sophia thought. She had forgotten her resolution to think positive thoughts about Connie.

Sophia made her way over to the slide projector, doing her funniest imitation of Queen Elizabeth's stilted wave as the kids clapped and whooped.

"Now we turn from the eighth graders to the sixth graders," Sophia told the audience. "Age before beauty, as they say." Should she really have said that? Too late now. At least she hadn't said, "I hope the seventh graders aren't feeling like neglected middle children." That was what she had said last year. She had received several complaints, except from the seventh graders themselves, who treasured their role behind the scenes. They got to be in charge of refreshments, which meant unrestricted access to snacks.

Sophia concluded her speech with "Congratulations, sixth graders. By structuring your own quest for answers to questions that made you curious, you have switched places with me and your other teachers, as we promised back in September."

"I bet that's the surprise," she heard a disappointed voice say.

"Dang, one day I just want a scavenger hunt surprise to be like an iPhone or a DSi," a girl replied.

The acoustics in the gym make these two voices easy to hear. Sophia giggled, wanted to make some joke, but couldn't think up something funny on the spot.

Victor saved the day. "Yo shorties, if you grow up to be scientists you can buy all the gadgets you want, and more."

Sophia thanked him, and ended her presentation with an old-fashioned quote:

A modest garden contains, for those who know how to look and to wait, more instruction than a library.— Henri Frédéric Amiel

Sophia lingered in the school garden on her way to unlock her bike for the ride home. It was twilight, and soon the mulched beds would bristle with green shoots. She remembered Lucy describing Scheherezade as "a master gardener of story seeds." Scheherezade accomplished an impossible task for a thousand and one sleepless nights. She had to deliver her numeric target, unlike even the most experienced and anal gardener, who can't predict, and doesn't have to predict, that every seed will germinate.

"Hi Sophia!" It was Barbara, with camera and tripod. Barbara photographed the school garden on a weekly basis, to document its changing nature.

"Is there enough light now?" Sophia asked, glancing at the darkening sky.

"For spring and summer, this is the best time of day," Barbara said, more to herself than to Sophia. "I go to a place in Pennsylvania in the summer where there are fields upon fields. When dusk begins to settle all the borders disappear. The grasses look like the ocean, even on a windless evening. There are so few distinctive shapes, it's as though the sky and the ground had switched places, as though the ground were as simple and uncluttered as the sky."

"You're poetic," Sophia murmured, She looked at Barbara's face, and saw Barbara's eyes were full.

Barbara's voice wavered as she replied. "You know Stephen wants us to repaint the brick walls out here, and put up murals just before graduation?"

"Yes."

"He's not doing it for graduation. He's doing it because Luscious LoCal wants to do a photo shoot out here with the kids."

"I know," Sophia said gently.

"I'm worried we will be putting up murals for the wrong reason. To whitewash his insecurity about the lawsuit, and the bad publicity we never even got. I'm worried that murals done for the wrong reason, out of defensiveness, will be too colorful and complicated. They will upstage the plants."

"Barbara, you have integrity. The murals will be as innocent and honest as the children's gorgeous faces," Sophia said.

Barbara didn't respond to this, just vented. "Luscious LoCal is going to use the photographs for their annual report. Stephen was concerned that the raised beds would look scraggly so early in the growing season, so he suggested the mural. Said he had great faith in a fresh coat of paint, decorated by our whimsical students. Can you think of anyone else in this community that would describe those kids as whimsical? Sounds a little too British to me, 'specially for someone who's not British as far as I know." Barbara rolled her eyes. "I'm sorry for sounding ornery. My brain ran away with my mouth."

"Don't apologize. It's refreshing to hear you complain since you're always so Pollyannaish—I mean, positive about everything."

Barbara blinked. Sophia thought she had offended her, but no, thank goodness.

"I do have a positive perspective," Barbara agreed. "First from practice, and now by force of habit."

Sophia pulled out a piece of scrap paper. "I'm going to write down what you just said." Barbara's insight was like Connie's quote *"Steer today to make tomorrow easier."* This fresh echo reminded Sophia of her desire to mend fences with Connie, rather than just slapping on a façade.

Chapter 28: Danny and Margaret and Messy Paint

Two chain link fences enclosed the front and back of Carver's school garden. Two brick walls lined its sides, and by the following Saturday—Mural Painting Day—the lower ten feet of the red brick walls had been painted white. Carver students were painting colors into the black-and-white symbols they had mapped out with Barbara earlier that week. The eighth graders were entrusted with higher ladders than the younger children, and with lettering.

Sophia planned to paint with the eighth graders for the whole time, because they would be graduating in three weeks. As she kept telling them with trite words, she missed them already. Her creativity hadn't returned reliably. Sure, she had written the "Responding to Prejudice" hunt with ease, but that was because she felt inspired by Tariq and eager to help Bernard, Rashid, and Hassan put a painful episode behind them. She wanted creativity to flood back into her. Instead, it trickled and itched.

Sophia felt tired. Were the paint fumes getting to her? She decided to stick to the path of least resistance. She would keep her eyes on the section of brick wall that she had assigned herself. This would be a zen-like, present-centered thing to do.

She dipped her brush in bright blue paint. She dotted one of the many feet of Graffi, the Graffiti-Toed Monster. This monster was a creature she had invented for the eighth graders one year earlier, and she had recycled it for this year.

Graffi gaped at the world through googly eyes in the middle of its octopus-head. Its legs were green vines, as tangled as the aash-e reshteh noodles from Nowruz. Each vine led to a three-toed foot. Some of the eighth graders were delicately painting words on to these feet. Their favorite words were the hardest ones from their three years' worth of vocabulary lists:

Curcurbit

Diatomaceous

Leguminous

Montmorillionite

Suffructicosa

"Who are those guys with Dawn?" a child asked.

Sophia turned and saw Stephen, Michael, and Ken Burnett. Ken was wearing the same tight Luscious LoCal t-shirt he had worn at the chili cookoff, except this time, there was nothing underneath it. How annoying that Ken and Stephen were here to "help." This meant Barbara would have to reassign some of the eighth graders to help Ken and Stephen attempt to be helpful.

"May I have everyone's attention, please," Dawn called out. She told the kids about Luscious LoCal's generous donation.

"Please thank them in person," she concluded.

Ken broke in. "But I want to thank *you*, Ms. Jordan and I want to thank all your parents for signing photography waiver forms that will enable us to document everyone's hard work today."

"And, I, personally, am going to paint a thank-you sign in

the lower-right hand corner of our North wall," Stephen said, putting his hand on Ken's shoulder. "Mr. Bennett has also funded the cost of our paint and brushes. Unfortunately, I haven't held a paintbrush since I was your age." This was directed at the kids, not at Ken. "Would any of you help me with my thank-you sign so the letters will be legible?"

Half the eighth graders' hands shot up. Sophia exchanged a glance with Michael, who inched closer to her until he was just a few feet away. His expression was dark.

"Are you okay?" she whispered to him once they were close enough to speak.

"No. I don't have a good feeling about this event. We're exploiting your kids," Michael said.

"Barbara, our art teacher, would agree with you," Sophia whispered. "And I think I agree, too."

"This garden should be an oasis from DC's unholy alliance of publicity and philanthropy," Michael said.

"Wow, did you come up with that line on your own?" Sophia heard her father's voice in her head: "Lawyers twist words faster than a clown with a balloon,'" but the voice was just her father's. She was sick of lawyer jokes.

"Yeah. It was easy to come up with because, well, uh, I've been playing around with words for the past few weeks. For a campaign at Luscious LoCal that I think you're going to like."

Sophia stiffened. Was he going to put her on the spot in some way?

"I mean it, Sophia. You're going to like this. I mean, no one's going to know it has anything to do with you and me, except for you and me. No one will guess our secret."

"Huh? Our secret?"

At this point, Dawn interrupted them to thank Michael for coming out to help paint, and to thank him for becoming part of the school community. She winked at Sophia as if to say, *I bet you two are dating*. Sophia wished this were true.

"I need to finish my unfinished project," Sophia told Dawn and Michael. She was feeling unresolved about both Michael and Connie, but she didn't want Dawn or Michael to sense this by ESP. She added, "By unfinished project, I mean I need to finish dabbing our monster mural with an infinite number of blue dots."

"I'll come over and help you soon," Michael told her, "But I want to hover around Ken for a while to make sure he doesn't try to rope one of your students into child labor."

"You think he's going to ask them to paint Luscious LoCal?" Sophia asked, grinning.

"More like making them PR footsoldiers."

Later, Sophia felt a tap on her shoulder as she worked. She turned around expecting to see Michael, but Danny and Margaret stood before her, dressed in matching overalls.

"Hi!" Sophia said. *Oh gosh*, she thought. *I wonder if they know Michael from law school*. Since Michael wasn't on Facebook, the fact that he hadn't appeared on Danny's friend list was inconclusive.

"We're engaged!" Margaret exclaimed. She was wearing latex gloves and tore off the glove on her left hand so she could thrust her ring in Sophia's face.

"Smashing!" Sophia said, feeling punched in the nose but no longer punched in the heart.

"I'm wearing gloves so I don't get messy paint on my three-carat ring," Margaret explained unnecessarily.

"I'm still on Carver's event mailing list," Danny said. "This school inspired me to be a better person, so I'm going to try to do some community service thing at least once a year."

"You mean WE'RE better people and WE'RE going to do community service TOGETHER," Margaret prodded.

"Yes dear," Danny said.

Sophia thought he was saying this ironically, but he didn't look ironic. He looked whipped.

"I'm sorry we won't be able to invite you to the wedding," Margaret said, "but we're trying to keep it under 300."

"300 dollars?" Sophia asked, though she knew Margaret meant 300 guests.

Michael joined her at this point.

"Do you three know each other?" Sophia asked, feeling nervous in her gut and gut brain.

"I think you were in my legal writing section," Danny said. "Nice to see you again."

Sophia exhaled with relief. They were mere acquaintances.

"I'm Danny's *fi-yahncée*," Margaret said, flourishing the last word.

Margaret and Danny walked away soon after, because the fiancée seemed eager to isolate her fiancé.

When Graffi was suitably poxed, Sophia and Michael walked around the garden, checking out what the other teachers were doing. Tariq and Sheryl were chatting as they added finishing touches to their respective creations. Tariq had empurpled nine phases of the moon.

"So clever," Sophia heard Sheryl tell Tariq, "because the school year has nine months."

Sheryl and Lucy had just finished painting an unintentionally butterfly-shaped sandwich. You could tell it was a sandwich from the "NO SUCH THING AS A FREE LUNCH" proverb above it. Sophia knew from her own efforts that it was as hard to replicate the pinched-in top of a bread slice as it was to draw hands and feet.

"Isn't 'NO SUCH THING AS A FREE LUNCH' a little harsh for schoolchildren?" Michael asked the teachers.

"It's a tie-in to the stories our seventh graders wrote about hubris," Lucy explained. "The scoundrels in those stories thought they were omnipotent enough to replace hard work with magic shortcuts."

"No such thing as magic beans," Sophia murmured. *No magic six words either.*

"Is that why you painted Peter Rabbit over here?" Michael asked. "Because he went after the free lunch?"

"That's not Peter Rabbit. It's the Velveteen Rabbit," Lucy said.

"The Velvet Rabbit? Sounds like a song by Jefferson Airplane," Michael said.

"Haven't you heard of the Velveteen Rabbit?" Lucy asked him. "The children's story?"

"No," Michael admitted.

Lucy told Michael the story about the stuffed rabbit who didn't mind growing old because his shabby, grungy appearance proved he had been loved. Love made him real.

"The Velveteen Rabbit is our school's mascot," Sophia said. "Because even though Peter Rabbit is more commonly associated with growing vegetables, the Velveteen Rabbit story challenges kids to hold on to what they have, instead of buying new stuff all the time. And the other moral of the Velveteen Rabbit is that good looks aren't everything. We have a hard time getting kids to try organic produce because it doesn't look as good as supermarket produce. It bruises, the skin cracks, and there are brown seams and mushy parts. Flea beetles nibble holes in our green leaves. It's tough to get kids to eat salad with those telltale holes."

"They are not fans of bug saliva?"

"Nope. Well, maybe Victor is a fan." Sophia turned and saw, for the first time, an unbroken view of the Graffi monster. At night, the blue dots would lose their color—might look red, might make Graffi look like he had the measles, though the dots she had hastily painted weren't uniform circles. Some were heart shaped, like bell peppers or apples. An orchard's worth of apples.

Sophia imagined the serpent in the Garden of Eden tempting her to "take a bite, discover the six words."

No, you don't have to do that any more, she told herself. *Go help clean the paint brushes.*

To close out Mural Painting Day, the eighth graders initiated Carver's call-and-response cheer:

"Curiosity is fuel!"

The sixth and seventh graders called back: "Grower's RULE!"

"Those are Carver's five words," Michael whispered in Sophia's ear. And impulsively, intuitively, Sophia decided to use this comment as a get-out-of-jail card.

"Oh, Michael. Forget about counting words. Both of us should. Those six words were horse sh— "

And at this very moment, when Sophia was finally going to come clean, albeit with a dirty mouth, she had the presence of mind to look over her shoulder, to see if anyone would overhear her say the word "horse shit."

John Simpson was right there.

He looked angry, as he always did. But right now he looked specifically angry. He looked as if he knew that Sophia's prefix "horse sh—" was going to culminate in the noun "horse shit." He wasn't attempting to veil the fact that he had been eavesdropping.

"Those six words were—hog wash." Sophia, amending the sentence without offense or defense. She gave Mr. Simpson an expectant look, raising an eyebrow just slightly in hopes of telepathically expressing two three-word sentences: "Take a picture. It'll last longer."

"Huh?" Michael whispered back. "What do you mean about hog wash?"

A pang of temptation stabbed Sophia. Did she need to clarify whether the six-word claim itself had been hog wash, or whether it would just be hog wash to say them to Michael, since he was so much cooler than the boy toys of her past

"Those six words were hog wash" was a six-word sentence, a perfect six-word sentence because it seemed like a throwaway line, but it had double meaning. Hog wash was something most people would think should be discarded, but farmers knew its worth. The analogy made her proud, and then on second thought, she thought it was convoluted, and she felt embarrassed. Her thoughts and feelings tossed like the waves of the Barbary Coste mural.

Then the images of Kira's diagrams of animal armor came to mind. The armor Sophia had donned for Michael had been as invisible a folly as the Emperor's new clothes—a façade rather than an outfit. She had tried to seem as engaging and farsighted in the course of her personal life as she tried to be when she composed scavenger hunts for Carver.

"So do you not know either?" Michael asked her.

"What?"

"Whether hogwash is one word or two?

"I thought and hoped just now that it was two words, and that it would count as two words. Michael?"

"Yeah?"

"You and I know there were never six magical words that

could control any guy. But this whole time we've known each other, I've been trying to come up with six witty-enough words to save face. Because I wanted to seem bulletproof in my cleverness, and lately it's been because, well..."

"Have you fallen for me?" Michael asked outright.

"I'm going to plead the Fifth on that," she replied.

They smiled at each other.

"Have you fallen for me?" she asked him.

"Like I'm going to tell you that now when you wouldn't answer me?" He shook his head and looked over his shoulder.

"Do you know the game 'rock, paper, scissors'?" she asked.

"Yes."

"Why don't we do the one-two-three thing, and instead of holding out our hands in rock, paper, or scissors, we'll answer the question at the same time so neither one of us will have to go out on a limb."

"Deal."

On the count of three, Michael said "Ye..." and only then did Sophia say "Yes," also.

"You cheated," Michael said. "Have you played this game before?"

"No," Sophia lied. "You know what? Actually, I have, but right now, I was more interested in your answer than the time I did it before."

"I'm glad you didn't lie to me," Michael said. "That 'rock, paper, scissors' trick is not the type of move a person thinks up on the spot."

He bent forward and kissed Sophia's forehead.

Angry looks from John Simpson transpired. Sophia checked out where the kids were in relation to Michael and her. All students were encircling the reception tables. They were about to dig into the delicious, healthful buffet they had prepared themselves, with Maggie's guidance.

The coast was clear, since Simpson was Michael and Sophia's only witness. Sophia gave Simpson a thumbs-up gesture instead of giving him the finger, and returned Michael's kiss.

Sophia invited Michael over that night for dinner. He wasn't so obvious as to show up at the front door with flowers, a suitcase, and a toothbrush, but she was sure they would also have breakfast together the next morning. She could tell because while they were making dinner they kept bumping into each other in her kitchen. They were clumsy and quick at first, then the touches lingered until they kissed. While they ate dinner, he was downright forthcoming not only about his past relationships, but about relationships in general. He asked about her romantic past. She answered his questions without bringing up Danny. While they ate sweet potato pie for dessert, she mentally crossed her fingers that he wouldn't defuse the sexual tension with a double entendre like "This wasn't the dessert I had in mind." Sophia didn't have many dealbreakers once she was very, very attracted to a man, but if a man sniffed a wine cork to judge the wine he'd ordered before tasting it, or if he made a double entendre about dessert, she ended the night with a handshake and a smile.

Michael ate his pie with a focus Sophia appreciated, and when he finished he said, "I've never eaten sweet potato pie, and I'm sure that if I ever have it again it won't be as good as yours."

"Thank you," she replied. "You're good at giving compliments."

The next day, Sophia couldn't stop thinking about the night before, but she didn't want to write about it in her journal. In the wake of having to hand over her diary during the lawsuit, she especially didn't want to describe the transition she and Michael made from kissing at the table, and onto the sofa, and then into her bedroom.

She just wrote:

Michael's in better shape and better in bed than I expected, though every guy has a flatter stomach when he's on his back.

That night and the next night, Sophia had dinner at Michael's and rushed home in the mornings to change so as not to be late for school. The fourth night, he suggested she bring over a change of clothes so she wouldn't have to dash off.

On the sixth day, they had yet another breakfast of leftovers from the night before, because both of them loved cold leftovers for breakfast. Michael asked, "Would you come by Luscious LoCal on your way home from work?"

"Sure," she asked, hoping he would unveil the mysterious campaign he had mentioned a few times since the mural-painting event.

"I want to show you something and tell you about something."

"Okay," Sophia said lightly. "I've got a lot on my to-do list right now since I haven't done any work the past few nights, but I can always make time to procrastinate. Should I come to your office?"

"No. Meet me in the produce section."

Chapter 29: Finally the Six Words Are Revealed

The smell assaulted Sophia as soon as she walked through the double doors of Luscious LoCal. Sweet refrigeration. Not something she could locate or isolate.

She texted Michael to let him know she had arrived. While she waited, she stared at the rhubarb stalks. They were a classic sign of spring, and a seasonal produce choice. She shifted uncomfortably. Although she knew each scarlet red stalk had been stripped of its poisonous leaves, the plant reminded her of pokeweed.

"I'm so glad to see you." Michael's forehead was moist and he was beaming.

He took her hand and steered her into the middle of the produce area. "Notice anything yet?"

"Only that we're blocking people," she said, shifting him out of the path of three carts pushed by customers who were clearly anxious to get back to their respective homes to make dinner.

"Okay, okay, I should be patient. Just tell me when you notice the change we've made," Michael said.

She scanned the shelves of oil and vinegar that lined the northwest quadrant of the produce department. She saw what she thought was a logo change on some of the shelf labels. About ten of them were color-coded light blue. She walked over to inspect the tags, but Michael touched her arm and said, "Not yet, I want you to see that they're everywhere."

Suddenly they were in another aisle, surrounded by soups, crackers, apple sauces, and the beginning of the baking supplies. Then he grabbed her hand again, and whisked her past tomato sauces and pastas until they came to an aisle of snack foods on one side and cereals on the other.

"Now you can look, he said, pointing to a shelf which featured at least six variations of oatmeal. One of them had the blue shelf label and she read the sentence above its price:

"This product is a sustainable choice."

"Oh Michael!" Sophia exclaimed. She looked for another blue shelf label. It bore the same sentence. She couldn't believe her eyes, so she checked a third.

"They're all the same," Michael told her. "A six-word sentence. You inspired that format, and also the content, with the seasonal produce scavenger hunt that you gave Ken Burnett at the chili cookoff. And that brave student of yours—"

"Tamika Lewis."

"Yes, Tamika, the girl who challenged customers to fill out survey cards, asking us to label sustainably-produced foods."

Sophia's spine tingled from the warmth of happiness. "You made my dream come true."

"I'm glad. I hoped so. Of course, at first I had to research the legality of making such a broad sustainability claim, because you know, there's a special corner in hell devoted to people who make groundless claims."

"Yes I do."

"...there's a blog you once mentioned, called Ethicurean which promotes the SOLE acronym: Sustainable, Organic, Local and Ethical. Ken's agreed to use those four criteria as our guideposts. We have you to thank for it."

She hugged him, then refused to take the credit. "This labeling campaign will be so much more effective than my seasonal produce scavenger hunt brochure would have been. Busy shoppers don't pick up brochures. They only read labels as they rush through the aisles. I need to make sure I point that out to the kids. We talk a lot about public awareness campaigns—not just the content of messages but also how best to convey them."

"Which brings me to something else I want to share with you," Michael told her. "Can we go sit in the café?"

Luscious LoCal's café was inviting. Sophia smelled bread baking, and tarragon. The orange walls looked painted with butternut squash soup, especially because someone had used a sponge to fleck them almost imperceptibly with a little yellow. Sophia remembered that Maggie's squash, carrot, and sweet potato soups had golden sheens from the mixture of olive oil and butter that Maggie added for a velvety finish.

As soon as Michael and Sophia had gotten their food, they slid into a currant-colored booth that would comfortably have accommodated four more people. The table was resinous, imbedded with shopping lists. She could only read a few words here and there. At first she thought they might be a sales gimmick, but she couldn't find a hint of product placement. In fact, most items were described in one word: bread, milk, flour, spinach, corn, grapes. Whoever had created this table had included all different styles of handwriting—bubbly, jagged, and flat, and words in languages that Sophia had to guess at from the

302

shape of their characters: Arabic, Korean, and what she guessed was Chinese rather than Japanese. The English and Spanish words were messily written, as inscrutable as prescription-pad directions. *Of course*, Sophia thought. *Everyone races through shopping lists.*

She looked up at Michael.

"So guess what?" he asked rhetorically.

"What?" she complied.

"This 'sustainable choice' campaign made me so proud I invited my mother to see it. I brought her yesterday. She met Ken, and everyone who was here that morning. Since getting to know you, I feel less rigid about maintaining the iron curtain between my personal and professional life. I told my mother I'd help her out with her campaign in every way I can, as long as my schedule permits." He took Sophia's hands in his. "You did something much better than what you said you could do New Year's Eve. You could never have controlled me, but your imagination and your spirit, and even your goofiness, have made my life more fun. You knock my socks off."

Sophia clasped the hands he reached out to her. "You knock my socks off too. And your six-word sentence, 'This product is a sustainable choice.' is outstanding beyond any six-word sentence I could ever come up with," Sophia admitted.

Michael said, "It may be more constructive, but romantically, your six words are pretty clever."

Sophia felt an opening in her chest when he said "romantically." As a teenager, she had felt this melting sense if a great song came up on the radio as she fiddled with the dial.

Michael continued. "I had trouble figuring out your six words, but as I worked to create 'this product is a sustainable choice,' I figured out your trick. As they say in romantic comedies, it has been right in front of my nose since the night I met you."

"Really?" The image that burst into Sophia's mind was of the Wizard of Oz telling Dorothy she had the answer the whole time. "But I never had a six-word sentence."

He interrupted. "Your six words were the boast!"

That couldn't be right. Because "I-can-control-any-guy-with-six-words" was eight words long. She realized this months ago.

Suddenly, she got it. The epiphany.

Sophia's original boast only required six words, not a complete six-word sentence. She could easily delete the first two words of that boast "I can," leaving her with six words: "control, any, guy, with, six, words."

Oh boy, she thought. *What Michael unearthed is so much shinier than my "I just want to be friends" cliché.*

"We started off strangely," Michael continued. "But I've come to feel both comfortable with you, and also curious about what you'll do next. It's a perfect blend of two feelings that don't usually blend."

When Sophia got home, she saw a message from Connie in her inbox.

I just found about the lawsuit. Why didn't you tell me yourself? I have three thoughts about this:

1) You picked the wrong time of year to harvest pokeberries.

2) Cover-ups are always more painful than mistakes. Just ask Bill Clinton, John Edwards, and Tiger Woods if you don't believe me.

3) Your mother didn't tell me about the lawsuit. I was eavesdropping on your parents and I got it out of them. Your mom told me you didn't want me to know because I am a source of stress to you, instead of a source of comfort.

It was a blow to hear this, especially since Persephone never criticizes me to my face. You and I both know your father has never been thrilled about having me around. Once, when I was being a know-it-all, and telling some dinner guest that Proserpina was the Roman name for Persephone, he said "Persephone is the pro in this house and you are the con."

You know that I view any conflict, any obstacle, as surmountable once its two opposing forces have been identified. I want to turn over a new leaf with you by telling what I think your clashing personality traits are, in hopes of helping you. I've intimated this before, but I want to state it simply and without rancor now:

You are both impulsive and defensive.

Since you were a child, I have feared your impulsivity. Because of my own anxiety, I made you feel guilty for it, instead of giving you a more constructive perspective. Impulsivity is unfortunate, and it often leads to missteps, but it is a fundamentally innocent trait. Most character flaws are expressions of innocence. People do them unthinkingly, automatically. Bo and your father never put the toilet seat down. We can't stand it, but they are unconscious when they do it and mean no offense.
It is my bad habit to give unsolicited advice and criticism. I wouldn't be surprised to find out you think of me as an evil

stepmother. And my relationship with you has forced me to admit I have a sadistic side. I bet I always will be somewhat sadistic, but please remember it is just one facet of my personality.
I do love you.

Sophia was shaking by the time she finished the email. Her journal was next to her computer. She opened it and began writing the rough draft of a reply. She didn't want to reply impulsively or defensively, and she was so grateful for Connie's six-word insight: *You are both impulsive and defensive.*

Sophia had known this subconsciously, but seeing it expressed succinctly make it conscious. In her journal she wrote:

My problem with Connie all along has been that she isn't the type of guru I can easily dismiss. I wish she had 20 gold Bentleys so I wouldn't take her seriously. When she criticizes me, it causes me angst because some of what she says helps me. I can't fully rebel, the way her own son did.

I may never be able to keep my slate clean, because I will never neatly subdue my flaws. No one can. But a lot of people aren't aware of their flaws, and now that I am I know what to work on. This generalization from Connie has always been true of me. I hope that going forward it won't be as true.

Sophia called Michael to tell him. She didn't have to confine her deepest feelings to her journal any longer.

The night before Carver's graduation ceremony, or rather the morning of the ceremony, the drum roll of heavy rain woke

Sophia at 3:24 am.

The yellow light from the old lamp near her bureau was still on. Part of her wanted to get up to turn it off. It was a waste of electricity, after all, but she was too comfortable to get out of bed, and she wished she could telepathically turn it off. Michael's back was to her. She dozed for a bit, then she opened her eyes again and watched his back expand and contract with his breath. The movement was as rhythmic as the downpour outside her windows. Maybe he felt her stare, or maybe she stirred, because a minute later he was awake too.

"Rain at night is my favorite sound," he murmured.

"Mine too," Sophia agreed.

"You okay? You didn't have a bad dream, did you?" he asked her.

"No."

"Okay. If you ever have a bad dream, wake me."

Sophia sighed with happiness. Her mom would have said the same thing to her. Meeting Michael had become a miracle. And not one of those miracles that Sheryl the math teacher had told her happened once a month. Michael was her once-in-a-lifetime miracle.

She was too happy to fall back to sleep. Happiness was like three cups of coffee, she realized. She jumped out of bed, switched off the lamp she had meant to turn off earlier, and then went into the front hall to retrieve the book she was going to quote from at the graduation ceremony later that morning. She was thrilled that the eighth graders had chosen her to be the graduation speaker. Since her demotion, she had spent more time substitute-teaching than holed up in her office with lesson plans. This meant she understood the students better than she ever had, and so she enjoyed them more, even the boisterous boys.

The book Sophia sat down on the couch with was Erich Fromm's *The Heart of Man*. Instead of lecturing the kids on all she had learned that school year, she would read them one page of wise Fromm. He believed that every time you act with integrity, you make it easier to keep yourself on the right track. Conversely, every time you take the easy way out, you increase the likelihood of weakness and self-entrapment.

Michael came into the living room, rubbing his face. "You're still up. Was I snoring?"

She smiled at him. "I can't sleep. I'm excited about you."

He came over to the couch and kissed her.

"Not that I'm underestimating my fabulousness," Michael said, "but maybe you're nervous about speaking at graduation. This is the book you're reading from, right?"

She nodded. "At this hour, I'm relaxed or tired or slow enough to contemplate it. I'm so grateful for your affection, and grateful that I'm working on a fresh start with Connie."

"Well, I'm going back to bed. Join me when you feel enlightened."

"Don't hold your breath," Sophia replied.

"I'm looking forward to spending the summer with you," Michael told Sophia as she parked the car a few blocks away from Carver. Parents with graduating eighth graders had filled all the parking spaces near the school.

"Me too," she said. The summer before had been solitary for her, except for two weeks with her family and some beach trips with friends. Sophia had focused on her tomatoes, cucumbers, purple basils, and peaches.

Michael and Sophia held hands until they reached the garden, and then Sophia let go. She explained, "Holding hands in front of middle schoolers is, from their perspective, as awkward as rolling around on the ground and groping each other in front of them."

Stephen approached Sophia just after she and Michael had sat down.

"Hi Michael. Sophia, can we talk privately?" Stephen asked.

"Sure." She followed him to the side of the garden.

"I heard you inspired Luscious LoCal's Sustainable Choices labelling campaign. I'd like you to return to full-time status in the fall. As vice principal. Dawn's going to be busy next year working on the possibility of adding on a high school."

Sophia croaked, "How amazing!"

"Keep it secret for now. So will you say yes to my offer?"

"Thank you, I'd love to be——." She paused for a second thought. Then she remembered the six-word sentence she had taped to the border of her computer monitor after re-reading Erich Fromm's advice:

Opportunities for Impulse Control Are Everywhere.

Sophia looked Stephen in the eye. "My impulse is to say yes right now, but I need to sleep on this before I let you know for sure."

At the end of the graduation ceremony, the eighth graders initiated Carver's call-and-response cheer for their last time:

"Curiosity is fuel!"

And the sixth and seventh graders, and Sophia and Michael, and everyone else called back.

"Grower's RULE!"

Acknowledgements

The first readers: Cynthia Harrison, Caroline Tolley, Nancy Coleman Wolsk, and Susan Zentay.

The teachers in my family: especially those with the last names Coleman Wolsk, Deutch, Hurwitz, Meringer, Oldknow, and Schotland. Mom, Dad, and Joey—I would need 300 more pages to thank you properly.

My teachers from National Cathedral School, Concord Academy, Brown, and Penn. You were so patient with me and your insights benefit me daily.

Thanks to writer and teacher Leslie Pietrzyk, whose quotes are taped to the wall behind my computer: "Write until something surprises you" and "The subconscious mind works things out in a miraculous kind of way." Thanks also to the writers in your novel-improving workshop.

Rhoda Trooboff got the ball(point pen) rolling. On walks, your attentiveness helped me solve problems with the drafts that I thought were unsolveable. *Solvitur ambulando* (Richard Mabey's translation: "you can work it out by walking"). Like Rhoda, Sarah Corson has been a role model for her creativity and generous joy.

Heather Sellers cured my research addiction with an eight-word line, "You already know everything you need to know."

Thanks to Ethicurean, the Common Good City Farm, Ed Bruske, and Karen Schacter for the engaging way you educate the public about physical and environmental health, especially the sustainable foods movement.

Thanks to my daughter Claire, nephews Kai and Eli, and niece Mai. When this novel was 600 pages of everything but the kitchen sink, thoughts of you kept me going. I figured that even if *Six Words* remained the width of *The Brothers Karamazov*, you would one day read or at least skim it.

Thanks to the community forum at CS for your invaluable formatting tips.

Thanks to Marissa Rauch Photography for making me look good, and to Jeremy for making me feel good.

www.ingramcontent.com/pod-product-compliance
Lightning Source LLC
Chambersburg PA
CBHW031250170626
46807CB00001B/69